PRETTY
desperate

Lacey Black

Pretty Desperate

Pine Village Series, book 6

USA Today Bestselling Author

Lacey Black

Lacey Black

Pretty Desperate

Pine Village Series, book 6

Copyright © 2025 Lacey Black

Cover Design by Y'all. That Graphic.
Photographer Regina Wamba Photography

Editing by Kara Hildebrand

Proofreading by Sandra Shipman, Joanne Thompson, and Karen Hrdlicka

Format by Brenda Wright, Formatting Done Wright

Published in the United States of America.

ISBN-13: 978-1-951829-64-3

Lacey Black

CHAPTER
one

KAMERON

24 Hours Earlier...

"Good afternoon, Mrs. Krokus. Thank you so much for taking the time to meet with me today," I say to the polite older woman on the sidewalk in front of her building.

She offers me a firm handshake, one that surprises me by how frail she appears. The woman is ninety years old and using a walker with tennis balls covering the back legs, but she shakes hands like a linebacker. "I'm intrigued, Kameron." She glances up at the building adjacent to my restaurant, Prime Steak House, and smiles. She's owned it for more than two decades longer than I've been on this earth. "It's been a while since I've seen her. Let's go inside."

I take the keys from her hand and make sure she has no trouble crossing the cracked concrete in front of the glass double doors. Slipping the key into the lock, I give it a turn, releasing the mechanism. My heart is hammering in my chest, the anticipation almost too much to bear.

I've wanted this building for years. Ever since I purchased the one next door and transformed it into a thriving steak house in downtown Pine Village, I've had my eye on it. My plan has always been to expand. My current location is quaint. The dining area is always full during the busy tourist seasons, and my kitchen is small. I built it to fit what I had. My dream has always been encompassing the vacant building to the south, since the north business is the clothing boutique, and I don't see them going anywhere. Purchasing another building somewhere else isn't an option, since there aren't any available in the downtown area, and starting with a new build at another location isn't financially feasible.

This really is my only hope at growing.

The doors are glass with an old wooden frame. I push open the first one and am assaulted by a musty scent, like I'm walking into a basement. I hold the door wide so Mrs. Krokus can get inside and let the heavy door fall closed behind us. For over ten years I've lusted after this building. I've made offers, I've called in favors trying to sway her, I've even dropped by to talk about it in person, but Mrs. Krokus hadn't been interested.

Until today.

Getting a wild hair up my ass, I picked up the phone and called her. Much to my utter shock, she agreed to meet with me, but it had to be between her afternoon nap and her dinner date at the diner with members of her church's Ladies Guild. I let her pick the time and prayed she'd show.

She did.

The old woman exhales as she glances around the empty space. "It's just how I remember it."

It's a beautiful building. With high ceilings very similar in style to my own and the original hardwood floors, it's full of light and love. And a lot of cobwebs and dust bunnies. "It's a great space. There's so much potential here, and I really think—"

"All business, I see," she interrupts with a chuckle. "We can get to that soon. First, I want to take a stroll around and see how she's fared over the years."

She extends her wrinkled hand my way, which I politely take. Mrs. Krokus leaves her walker behind and leaning a bit of her weight against my arm, starts to walk toward the back wall. "My Louis purchased this building for me in nineteen sixty," she informs me, a far-off look on her aged face. "Back then, it wasn't standard for the women to work the way the men did. Women were mostly home, raising children and keeping the house. Well, I had dreams, and my Louis wanted to help me achieve them."

We stop in the middle of the room.

Lifting her frail hand, she points to one of the closed doors. "Back there was the storage room. There's a utility closet in there with a water heater that's older than you," she says with a chuckle. "I had two dressing rooms on that wall," she adds, turning slightly to the left and indicating where the rooms were located. You can still see the different colored wood on the floor where they once sat. "Families shopped for their Sunday attire, men found work clothes, and ladies would pick out pretty dresses. I even stocked some beautiful linens and tapestries for the home. It wasn't a big store, but it was mine and I loved it."

A smile spreads across my lips as she tells me about the store she once owned. She gives me a brief overview of the layout for Krokus Clothing before turning her attention to me. "Department stores were a thing in the sixties, but we didn't really feel it until the eighties when shopping malls started popping up. One was built in Hudson, and all of a sudden, families were willing to travel a little farther for a bigger selection at a fair price. Not to mention, food courts with all sorts of options. The teenagers flocked to them as a place to shop and hang out. They were all the rage back then, and unfortunately, our little store felt it.

"I raised my family here, while running a successful business. All three of my children worked here through their teenage years, because family was so important to me." She turns and meets my gaze. "Still is, Mr. Markley."

"I, uh," I start, clearing my throat, "I don't have any family left in town. It's just me."

She gives me a knowing little grin. "I remember your family. Your parents were around the same ages as my own children."

I nod, swallowing over the lump I get in my throat when I think of my parents.

"They've been gone for several years now."

"They have. They passed when I was living in Chicago."

Patting my hand in a very grandmotherly way, she says, "Terrible accident that was."

Again, I nod, unable to speak. I'll never forget that phone call. In one moment, both of my parents were taken away in the blink of an eye. That's when I knew I needed a change. The city life wasn't for me anymore. I wanted to go home.

"I'm sure they'd be very proud of you."

"I'd like to hope. They were huge supporters of my desire to go to culinary school and eventually own a restaurant."

She glances around the empty building. "They'd love your restaurant. I admit, I'm not a regular patron, but I've been a few times for special occasions when my kids come to town. You have a great atmosphere and menu. I can understand your desire to expand."

Here we go...

My heart taps a little harder in my chest as excitement sweeps in. "Yes, ma'am. I love my current space, but it's a little tight. I'd love to tear out the wall here," I inform, sweeping my hand toward the bricks separating our two buildings, "and add a dozen more tables. I'd even be able to open up the kitchen area and double that space. I have drawings too, based off the old city engineer's drawings from back in the day. I understand it might not be completely accurate, but the square footage is the same, and that's really what I was looking for."

"I won't sell to you."

My bubble pops, completely deflating me.

If she didn't want to sell, why the hell are we here?

"I'm sorry?" I ask, hoping I misunderstood her.

The smile she's been carrying since stepping foot inside this building slips, and a serious look full of concern takes its place. "Please forgive me, Kameron. You seem like such a nice young man, but I don't feel like this is the right partnership."

I want to drop her hand and start pacing, but her walker is over by the door, and the last thing I'd want is for her to fall. "I don't understand," I say, running my hand across the back of my neck in frustration.

She gives me one of those grandmotherly smiles, one that's all warm and full of affection, but I don't feel the glow over my own confusion and devastation. "Let me try to explain it a little better," she says, pushing off my arm and taking a step toward the very center of the room. I wonder if I should go get her walker, but she appears to be okay, so I let her be until she tells me otherwise.

"This place, it holds a beautiful magic within the walls. It was built on love, cultivated on it. Families blossomed right here where I stand. That's the real legacy of Krokus Clothing." She spins around and pins me with a look. "Don't you see? The next owner of this building must hold the same values my late, dear husband, Louis, once held when he risked it all to purchase this building. He wanted it to be a place families would come together, but it was more than that. He wanted to watch families grow within too. Our family."

All I can do is stare at her, because she's making absolutely no sense. How can her family continue to grow if her children and grandchildren are gone? Why keep this building if it's going to just sit and fall apart? You might as well tear it down and build a parking lot if she's waiting on her family to come back and make something of this place. I can't imagine seeing this building dilapidated and a tax and utilities burden to her in this stage of life was anything Louis wanted for his widow after he was gone.

Clearing my throat, I collect my thoughts, trying to be polite and not let my frustration show. "Mrs. Krokus," I start, but she cuts me off.

"Dorothy, please," she says with a smile.

"Dorothy," I state, lifting my chin. "My restaurant expansion would be all about families. These walls would be bustling again, filled with families of all ages who are here to dine. It would be the centerpiece of this place," I assure her.

She grins. "I do understand that, but…this place won't be built on love, Kameron. Don't you see?"

No. No I clearly need fucking glasses, because I do not *see.*

Trying to tamp down my frustration, I insist, "No, I suppose I don't." I need her to explain it a little better than this.

"I promised my Louis that when I was ready to let this piece of our past go, I would sell it to a family, one with a vision as beautiful and forever as ours was."

A family?

"These walls are ready to hear laughter again. The kind of laughter that comes from love." She spins around and pins me with a look. "You're single, Kameron."

My mouth drops open.

"There is another offer on the table for this building. A husband and wife with two adorable little ones. They want to bring a home goods and décor shop to town, featuring some local artisan wares. I think it's a wonderful idea," she says.

"Home goods and décor?" I whisper, mostly to myself as I gaze around the empty space.

My dreams seem to be going up in flames with each passing second. Mrs. Krokus isn't going to sell to me because I don't have a family? A wife? A girlfriend?

Unless…

"I've been seeing someone," I blurt out, catching even myself off guard.

She turns and pins me with a look. "You have?"

I nod insistently. "Yes, I've been dating someone for a few months now."

"Well, that's wonderful news!" she proclaims, shuffling toward me. She places her hand on top of mine. "Is it getting serious?"

I nod again. "It is."

Reaching up, she places her hand against my cheek. "This makes me so happy for you. I hadn't heard you were seeing anyone."

"We've been keeping it pretty quiet. Low-key. You know how this town gets," I say, my head spinning as I fabricate a story on the fly.

"Yes, I do. I can understand and appreciate wanting to keep it to yourselves until the time is right." She turns hopeful eyes my way. "And is that now? Is the time right for you to step out together? Show the world your love?"

My throat is completely dry, my brain is ready to explode. I know what I'm doing is wrong, but I can't seem to stop. I've wanted this building for more than a decade, and now she's finally willing to sell. Only, she doesn't want to sell to someone without the prospect of a family on the horizon. It's completely ridiculous and absurd, but what can I do?

Besides, it's one little white lie.

No big deal.

"It is." Just saying those two words is like raking my vocal cords over sandpaper.

"Oh, how wonderful!" she proclaims with a little clap of her hands. "I want to meet her."

What?

"What?"

"I would love to meet the woman who finally stole your heart, Kameron. If you're finally ready to step forward with your relationship, then it's only fair that we meet. You want to purchase this building, correct?"

I nod, unable to find words.

"Then we shall all get together, say for dinner soon?"

"I'd, uh, well, I'd have to ask her if that works for her schedule," I say, running my hand down the back of my neck nervously.

"Of course. What does she do?"

"She owns a business. Here. In Pine Village."

For fuck's sake. Really, Kameron? That's the best you can come up with?

At least pick some fictitious woman from a neighboring town like Hudson. Now, I have to find a girlfriend in my hometown of two thousand, knowing the single dating pool is getting drier and drier by the day.

"Which one?" she asks eagerly, ready to put the pieces of my lying puzzle together.

My mind spins. I'm at a crossroads. I should end this now, confess that I lied and walk away from the building. It'll be sold to another family and a home goods and gift shop—or whatever in the hell they were going to put here—will open instead of my restaurant. It would serve me right for outright lying to this sweet old lady in an attempt to purchase her building. I'm the worst kind of asshole, but I can't seem to get past the tip of my own growing nose right now to right this wrong.

Or I could cultivate this little white lie and grab hold of my dream. It's the first time it's been even an option for me. Right this very second, it's dangling before me, like a carrot to a horse, and all I have to do is take a bite. So I need a girlfriend. I can do that. It's not forever, right? Just a short period of time to help me get this building. Someone I trust with the truth and will understand and appreciate my drive for success. Someone who does own a business in town and is just as determined and driven as I am. Someone with acting skills who can sell this lie until it's time to walk away.

Someone like my friend, Jillian.

Not that Jillian's really a friend. We have mutual friends, really. Sure, we're on friendly terms, but it's not like we hang out or anything.

But Jillian fits the bill.

She owns a business here in town, and as far as I know, she's not dating anyone.

Plus, she's fucking gorgeous and fake dating her wouldn't be a hardship.

I know what I have to do.

I just have to convince Jillian to lie with me.

"She owns the bakery," I blurt out, feeling heat creep up my neck.

"Jillian Kirby? Oh, what a lovely young woman. Her cinnamon rolls and scones are simply divine," Dorothy says, looking quite pleased. "I'm so happy to hear you two are dating."

"Thank you," I somehow spit out over my Sahara-dry throat.

"I'd love to meet with you both. Soon. Maybe next Sunday? The bakery is closed, so it would be easier for her. I know your restaurant is open, but surely you can slip away for an hour or so to appease an old woman."

"I can."

"It's set then. Let's say five o'clock? We can dine in your restaurant so it's more convenient for you. You can show me your plans for this space, and we can work out any details needed. After that, if we can agree upon a price and terms, I'll be in contact with my lawyer."

If it's possible, my heart sinks and soars at the exact same time. I'm ecstatic for the opportunity, yet completely shocked at how I'm getting it.

And maybe a little worried at the extent at which I'm willing to go...

"That sounds wonderful, Mrs. Krokus. I'm sure next Sunday at five will work beautifully," I say, my entire body hot, despite the fact the room is not.

"Great. Now, if you'll excuse me, I need to get to the diner."

I escort the older woman to the door, where she retrieves her walker. Together, we exit the building, and I secure the door behind us. "Thank you, Mrs. Krokus."

"No, thank you, Kameron. I look forward to sharing a meal with you next weekend," she says with a smile.

"Me too. And I'm sure Jillian will be ecstatic."

My gut churns.

"Enjoy your holiday weekend," the old woman says before starting to shuffle toward the diner down the street.

"You too," I holler, throwing her a wave as she goes.

My head tells me I need to stop this. A lie of this magnitude won't have the outcome I expect, that's for sure. I'm deceiving a sweet old woman to get her building. A building I've wanted, lusted after for more than a decade, but still. It's not right.

But...what if it is right? What if this is exactly what I'm supposed to do? Not the lie itself, but the determination and hard work to achieve my dream. I've never been afraid of going after what I want, and I'm not one to back down from a challenge.

That's what this is.

An obstacle put in front of me. One I need to consider and figure out. Like a puzzle. Dorothy has terms for selling the building, and I can find the solution to achieve what I'm after. It's actually quite simple.

I need to go secure a girlfriend.

CHAPTER
one

Jillian

Present Day

I almost have this recipe perfect.

As soon as I have it where I want, I'll add it to my digital cookbook. Then, I'll be one step closer to fulfilling my dream. Not that owning my own bakery and coffee shop isn't living my dream, but I've always wanted to produce my own cookbook. Maybe even have my own cooking blog or YouTube channel, like Ryan. Someday, I'll be brave enough to talk to her about it. I haven't known her that long, but she's become a great friend in a short amount of time. I'm certain she'd offer me any tips or tricks she can to get me started.

I slip the pan of pastries into the oven and set the timer. I have thirteen minutes until I need to pull my latest creation from the oven, and usually I'd use the time to start cleaning up my workspace. Of course, my workspace tonight is my kitchen counter at home. Usually, I do all my creating in my bakery kitchen, having plenty of supplies and oven space to play.

However, tonight was a rash decision to bake. I had just returned home from having dinner with my parents, and that always goes about as well as you'd expect. Not that I don't love my parents—I do—but they're ready for grandbabies, and I'm their only hope. The problem is I'm thirty-seven and don't even have a boyfriend. I've spent every waking hour over the last decade, pouring myself into my business. Sure, having a boyfriend sounds nice—more than nice, actually—but the reality of it isn't so easy. I work a lot and the only men I meet on a daily basis want me for my cinnamon swirl bread and banana chocolate chip muffins. Oh, and the caffeine. They definitely want that too.

So those grandbabies my parents want? They're starting to get real restless and vocal in their disappointment. Tonight's dinner wasn't any different, except this time they took it a step further. Tonight, while enjoying honey-glazed pork chops, roasted brussels sprouts, and creamy mashed potatoes, they offered up a list of available, single men in Pine Village.

A list!

Typed up and printed out on my dad's company letterhead.

I almost threw up my food right then and there. I couldn't get out of there fast enough.

That's the reason I'm baking on a Sunday night instead of relaxing and preparing for the busy week ahead of me. I glance at the timer on the oven. Five minutes left. Just as I grab the container of sugar to place in the cabinet, there's a firm knock at my door.

Hesitantly, I move toward the entryway. I'm not expecting anyone, especially at this point in the evening. All my friends would have texted or called first, so chances of the visitor being one of them are slim to none.

As I reach the door, I go up on my tiptoes and peek through the security hole. My mouth falls open when the individual on the opposite side comes into view. "Kameron?" I find myself asking, reaching down and releasing the lock.

"Hey, yeah, sorry to just drop by like this," he says, glancing over my shoulder into my house.

"Are you all right?"

He sighs and shakes his head. "No, not really. I need your help."

Worry fills my chest. I've known Kameron practically my whole life. He's a few years older than me, but we grew up down the road from each other. He may not be one of my closest friends, but if he needs something, I'd readily help. "Okay, what's up?"

He levels me with an intense look, his blue eyes full of anxiety as he drops a bomb straight in my lap. "I need you to be my girlfriend..."

I stare back at him for one, two, three seconds before bursting into laughter. "Right," I say between fits of giggles. "Okay," I add with a playful eye roll. Of all the years I've known Kameron, I've never really known him to be so funny. Serious and inquisitive, sure, but never one to joke.

Kameron sighs and closes his eyes. "I'm dead serious, Jillian. Can I come in?"

The smile I wear slowly falls from my face when I don't see a flicker of humor in his gaze. "Uhh, yeah, sure," I mumble, stepping back so there's room for him to pass through the doorway.

He steps inside my small home for the first time ever and glances around. There isn't much to it, not that I need a lot of space. I live in an eight-hundred square foot, one-bedroom home. The majority of my time is spent at my bakery. Here, I eat a little, sleep some, and shower before heading back to the business I pour my heart and soul into.

With a strong exhale, Kameron turns and faces me. "I need you to be my girlfriend."

"You keep saying that," I grumble, trying to wrap my head around his words. He's not asking me out. No, this is way more...businesslike.

He levels me with a serious look that has my heart hammering in my chest. "I'll explain everything, I promise. Can we sit?"

Just as I nod, the timer on my oven dings. "I'll be right back," I reply, practically running into the kitchen to retrieve my latest creation. Slipping oven mitts onto my hands, I open the oven door and inhale the sweet aroma of the salted caramel treat and remove the pan, setting it on the trivet.

"What's that?" Kameron pokes his head over my shoulder, taking a whiff.

"Salted Caramel Blondies." I can't hide the pride in my voice, even though I have yet to taste them.

His dark eyes fill with excitement. "Can I have one?"

"They're too hot right now," I insist, turning to face him. Of course, he's still standing directly in front of me, our chests practically touching. I catch another scent heavy in the air, and that's his cologne or soap or aftershave. Something. It's woodsy and intoxicating, and it takes all my self-control not to lean forward, press my nose to his neck, and inhale.

Maybe diving into those blondies now isn't such a bad idea...

Meeting his stormy eyes, I add, "Besides, I don't think I'm going to like what you have to say, so I reserve the right to share my blondies until later."

The corner of his mouth curls into a smirk. "Deal." Kameron walks over to my little dinette table and has a seat. "Though, I'm sure you won't like what I have to say either." He takes a deep breath and adds, "Just promise me you'll hear me out completely."

I don't want to agree to that at all, but it seems fair. "All right," I reply, taking a seat across from him.

He takes a deep breath and starts, "It's been my dream since moving back to town and opening my restaurant to expand. I'd love a bigger space for more patrons, but when I purchased my building, I made do with what was available. Ever since, I've made contact and inquired about purchasing the empty building to the south of my restaurant. Yesterday, the owner finally agreed to meet with me."

"Mrs. Krokus, right?"

He nods. "Yes, that's right. She decided it was finally time to sell the building. However…" He pauses and glances around. For what, I'm not sure. He leans forward, lowers his voice, and drops the bomb. "She will only sell to someone who is family-oriented, which means I need a girlfriend for the next few months, until the deal is done."

I lean back in my chair and stare back at Kameron. He's a gorgeous man. Like standing on the surface of the sun hot. I've crushed on him off and on for the last couple of years but never told a soul about it. Now? Well, he's still hot but with a side of crazy. "Have you been drinking?"

"No."

"Did you fall and hit your head?"

"Of course not," he scoffs, shaking his head.

"So, let me get this straight. You want me to be your pretend girlfriend, so you can scam some sweet little old lady out of her building." My face surely shows the horror which I feel.

"No!" he insists but then pauses to think. "Well, sort of. But it's not like that."

"How is it?" I ask gently, trying to understand.

He exhales and shakes his head. "I really, really want this. I've worked my ass off since culinary school for this. I've paid my dues, worked my way up to what I have now. It's not easy, as I'm sure you know. It's hard fucking work, day in and day out. I don't sleep, I don't leave my restaurant. I live, breathe, and eat Prime Steak House. It's all I want, all I know."

My throat gets a little tight at the determination and passion pouring from his words. Why? Because I do understand. Probably better than most. I've paid my dues too, worked at a variety of places since graduating high school. Some good, some not so much. I pushed myself to take some online business classes at night, earning an associate's degree in business to help prepare me for one day owning my own bakery.

I'd always loved to bake. It was my stress reliever. In high school, I'd make rolls and muffins and sell them out of my parents' kitchen for fifty cents each. I never really knew what I wanted to do in the future, so instead of paying for schooling, I entered the workforce. I have worked a variety of jobs over the years. Secretary, server, cook, and advertising sales for the local newspaper. Hell, I even cleaned houses for a short time. But it was always baking I came back to.

I'd make cakes for birthdays, weddings, and anniversaries, trays of cookies, bars, and brownies for office parties. I had my food service license and was registered with the county to sell baked goods from my home, but it wasn't enough. In the back of my mind, I saw something bigger for myself. I had a dream, and that picture was starting to take shape.

So if anyone understands what it takes to live a dream, it's me. I've been there too.

But I didn't need a fake boyfriend to get it.

Though, I was able to save, thanks to the busy summer tourist season, but it'll be a few months before the winter crowd arrives. Did I save enough? Spring and fall aren't always the easiest when you own a small bakery that's reliant on foot traffic to pay its bills.

Clearing my throat, I reply, "I can understand your passion, Kameron. Really. I get it. Owning a business in this town can be challenging."

He nods. "Incredibly so. But I've got a solid foundation. I have roots that run deep in this town, and I don't want to be anywhere else. I want more space. I *need* more space. My kitchen is tiny and storage is practically nonexistent. I had to build my restaurant for the space I had, not what I needed. I need to grow. I'm stunted." He holds my gaze, his dark eyes burning with an intensity I can feel clear down to my toes. "I need this, Jilly. I need your help. You're the only one I can ask, and I know this is huge."

Jilly.

No one calls me Jilly. Not anymore. My parents did when I was little, but I put a kibosh on it back in junior high. It was embarrassing to me, having your parents holler your nickname at track meets and at the end of plays. Classmates picked up on it and used it against me, teasing me mercilessly my entire sixth grade year. That's when I asked them to stop, explaining how much I didn't like it, and for the most part, they abided by my wishes. Every now and again it'll still come out, but they usually refer to me by my given name.

Hearing Kameron use it doesn't have the same effect it did when I was younger. In fact, it's quite the opposite. The name Jilly rolling off his tongue is more intimate, like an aphrodisiac that goes straight to my underused, undersexed girly bits and pieces. Even my nipples seem to want in on the action, pebbling hard against my cotton bra and T-shirt. I have to shift in my seat and tug on my shirt to keep that tidbit of intel to myself.

"I don't know," I find myself saying. "I don't want to lie."

"I don't either," he insists. "It's not my style, but I'm against the ropes here and am out of options. Think of it as...acting. Like you did in school."

That makes me sit up straight. "How did you know I did theater?"

He shrugs his strong shoulders. "I was in the play my senior year, and I remember you."

I remember him too, but probably not for the same reason. He was so gorgeous, so much more than the rest of the boys in school. He was a senior when I was a freshman. We never talked, never hung out. But that didn't mean I didn't lust after the hot upperclassman, especially during the spring play.

"You were one of the leads."

I nod. I was the lead all four years. I loved art, loved drama, loved the stage. Of course, I never wanted to go past high school, never thought I'd make it in the cutthroat world of acting. I had fun, participating in all the plays throughout school, and then moved on.

23

But that one year, I remember Kameron. He had a small part in *Clue: On Stage*, a high school stage version of the popular Hasbro board game. I played Miss Scarlet, while Kameron had a role as an extra who made only a couple of appearances. We never interacted, on stage or off.

"Just think of it as a part. You be my pretend girlfriend for a bit, and you'll be paid for your time."

My jaw drops. "Paid? Like…a prostitute?"

He blanches at my question. "No, of course not. I wouldn't expect…that." I can't believe it, but Kameron's face turns a lovely shade of red.

"I can't take money, Kameron," I insist, knowing it's true. Even if I need it, I wouldn't be able to accept it. Not when my "acting" job was based on a lie.

"Okay, fine. What else can we work out? There has to be something you want or need?" he insists, leaning a little closer as he waits.

I think about my bakery, how difficult it can be to make ends meet from time to time. How there's always something I need to spend what savings I have on. Work on my fridge, oven, a roof leak, and new display case. All things I've had to dip into my savings to pay for over the last almost-five years. Not to mention the cost to self-publish my cookbook. I know I'll need a good chunk of change for that too.

Of course, the dream would be to have it published through an actual publishing company. The promotional resources alone would be well worth the investment, but I'm not ready to pitch my idea quite yet. Not only do I need a few more recipes, but I'm not sure my heart can handle the rejection.

"I can see your gears turning," he says, interrupting my thoughts. "Lay it on me."

I need something to help sustain me during the slow seasons, and an idea starts to take shape. It might just help me achieve both dreams. I could make enough to save during spring and fall, and also put money away to produce my cookbook, while continuing to do exactly what I love to do.

"I want to contract with you to provide exclusive desserts to Prime."

He seems surprised by my request. "You do?"

I nod eagerly. "I can provide dessert options each week or on a mutually agreed upon schedule. I would offer different desserts than what I sell in my bakery, more gourmet, decadent choices that fit your menu and prices. I'd even deliver."

"Deal," he replies instantly, as if he didn't even have to think about it. "Actually, I feel terrible for not considering this sooner. Those cheesecakes you made for me were a hit."

I can't help but smile.

But that smile falls off my lips just as fast. Could I lie to everyone, including a sweet old woman? For a business contract? For a little more cushion in my bank account?

No, I don't think I can.

"Jillian," he starts, dropping his voice and leveling me with a vulnerable gaze. "You're my only hope. I can't do this without you. Please."

I drop my head to the table, mostly to avoid those dang intoxicating eyes. They're the prettiest shade of blue, the color of the ocean under a brilliant summer sun. All I know is I can't think straight when looking at them. They make me want to go along with this cockamamie scheme. And that's exactly what this is. An absurd, ridiculous, outrageous idea that shouldn't even be on the table.

But it is.

"This is insane," I murmur, mostly to myself.

"It absolutely is," he confirms, yet not backing down from his massive request.

Lifting my head, I meet those damn eyes once more. They're pleading with me, and I realize, right now, in this moment, I'd agree to about anything. Including being his pretend girlfriend for an undetermined period of time.

It's quite possible I've lost my marbles.

Especially when I say the words I never thought I'd speak. "I'll do it."

CHAPTER Two

KAMERON

Relief.

That's what I feel the moment she agrees to my crazy idea.

"Thank you," I whisper, my nose catching another whiff of those blondie bars she made. "Are they cool yet?"

Her eyebrows pull together in confusion. "What?"

"The blondies," I state with a wink, standing up and heading over to where Jillian left them cooling on the counter.

I grab a large knife out of the block beside the stove, but before I can start slicing into the delicious smelling treats, Jillian is there. "Don't you dare use that," she says, carefully taking the knife from my hand and replacing it in the block.

I step back, but not because I want to. In fact, I rather enjoy being close to the adorable Jillian Kirby. She smells like sugar, her dark hair hitting just below her shoulders. It looks soft, and my fingers itch to slide through the strands. Not to mention the pale green T-shirt she has on with a pair of leggings. Leggings. A man's Kryptonite. And hers look pretty fucking good too. The black material hugs her round ass and thighs, begging for my palms.

She pulls open a drawer and removes a different type of knife. This looks like a hard plastic and cuts smoothly as she slices into the blondies. Using a small spatula, she removes two pieces and places each one on a small paper plate. "Here."

I take the treat, anxious to dive in. "Only one?"

She rolls her eyes before returning to the table with her own plate. "You can have more if you like it."

"Why wouldn't I like it?" I ask, taking my seat across from her.

She lifts her shoulders, her focus on the dessert on her plate. I fully expect her to pick it up and take a bite, but that's not what she does. I watch, mesmerized, as she scrutinizes the blondie with a very critical eye. I have no idea what she's doing, but it's fascinating to witness.

Finally, she lifts the treat and inhales. It's not a deep sniff, but she's definitely taking in the aroma of her baked good. Then, she leans forward and takes a small bite. I mean a *small* bite. Like the type of bite a toddler would take if you were offering them broccoli. It's full of hesitation, but the moment the treat hits her tongue, her eyes light up. She chews slowly, as if dissecting and cataloguing her work before she swallows.

Catching me watching her, she asks, "What?"

"You tell me."

She glances down at her plate and realizes what I was referring to. "Oh. Sorry. This is a new recipe. If it's good enough, I'll add it to the bakery this fall." Something flashes through her eyes. Clearly there's more to it, but I don't feel comfortable pushing.

Lifting my own blondie, I take a healthy bite, one much bigger than the dainty one she took. The flavors explode on my tongue in a delicious combination of salty and sweet. It's still warm, the caramel gooey and rich, but not overly sweet. "These are great."

She beams. "Thank you."

I finish my first bar and grab another. As I sit down to enjoy more dessert, I ask, "We can iron out all the details soon, but is there anything we need to discuss right now?"

She considers my request and nods. "Actually, yes. I want this to stay between us. I don't like the idea of lying to my friends and family, but I think we have to be consistent. It'll be less likely people find out about the lie, you know?"

I dip my chin, completely understanding. "I agree. It'll be between the two of us. No one else."

A loud sigh fills the room, and she places her half-eaten treat back on the plate. "I really don't like this," she murmurs, almost to herself. "I hate the thought of lying to everyone, Kameron."

"It's temporary," I assure her. "We'll go public with our relationship after we meet with Mrs. Krokus next Sunday. That's when the details of the sale will be discussed, and I'll have a better idea of how long we have to keep this charade up."

"We can't just end it right after," she says absently. "Everyone will know something is up."

I get what she's saying. "Yeah, you're probably right. We'll have to at least keep it up a couple of weeks after I close on the building."

She doesn't say anything for a couple of minutes, but I can tell she's thinking. Probably overthinking, if I had to guess. Not that I blame her. I can't imagine being in her shoes right now. Hell, I don't even like being in my own shoes. But I feel up against the wall, and even though I don't like it, I don't have much of a choice.

"Next Sunday. Okay, so that gives us a week to, you know, figure this out."

"We'll keep it simple, Jilly. We both have demanding jobs, so we probably won't even see each other much."

She holds my gaze, those green eyes both assessing and understanding. "True. But won't that be weird?"

I shrug, truly having no clue. It's not like I date a lot to even know what constitutes weird or not. My last girlfriend only lasted a few weeks because she got a job offer out of state. With her impending move, and the fact there was no way I was going anywhere, we opted to cut ties and not force any long-distance relationship.

"You can swing by the restaurant for dinner, if you want. I usually just take a quick dinner break when it's slower, but I could try to work it around your schedule. And I'll drop by the bakery in the mornings on my way in and grab a cup of coffee. People will at least see us visiting each other's place of business." She doesn't mention the fact my restaurant doesn't open until mid-afternoon weekdays, and the fact I go in between eight and nine every morning is reflective of my commitment.

Or of my obsession.

"Yeah, I think that will work."

I push away from the table and stand up, enjoying the last few bites of my blondie before tossing my plate in her trash can. When I meet her gaze, I offer an honest, "Thank you, Jillian. Truly. I appreciate what you're doing for me, and I'm honored to work out a deal to purchase your desserts for the restaurant. Honestly, I'm a little embarrassed I haven't thought of it before now. I've used the same company from St. Paul since I opened, or I whip something up myself. I want to support another local business."

She stands and offers me a small smile, one that's full of gratitude and makes her eyes shine brighter than emeralds. That one gesture reaches into my pants and caresses my balls.

What?

I mean, Jillian is beautiful, but I've never felt any strong pull toward her.

Yet, seeing her now, casually dressed in the middle of her kitchen while she perfects a recipe for her bakery has me all sorts of confused. Sure, I consider her a friend, but right now, I'm entertaining thoughts that aren't exactly friendly, if you know what I mean.

"Here," she states, walking over to the counter and placing several bars onto a paper plate. She wraps it with paper towel and hands it over. "I'd never be able to eat a whole batch by myself. Well, let's just say I *shouldn't* eat a whole batch by myself." She giggles.

Giggles.

And my balls? They're fucking aching with need.

"Thanks," I reply, needing to turn away so she can't see how the noises she makes affect me.

Jillian follows me to the door and before I can exit, she stops me. "One more thing."

Turning around, I give her my complete attention. It's when I notice a light blush creeps up her neck, staining her fair complexion with a pink hue. "Yes?"

"Umm, so what about..." her words trail off and she closes her eyes. "Gosh, this is embarrassing."

I have a feeling I know where she's going with this, but I wait her out, nonetheless.

"What about *other* relationship stuff?"

"Like?" I have to fight to keep my grin off my face.

"Like kissing and other shows of affection. I mean, if we're in a relationship, people will have to believe it, right? We can't just stand next to each other for a few months and assume everyone believes there's chemistry."

"You don't think we have chemistry?" I ask, taking a slow step toward her.

She lifts her shoulders. "I don't know," she insists, throwing her hands up in the air. "Maybe? It's hard to tell just standing here."

"You're right," I agree, stepping into her personal space. I slide my free hand around the back of her neck and hold on, letting my fingers slip into the silky strands of her dark hair. Bending down, I press my lips to hers gently. The softest gasp slides from her mouth as my tongue delves inside, tasting her for the first time.

I could easily deepen this kiss. This kiss is the preamble to something spectacular. I can feel it. But now isn't the time. The last thing I'd want is to freak her out any more than I already have.

Pulling back, I open my eyes and stare at her lips, swollen from my kiss. "I'd say we're fine on chemistry, Jilly."

She clears her throat and opens her eyes to meet mine, seeming a bit dazed. "Oh, uh, yeah."

I can't stop a playful smirk from crossing my mouth as I stand tall and take my hand from her neck. I'm surprised I didn't drop my blondies in my desire to explore our chemistry. "I'll be in touch, Jilly."

"Bye," she murmurs, her eyes still glossy with lust.

I force my feet to move, walking out of her house and heading toward my SUV. With each step I take, I feel her eyes follow. I don't know if that's a good thing or not. Taking that kiss into consideration, I'd like to think her thoughts are positive, but I did just ask her to lie to everyone she knows for a specific length of time and pretend to be my girlfriend.

She could easily tell me to get fucked.

I hope she doesn't, because I wasn't lying when I said I needed her. I can't see pulling this off with anyone else. I need someone I know and trust, and even though I'm not super close to Jillian, I feel confident in placing my trust in her. We have mutual friends, one couple being Blair and Gabe. I went to school with Gabe and have considered him a friend most of my life. Since she moved to town, I've gotten to know Blair too, and feel like she's good people. That extends to other mutual friends we share.

I'm lost in my thoughts as I drive back to the restaurant. My place is open Wednesday through Friday evenings for dinner and both lunch and dinner on Saturdays and Sundays. I left my sous chef in charge of the kitchen so I could run and speak to Jillian, with the understanding I'd be back to help close. I wasn't sure how long my impromptu meeting with Jillian would go, but I'm pleasantly surprised it took less than an hour to convince her to help me.

Pulling into the alleyway behind the businesses along Main Street, I park in my designated spot beside the back entrance. I climb from my vehicle, grabbing the plate of sweet treats, and make my way inside. The rear entrance is used by employees and for emergencies, so I use my key for access. Immediately, I'm assaulted with the pleasing aroma that comes from my kitchen.

I pass the employee break room and hit my office. The door is locked, as it always is if I'm not in it. The only people who have a key are Marlin, my number two and sous chef, and Veronica, my dining room manager. She's the face of my business, dealing with waitstaff and customers, while Marlin and I try to stay behind the scenes. I'm in constant contact and have control over what happens out front. Veronica has control to a degree, but big decisions are mine.

I try to make appearances when I can out in the dining room too. It's good for business if patrons see me. I always take a few minutes to ask customers how their meal is and thank them for stopping by. I can't always get out there during the highest volume of customers, but I still make an attempt the first chance I get.

Now would be a good time to do that.

It's Sunday evening, so it won't be completely packed. I set my blondies on my desk and head toward the dining room. I offer a smile to the two servers who are busy refilling drinks and delivering plates of food. Spotting Veronica at the hostess stand, I start in her direction, stopping by a couple of tables to greet customers as I go.

"You weren't gone very long," she says when I reach her side. "Couldn't have been that hot of a date."

I snort. "Date. Unless you're referring to the date on a calendar, I'm afraid I don't know what you mean."

She grins, shaking her head. "You know, it wouldn't hurt you to go out every now and again. You can have a life, as well as a successful business."

"I'm well aware," I counter.

"That's why you have Marlin and me," she goes on, her eyes always scanning the room.

"I'm aware." I glance around the room. It's not super busy. Not only is it Sunday evening, but it's also Labor Day weekend to boot. Most are out enjoying the last bit of summer fun they can get before the weather transforms into fall. The locals will still be here, but I'll have a little less out-of-towner foot traffic. "Everything going well out here?"

"Of course it is," she boasts. Veronica runs a tight ship, ensuring excellence to keep the customers happy. "A birdy saw you entering the empty building next door yesterday."

I slowly nod, trying to decide how much to say. Recalling Jillian's request to keep our deal private, I opt to wait to share the news about the potential building purchase until I know more. I guess Mrs. Krokus could still back out, and the last thing I'd want is for people to expect a deal to come down the pipe, but nothing transpires. That's another reason I don't want to take our fake dating relationship public yet, until we know this building sale is truly in the works.

No reason to get everyone all worked up if the deal doesn't work out.

"Just checking it out," I state.

"It would be a great space for extra seating. You could open up the wall between the two and really make it into something special." She meets my gaze. "Not that it's not perfect the way it is, but I know you'd love to have a little more wiggle room in both the dining room and kitchen."

I nod, refusing to take the bait. "There's some salted caramel blondies in my office."

Her eyebrows shoot toward the ceiling. "You take up baking in your spare time?"

"No, Jillian made them."

Her all-knowing eyes feel like laser beams. "Jillian? From Flour Power Bakery?" A Cheshire cat grin spreads across her pink lips. "Really?"

"She was trying new recipes for the bakery, and I was lucky enough to get a sample," I say, hoping that's the end of it.

"A sample. I bet you did," she adds with a whisper.

"Anyway, I'm gonna head back and help Marlin tear down," I state, turning the conversation away from Jillian and back to work.

34

"All right. I think we're done seating new tables, and the last two checks are in the kitchen now."

I lift my chin in acknowledgment and turn to retreat to the kitchen. As I go, I stop by a few more tables and greet the diners, happy to see the townsfolk enjoying their meals. Tonight's special was a sweet and spicy pork chop with mashed red potatoes and fresh asparagus. I spot a few specials in the dining room, which lets me know to keep it in rotation.

Making my way to the kitchen, I nod in greeting to the kitchen staff. Tucker, the dishwasher, is busy loading up the machine with dirty dishes and silverware, and Marlin is finishing up the last dinner plates before sending them out with the server.

"Hey, boss."

"Evening," I reply to the only other man I trust to run my kitchen.

"Been somewhat steady since you left, considering it's a holiday weekend," he says, tapping the bell to call the server.

"That's good. You never know how these weekends will turn out."

I nod in agreement. "I'll be in my office for a bit. Holler if you need me."

"Will do," he replies, turning his attention back to his work.

The thing is, I know he won't holler. He doesn't need help. Even if the place was jam-packed, he still wouldn't ask for assistance. Marlin is cool under pressure and gets the job done. He's an incredible asset to Prime Steak House. Honestly, I'm surprised he's still here and hasn't been scooped up by some big Michelin star restaurant. I've told him as much, but he swears he's happy here. He prefers the slower pace of our small town, and as long as he's content, I'm good.

The first thing I see when I enter my office is the plate of blondies. I want another, but I've already had two. Instead, I'll save them for the staff when they're closing down the restaurant.

My mind goes to Jillian. Beautiful Jillian with the bee-stung lips that taste like sugar. I wasn't lying when I said we had chemistry. We have it in spades, and all I want to do is explore it a little more. More kisses. More...everything.

But I need to keep a clear head. We're in an unofficial business arrangement, and that's the way it needs to stay. Sure, I can enjoy the kisses and any other PDA we engage in, but that's it. That's where I draw the line. I have to keep the personal and the business aspect separate. Shouldn't be too hard, really.

Liar.

CHAPTER
Three

Jillian

By Wednesday morning, I'm having a nervous breakdown. Even Lisa, my weekday part-time employee, has noticed. She's watching me, waiting for the moment I completely meltdown.

Why, you ask?

Because I can't stop thinking about the kiss.

Oh, and the fact I'm about to lie to everyone I know and love. But also the kiss.

It consumes my every thought, both waking and not.

So much so my vibrator is getting a workout. In just three short nights, I've used that bad boy five times, and I still feel unsatisfied. I'm starting to wonder how I'm going to survive fake dating this man, to be honest. He seems to set my nerve endings on fire. Not to mention what he does to my panties.

I toss the burnt cookies into the trash and prepare to start over. Cookies are a huge hit for my business, especially after the breakfast crowd winds down. Not only are they easy to make, but they're also great for grab and go. Offices will pick up a dozen for staff, or those having lunch at the Mexican restaurant or diner will stop by on their way back to work and pick up an afternoon snack.

I'm mad at myself. I was so distracted, thinking about the kiss I have no business thinking about, I forgot to set my timer. I *never* forget to set my timer. Ever. It's one of the main steps in preparing baked goods.

Grabbing the dry ingredients, I start to prepare another batch. Just as I'm tossing chocolate chips into the bowl, I hear, "Jillian, you have a visitor."

I glance up and find Lisa standing in the doorway separating the front of the bakery from the kitchen. "What?"

She steps aside, awarding me sight of the man standing off to the side of the counter. Kameron is looking at me over Lisa's shoulder, holding a steaming cup of coffee.

"Oh, uh, he can come back," I say, my brain scrambled the moment I spot him standing there.

She grins and wiggles her eyebrows. "Go ahead and go on back," she says to Kameron, blatantly checking out his ass as he passes by. She meets my gaze and mouths "Oh my God!" before returning behind the counter to help customers.

Kameron slowly approaches, glancing into the trash bin beside the island workstation in the middle of the kitchen. "Problem?"

I huff. "Even cookies come out bad every now and again." I refuse to tell him the real reason for my cookie flop.

"I can understand that," he states, leaning against the island and sipping his coffee. My eyes are drawn to his free hand, how big it is sitting casually on top of the stainless-steel island. His fingers look strong and deft, and I can imagine him using them for...*other* things. Inappropriate things.

"What brings you by?" I ask, my heart hammering in my chest. I'm usually a pretty calm and collected woman, but being around him since the kiss is messing with me.

"Well, I was thinking last night," he starts.

Sure, he was thinking, while I was masturbating...

"I wanted to see if you were available for dinner tonight."

My heart? It literally stops beating in my chest. I fully expect to drop dead any moment from shock. "Really?"

He nods, taking another sip of coffee. "I have to work, but Marlin can man the grill for a bit while we talk."

Talk. Right.

"Sure, that sounds fine," I reply with a bit too much pep. I sound like I just downed a few shots of espresso.

"I figured we need to just discuss our lives a bit more, you know? We have to make this believable, so I need to know more about you," he reasons.

"That makes sense," I agree.

"Okay, good. What time do you want to eat?"

"Umm, well, I usually eat a little on the early side, since I go to bed around eight."

His eyes widen. "Eight? At night?"

"Well, I don't go to bed at eight in the morning," I retort, unable to hide my sarcasm or my grin.

Kameron shakes his head and laughs. "Yeah, that was a stupid question. It just surprised me. My restaurant is still going strong at eight."

It's probably the first time either of us has truly considered the differences in our businesses. While we are similar in certain areas, we're worlds apart in what we offer on the menu and the hours we keep. Fake dating this man might be more complicated than I originally expected.

"Well, you know what they say, opposites attract," he adds with an uncomfortable chuckle. Clearly he's noticing one glaring difference in our businesses too. It might be hard to date someone— even fake dating—when the hours he's available are night and day different than when I am.

"It's only for a short time though, so I'm sure it'll be fine. We really only have to convince them we're together for a few weeks or months, right? We can easily stay in the getting to know each other phase."

He nods in understanding. "I think you're right. Anyway, what time would you like to eat tonight? And do you have any dislikes or allergies?"

"Not really. I've eaten at your restaurant before, and I don't think there was anything on the menu I wouldn't eat. Except fish. I don't mind shrimp, but I'm not a huge fish girl."

The corner of his mouth curls up in a smirk. "You haven't had any of my fish. I assure you; you'd like it."

Something tells me I'd like anything he placed in front of me.

"I'll steer clear of fish for tonight, but one of these days, I'll make you some of my specialties," he states proudly, as if knowing I'll like them over any previous fish dish I've ever tried. "You pick the time."

"Is five too early or inconvenient?" I ask.

"No, that's fine. We'll start to pick up a bit around six, but since it's off-season now, it won't be too bad. Marlin can handle it in my absence."

"All right, five it is."

"I'll tell Veronica to expect you."

"Sounds good," I say, reaching for the bowl to mix the ingredients together.

"Too bad I wasn't a little later, huh? I could have stolen one of those cookies on my way out," he says with a playful grin and a wink. "Have a good day, Jilly."

"Bye." I admit, when he turns around and walks out of my kitchen, my eyes land firmly on his ass. It's a phenomenal rear end, one you could probably bounce a quarter off. Unlike mine, which has a little extra jiggle, thanks to all the dessert sampling I do.

Lisa comes scurrying back here the moment Kameron exits the building. "Please tell me that was personal," she murmurs with a wicked glint in her eyes.

I shrug, not wanting to get into it right now, but know I'll have to start the lie at some point. "We've been...talking." That was the best way to describe it.

"Good for you. Any man who can cook the way he can moves right to the top of the list."

I don't comment, just keep my focus on my cookies so I can get them in the display case. It won't be long and customers will be stopping in, looking for them.

"Oh, there's someone else here to see you," she says, grabbing my attention once more.

"Really?"

Two visitors in one day? That's unheard of for me.

"Yeah, some guy named George Riley. Not as good looking as Kameron, but he's wearing a suit and has that intense banker appearance," Lisa says with a shrug.

Grabbing a hand towel, I wipe off my hands. "What the hell is an intense banker appearance?" I ask.

That question seems to stump her a bit. "I'm not sure. Maybe not so constipated?"

I roll my eyes. "I really only know one banker, and that's Mr. Jefferson." His family has owned the local bank since it started in the nineteen fifties. I think his grandson is one of the loan officers now, and his son vice president.

"Me too," she concedes. "Anyway, George Riley's out here for you."

I nod and follow her out of the kitchen. The man standing at the counter isn't anything like Kameron. Where Kameron has that tall, dark, and handsome thing down pat, George is anything but. He's not nerdy per se, but he definitely screams office guy. Lisa's right, he screams banker in his gray department store suit and red tie with what appears to be a stain on it.

"Miss Kirby, I take it?" he asks, pushing his glasses up on his nose and offering me his hand.

"Yes."

"I'm George Riley."

I wait a few seconds, hoping he gives me a little more information other than his name.

"Your parents didn't tell you I was stopping by?"

My parents?

"Uhh, no, they didn't. Is everything all right?"

"Oh, yes. We go to church together," he offers in way of explanation. He glances around. "Would you like to sit?"

I turn toward the front windows, to the small bistro tables, which are empty. "Sure," I reply, heading over to the farthest table. If I'm about to have bad news delivered, I don't want an audience.

"This place is cute," he says after taking a seat across from me.

"Thanks." I still have no clue what he's doing here, but I don't have a good feeling.

"Well, if your parents didn't mention I was stopping by, this is probably a little awkward for you."

I swallow hard and knot my fingers together on my lap. "A little."

"Your parents thought we should meet."

I feel my mouth fall open and dread fill my entire being. "My parents?" I whisper, knowing what's to come, but praying I'm wrong.

He gives me a sheepish grin and shrugs. "I'm their accountant. They wanted me to stop by and meet you, said you'd be expecting me. They offered a coffee date."

My eyes are about to pop out of my head. "A date? But I'm working."

He shrugs. "They said you'd be willing to take a break for a bit. I apologize if this is blindsiding you."

My mouth resembles a fish out of water. I don't know what to say, what to do. My parents sent a strange man into my business for a…date? When they were talking Sunday about setting me up, pushing for the whole marriage and grandkids thing, I never really expected them to follow through with their suggestions. Believe me, they've offered lists of available, single men in both Pine Village and neighboring Hudson in the past, and now here we are.

Sitting right smack-dab across from George, their accountant.

"Umm, listen," I start, trying to figure out how to let him down easy. "I appreciate you taking the time to come in and see me."

He gives me a small, slightly uncomfortable grin. "I feel a but coming…"

"*But*," I start, my brain spinning. Sure, I can tell him I'm just not interested. While he appears to be a decent-looking guy, he doesn't exactly *do it* for me. I'm not attracted to him, and even if I was, I don't want to be set up by my parents.

How embarrassing…

Kameron pops into my mind. Oh, I'm very much attracted to the gorgeous chef, and it hits me like a ton of bricks to the abdomen, I have an out. One I probably never would have used until today. "Actually, George, I'm seeing someone."

His face falls. "Oh. Your parents didn't tell me that," he insists, taking a sip of his coffee.

"It's new," I quickly reassure him. "We haven't really gone public with it, which is why I haven't said anything to my parents about him."

He watches me, probably trying to gauge my sincerity where my sudden boyfriend is concerned. If I were in his shoes, I probably wouldn't believe it either. It looks too convenient, too made up.

Clearing his throat, he nods. "I understand." He takes a longer sip of his coffee before averting his gaze. "I'm sorry to have bothered you while you're working."

"It's okay," I reply politely. "I'm sorry you made a wasted trip here."

He shrugs and gives me a sheepish grin. "I don't know if it was wasted. I get to enjoy an excellent cup of coffee and sit with a pretty lady for a bit."

I give him a genuine smile.

"And as amazing as your parents said your pastries are, I'm definitely going to indulge a little and grab some to-go. My assistant will appreciate the sweet treat."

I can't help but smile wider at his polite regard for his assistant. "Does she have a favorite? I'd be happy to box up a few things for you."

We stand up and make our way to the counter. George looks over today's offerings and selects a small variety of four pastries. "They all look delicious," he says as I slide the small white box over the counter.

"All made fresh this morning," I boast, even though he didn't ask. It's one of my big selling points at Flour Power. Nothing is carried over and sold the next day. All freshly baked with only the best ingredients.

"How much?" he asks, taking the offered box.

I wave my hand. "It's on me."

"Oh, no, I insist," he pushes, pulling his wallet from the back of his pressed slacks.

"Really. An apology, of sorts, for the confusion today." I rock back on my heels, needing the movement to keep myself occupied.

"Well, thank you," he starts, glancing around the bakery. There are two women and a small child not too far away, enjoying cinnamon rolls and coffee drinks. Leaning over the counter, he adds, "I was hoping for a second date, but I suppose the pastries are a solid trade-off."

I give an uncomfortable chuckle. "I'm glad you think so."

He shrugs and turns to leave. "Oh, one more thing. Who does your taxes?"

"My—"

"Your taxes," he says, slipping something from his pocket and setting it on the counter. "If you're ever looking to switch accountants, my office is in Hudson." With that, he turns and leaves the bakery.

And I'm standing here completely flabbergasted.

"What was that?" Lisa asks, standing directly to my left.

I sigh and shake my head. "My parents."

She looks baffled as she looks from me to the front door. "I don't understand."

"My parents sent him. Like...for a date. A coffee date."

Her eyes widen like saucers as her mouth falls open. "What? Are you serious?"

"Yep," I insist, popping the P. "Apparently, they made good on their promise to find me an eligible bachelor to date. That was George, an accountant from Hudson," I state, holding up the business card. "Of course, my parents conveniently forgot to tell me they were sending someone by, so I was completely caught off guard."

"Oh my God," Lisa bellows, covering her mouth with her hand. "You're serious?"

"As a heart attack."

"That's messed up," Lisa says, glancing at her watch.

I sigh, worrying about the conversation I would now have to have with my parents. I had hoped what I said on Sunday would get through to them, but apparently not. I don't want them to set me up. I want them to respect my decisions and not project their wants onto me. They *want* to see me married. They *want* grandkids. They're tired of waiting for me to achieve this on my own, so they're sending "dates" to my place of business.

"I need to get the cookies finished," I state as the bell chimes over the door, alerting us to an arriving customer.

"Go. I'll handle up here," she says, turning her attention to the group of four ladies approaching the counter.

I return to the kitchen and wash my hands. My mind is spinning as I grab the bowl of dry ingredients and add the wet. Once it's all inside the bowl, I place it under my big mixer and start the machine. Retrieving a fresh baking pan, I prep it for the cookie dough.

Maybe this deal with Kameron isn't such a terrible thing after all. I mean, I knew I'd be able to use it to my advantage where my parents are concerned, but now it's more blatantly obvious. I need him as much as he needs me. Not only will I get a contract to provide the desserts to his restaurant moving forward, but he'll be able to get my parents off my back, even for just a short time.

A very welcomed short time.

I hate the idea of lying, but if it keeps random dudes from showing up at my bakery for a "date," well, then so be it.

A girl's gotta do what a girl's gotta do.

CHAPTER *four*

KAMERON

"Kam, your guest is here."

I glance up from the grill, ignoring Veronica's wide grin, and nod. "I'll be right there."

"I'll send Nicholas over to get her a drink," Veronica says before exiting the kitchen and returning to the dining room.

I put the finishing touches on dinner before plating our entrées and adding the sides. "You got this?" I ask Marlin, who just rolls his eyes.

"Does a bear shit in the woods?" he asks, practically pushing me out of the way to work on another order.

"I assume so, but I've never witnessed it," I tell him, placing both plates on a tray. Before I go anywhere, I wash my hands well. I also take a moment to check over my appearance in the mirror above the sink. There have been plenty of times where we have a splatter of this or a swipe of that across our faces. We try not to touch anything, especially our skin, while cooking, but splatter happens.

"I'll be in the dining room," I tell him, retrieving the tray.

"Is she pretty?" he asks, waggling his eyebrows.

Now it's my turn to offer an eye roll. "Stop being a Nosy Nelly."

He barks out a laugh. "You haven't had a date in two years, and I'm not supposed to be nosy? Get the hell out of here."

Shaking my head, I ignore any further comments and head for the dining room. Jillian is sitting in the back corner, a small four-person table offering the most privacy. I figured this way we'd be able to talk openly without having people walk past every two seconds and overhearing. And since I'm actually sharing a meal with someone of the opposite sex, people will be curious, especially my employees.

The first thing I notice as I approach the table is how pretty she looks. Her dark hair is both up and down, with the top half pulled back to keep it out of her face. She's wearing blue jean capris and a fitted black shirt that accentuates her curves, and her feet are covered in some sort of strappy sandal. Even in the dim lighting of the restaurant, I can see the light purple coloring on her toenails. I never really thought of why women are so obsessed with painting their nails, but when I see her light purple ones, I get the appeal. In my world, toes aren't anything I ever want to see, but right now, I kinda want to see them wrapped around my neck as I do inappropriate—and very pleasurable—things to her body.

Clearing my throat as I reach the table, I offer a brief, "Good evening."

"Hi," she replies, almost shyly. Her green eyes move to the tray I'm carrying, and she adds, "Oh my heavens, that smells amazing."

"Well, I hope it tastes as good as it smells." I place the first plate down in front of her and the second at the other seat.

"Here you are, Jillian," Nicholas says as he places a glass of red wine in front of her. "Can I get you a drink, boss?"

"I'll have what she's having," I reply, even though I don't usually drink while on the clock. But I'm the first one to admit when food and wine pairings are on point, the flavors of both are enhanced.

Nicholas nods, returning to the wine bar to retrieve my requested glass.

"What are we eating?" she asks as I take the empty seat across from her.

"This is steak au poivre with roasted red potatoes and steamed green beans. I took a chance that you'd be comfortable with that. The steak is medium to medium well, so if you'd like me to grill it just a bit longer, I can do so. You can always add more time on the grill, but you can't take it back. If I don't know someone's preference, I stick to a medium cook."

"That's perfect, actually," she replies, reaching for her fork and knife.

She slices into the cut of meat easily, which is one of the most important aspects of cooking. If the meat isn't a good cut, it doesn't matter how amazing the recipe is. I watch, waiting for her to take her first bite. The fact she doesn't think twice to eat what I put in front of her is a huge turn-on. I know food, and she trusts me enough to not ask many questions. It's as if she knows her food is going to be exquisite.

Dipping the tip of her steak into the cream sauce, she takes a bite. "Oh my God," she sings, covering her mouth with her napkin since she's still chewing. Her eyes light up as the flavors hit her taste buds. She's practically grinning as she chews and swallows.

I preen at her praise.

She takes a sip of her red wine. "What is it? The au poivre?"

Placing my own napkin in my lap, I reach for my silverware to slice into my own meat. "It's French. It's a fresh peppercorn cream sauce made with cognac and cream. The key is to keep the peppercorn from becoming overpowering. You want it to flavor the meat and the sauce but not become the main ingredient. You want it to enhance the flavor."

She stabs a piece of green bean with her fork and brings it to her mouth. "I think you accomplished that feat."

"It took time to perfect the recipe, but it's one of our most popular dishes."

"I can see why," she states.

Nicholas delivers my wine and tops off Jillian's water glass. "Anything else I can get you two?"

I glance to Jillian, who shakes her head. "I think we're set, Nicholas, thank you."

He nods before heading off to another table.

"How was your day?" I ask, finding I truly want to hear the answer.

"It was good. I always enjoy the slower times after the busier tourist seasons, but it can be hard to adjust to making less product again."

I nod, stabbing a piece of steak with my fork. "I understand that. I have to cut back on what I order, which does take some adjustment."

"But you have a solid business. Even in the off-season, your parking lot is always full."

The corners of my mouth curl up. "It's taken some time, but yes, I have built a solid foundation. The first few years were harder, that's for sure. But the people of Pine Village and surrounding towns have found the value in a nice sit-down restaurant. The diner is great for comfort, homecooked food, usually when you're on the go or have limited time. Same with the Mexican restaurant. Everyone loves tacos. Hell, I love them. I frequent both establishments too. My steak house is a step above those. The meals more gourmet, the dining experience classier. And the menu has been tailored to offer staples, like prime rib and filet mignon to other dishes that force a diner to step outside of their normal comfort zone."

"Like steak au poivre," she says, smiling.

"Exactly."

"But you still offer other things besides steak. I've had your stuffed chicken breast and honey-glazed pork chops before."

I nod. "I do. Not everyone likes beef, so even though this is a steak house, and most of what I offer is beef-related, it's important to have other choices too. Just no cheeseburgers. You wouldn't believe how many times I get asked if I can whip one up real fast."

Her eyes sparkle like emeralds as she laughs. "Really? I'd never ask for something not on the menu."

I shrug. "I get it. The request is usually coming from someone under the age of sixteen."

"Well, I think you have a great place here. The menu has a wonderful variety, and the food's exquisite," she says, taking another bite of her steak. "I've never had something I haven't thoroughly enjoyed."

"Thank you."

She glances around, noticing how the restaurant is starting to fill up. We only have twelve tables available, thanks to the smaller building. Most tables are for parties of four, but there are a couple of two and six-seater tables. We can comfortably seat a party of twelve together, but it really cuts into the open space. In the summer or winter, when traffic is heavy with tourists, we can fill up quickly and that's why this potential building expansion is so important to me.

Leaning forward, she drops her voice as she says, "I can see why you want the building next door."

"If I kept this space for the rest of time I owned the restaurant, I would be content. But, I can admit, I want more. I can still grow this business without it becoming overwhelming. Adding the building next door would double our potential seating. Friday and Saturday nights, we wouldn't have to turn away customers because we're full."

"That's a good problem to have," she says with a little giggle, cutting into a roasted potato.

"It is, but I always feel bad. Especially when the dining room is full of out-of-towners, and someone local is trying to get in. That's why we always recommend reservations during the busy season. Summer isn't quite as packed as the winter months, especially with people grilling out all the time, but they do finally get tired of burgers and dogs over the open fire and come into town for something different."

She nods in agreement. "Same. I have to count on those people getting tired of their eggs and coffee at the campgrounds and venturing into town for some of my pastries and gourmet coffee options."

"See? We're not so different after all," I reply, holding her gaze.

We sit in comfortable silence for a minute, both enjoying the food in front of us. I find Jillian's company quite pleasant, even if we're not filling every second of the time with words. Unfortunately, there was a reason I invited her to join me, and we should get to it. Now that the restaurant is picking up, I don't want to leave Marlin alone for too long, and I know Jillian can't stay all night, talking.

Clearing my throat, I say, "One of the reasons I invited you here was to get to know you a little better, but also to discuss Sunday."

Jillian seems to sit up a little straighter in her seat as she reaches for her wine and takes a hearty sip. "Right."

"I know a little bit about you, since we both grew up here. I know about your business, and I think we can easily say that's one of the draws we have to each other. We both understand what it takes to make a successful go of it, even if our businesses are different."

"Agreed," she says, abandoning her fork. I can tell this conversation makes her uncomfortable, but what I'm not sure of is if it's simply because it centers around a lie or if she has things she'd rather not discuss. Either way, I get it. I'm not exactly looking forward to telling her about my past, especially since no one knows about it. I'm taking a huge step forward on the trust scale by sharing it, but I do feel it's necessary. In order to make it believable, I feel we should both know all the details.

Eventually.

I'm not saying we have to know each other's biggest, darkest secrets right this moment, but as the relationship progresses—fake or otherwise—there will be things we'll have to discuss, because it would be natural that a boyfriend would know his girlfriend's dating history. And vice versa.

"I think we have a little bit of a grace period in the beginning. The fact we would only know the basics wouldn't be too far-fetched. We're getting to know each other, right?"

"Right," she agrees, nodding her head insistently.

"One of the things we should talk about is affection."

She swallows hard. "Affection."

"Yeah, you know, hand-holding and touching. I don't want to make you uncomfortable, but I think there should be some sort of touching if we're dating. We've already proven the chemistry is there, but I may reach over and take your hand or brush your hair off your shoulder, and I wouldn't want you to flinch."

She takes a deep breath. "I can do this."

I can't help but crack a smile. "Are you talking to me or yourself?"

She grins and shakes her head. "Both, maybe? I'm not worried about you touching me, Kameron. Not in the sense you mean."

"No? Then what are you worried about?"

I don't miss the way her cheeks turn pink in the cutest blush. The same thing happened after the kiss we shared, and I'll be damned if I don't start to get hard. All I want to do is kiss her again, and that's probably the last thing I should do.

She exhales and takes another sip of her wine, as if she needs the liquid courage to get this part out. When she sets her glass back down on the table, she leans in a bit and meets my gaze. "I'm comfortable with you, Kam. Maybe a little *too* comfortable."

"What does that mean?" I ask, wanting a sip of wine, but not wanting to take my eyes off this woman for a single second.

"I liked you kissing me. Maybe a little too much." That blush? Oh, it's a deep crimson shade that spreads down to her chest, to the hint of cleavage I see at the V-neck of her shirt. "I'm fine with you holding my hand or brushing my hair off my shoulder, Kameron, but you need to be ready for my reaction."

My mouth goes dry, and my balls start to ache. "You're reaction? Do tell, Jilly," I whisper, leaning closer.

"I'll probably want to touch you too, maybe run my fingers through your hair. I'm a reactive person. I like to touch and be touched. Even if it's for show, I'm a touchy-feely girl, so you should probably be ready too."

She's a damn black widow spider, and I'm trapped in her web, lost in the sea of her green eyes and full pink lips. I want to taste the wine on her tongue and feel the heat of her touch, even though I know I'll get bitten.

"Chemistry," I murmur, replaying that kiss for the ten-thousandth time.

She shrugs and gives me a coy little grin. "It's there, Kameron, but I also understand what this is. It's a business agreement, right? So chemistry or not, we have an expiration date."

I can't stop my smirk. "So, let me get this straight. We have chemistry, and you're okay with me casually touching you, holding your hand, and maybe kissing you during the duration of our fake relationship. Not only are you okay with it, but you will reciprocate and be just as affectionate."

She nods. "Correct."

"Sign me up, darlin', because the next few months are going to be pretty interesting."

She pushes her plate aside and finishes off her wine. "If I'm being completely honest here, I have to put a little bit of my heart into this. I'm not saying that to freak you out, but it still bothers me that the whole thing is a lie." She holds up her hands when my mouth opens. "I understand why, and I'm okay with it. But, if I'm going to play a part, I have to put a bit of heart into it. That's how I acted in school. I'm looking at this role like any other I've had." She drops both hands onto her lap, and her shoulders look tense.

I can't help but reach under the table and take her left hand. Her skin is soft as I entwine my fingers with hers, and I didn't feel her flinch or jump at the contact. It's just as she said. She's okay with me touching her, even if she's looking at this professionally. "I can respect that, Jillian."

And I can. I'm glad she's honest and upfront, and it makes me like and appreciate her even more than I did before.

As a friend, of course.

I might have to remind myself of that every now and again, but I could easily see why a man could fall for a woman like Jillian Kirby.

For real.

She's gorgeous, hardworking, and driven, loyal to her friends and family, and kisses like you're the very air she needs to breathe. She's the breath of fresh air I didn't realize I needed in my life.

Yeah, she's not the only one who needs to remember this relationship is fake.

I haven't had many relationships since returning to Pine Village, mostly because I don't have the time. My schedule is crazy and even though my restaurant is only open five days a week, it's still a huge commitment. There's so much more to it than just grilling some steaks and steaming some vegetables. Women I've tried dating in the past don't see past the superficial of owning a steak house. They want a man who's present and available, and for me, that's hard.

But Jillian gets it. She's just as committed to her bakery. She works long hours six days a week, including getting up way before the birds because that's what it takes to make her business work. Yeah, I have mad respect for this woman, and I look forward to getting to know her better.

"Good," she replies, releasing a long breath and squeezing my hand. "Now that's settled, what's for dessert?"

CHAPTER
five

Jillian

"Excuse me, what's this I hear about you having dinner with Kameron?"

I sigh into the phone. I shouldn't be surprised to be receiving this call, but I am a little shocked it took almost twenty-four whole hours to get it. The Pine Village grapevine is legendary for its swift action in spreading any sort of gossip, and why I thought I would be immune is beyond me.

"It was just dinner," I insist to my newest friend, Ryan Marcotte. Ryan and I met earlier this summer, when she rented Marcus's cabin for a month-long getaway. Turns out, Ryan is *the* Ryan Marcotte from the popular TV show *Ryan's Reality*. Plus, she has her own YouTube channel and makeup line.

But that's not why we love her. She's a great friend. While she was hiding away in the woods, we got to know the real Ryan, not the one the media portrays or the one she pretends to be on television. She's sassy, yes, but so kind and caring. We've really gotten to know her over the last few months, and I'm so glad she's here to stay. Very recently, she moved in with her boyfriend, Marcus, who owns the auto repair shop in town, and she's running her business and making YouTube videos from here.

"I had *just dinner* with Marcus once. There was sex, Jillian. Lots of sex."

I roll my eyes, even though she can't see it. "Stop it. We're friends," I insist, adjusting the phone on my shoulder while I start the dishwasher.

"Mmhmm," she sings.

Then I think about the lie we're about to tell, and I know I can't keep this "friends" façade in place too much longer. In a matter of days, it'll be all over town that Kameron and I are dating.

Clearing my throat, I decide to stick to the truth as much as I possibly can. That's the only way I'll get through this. "He's...cute."

"Uhh, yeah! He has that whole smoldering intensity thing going, but with an easy smile. He's like The Rock in that *Jumanji* remake. It's practically one of Kameron's superpowers!" she proclaims, yelling into the phone.

"Lord, woman, chill out. All I said was he's cute."

"And you'd be right. But I also caught the underlying words you didn't say."

"And those would be?" I ask, almost afraid to hear the answer.

"That you *love* him and want to make babies!"

I laugh. Hard. "You're nuts."

"Yeah, that's true," she agrees easily with a giggle. "Listen, Jillian, I don't know him well, but he seems like a nice guy. Marcus talks highly of him, so I put a lot of stock into that. Marcus doesn't like many people. All I'm saying is if you want to date him, you should."

"I'll take that under consideration," I reply with a small smile. I'm glad my friends approve.

"I think you should do one of those dating profiles."

"What?" I bark out a laugh. "I'm not doing online dating."

"Why not?"

"Because it's…"

Embarrassing?

Not necessary?

How do I answer that?

"I get it," she replies without me actually giving an answer. "It's not for everyone."

"Says the woman who has a ton of online presence," I tease.

"Yeah, but that's different. My face is all over social media, but not in regard to dating. Though, I've had plenty of guys—and a few girls—slide into my DMs. And I'm pretty sure I've been catfished a few times too. My face shows up on dating profiles, but it's not actually me."

"That's…creepy."

"Totally. I don't even check my direct messages anymore. There are a fuck ton of weirdos out there, Jillian."

I snort. "And yet, you thought I should give online dating a try," I reply dryly.

"Only if you wanted to. Some people find forever love on those sites."

"Very true, but I won't be one of them. Besides, who needs online dating when your parents just send you eligible bachelors to your place of business."

I'm met with silence.

After a few very long seconds, she finally asks, "Are you serious?"

"Unfortunately," I grumble. "My parents—I love them—but they, well, they're ready to be grandparents, and I think they believe if they send me single men, I'll fall madly in love with one of them and start popping out grandbabies."

"Wow, that—"

"Yep," I reply, popping the P. "I don't know if you knew this or not, but I was married before," I say, taking a seat on my couch and getting comfortable. Even though my other friends know, I've not had this conversation with Ryan, so I expect she's going to want to hear all the dirty details.

"Tell me," she encourages.

"You sure you have time for this story?" I ask.

"Yes. Marcus is on a tow call, so it's just me and Buddy here. I'll put you on speaker, so he can hear too. He loves it when he's included on phone calls."

I blink slowly, gauging her seriousness. "Umm, okay."

"You're on speaker. Say hi to Buddy!"

"Hi, Buddy," I greet Marcus's rescue dog.

"His tail is wagging. He says hello. Now go on."

"All right, anyway, I was married in my mid-twenties, but it only lasted about nine months."

"Really? Why? Did he cheat? Was he a dirty, lying cheater who slept with your best friend?"

"What? No."

"Oh. Good."

"You watch too much reality TV," I insist.

"Yeah, it's probably the fact I grew up around all that drama. Sorry. Go on."

"His name was Davis, and we met while I was working as a receptionist at a medical office in Hudson."

"You worked as a receptionist at a medical office?" she asks, genuinely surprised.

"I've pretty much worked everywhere," I tell her. "I didn't really like school, and never really knew what I wanted to do with my life, so I did it all. Anyway, he worked at the insurance agency next door, and we'd see each other all the time on the sidewalk and at the deli right down the block. We started talking, and eventually, dating."

"Okay, seems normal so far. Then what happened?"

"We seemed to have a lot in common and dated for about a year and a half when he proposed. I accepted, and we were married almost a year later. I never once pushed him for a baby. He knew my dreams were to eventually become a mother. We had discussed it before we ever got married, but almost nine months into our marriage, he decided he didn't want kids."

"Shut the front door," she proclaims, earning a bark from Buddy. "See? Even Buddy says that's bullshit."

I can't help but smile. "I wanted to discuss it, but it was useless. He—*and I quote*— changed his mind. That was that."

"How do you change your mind?" she asks, almost absently, as if she's trying to understand.

"He thought the urge to become a father would magically appear after we were married. It was the most logical next step, right? But it never happened, and the longer we were together, the stronger his desire to *not* become a dad grew."

"Wow."

"Yeah. So, he moved back to Hudson, and I stayed in Pine Village in our house. I ended up quitting my job over there, since I really didn't want to run into him all the time and found one here."

"When did you open your bakery?"

"It'll be five years this December."

"I'm so proud of you," she says. I can hear the smile in her voice.

My throat is suddenly dry, and it's hard to swallow over the lump. "You are? Why?"

"Because you didn't back down from one dream, even if it meant starting over. And then you put on your sassy big girl panties and went after your other dream. You're a total badass, Jillian Kirby."

A smile spreads across my face. "I am?"

"Totally. That Davis guy doesn't know what he's missing, but lucky for you, that just means he's out of the way so you can date hotties in the area. Like Kameron."

A snicker slips past my lips. "We'll see."

"Yeah, we will see. So, you were married once before, dangled the grandbaby carrot in front of your parents' faces, and then ripped it away. That's not your fault, you know."

I sigh. "Yeah, I know, but they're getting anxious, and since they think I can't find a man on my own, they've decided to send them to the bakery. Their first attempt at insta-love was their accountant."

"Oh my God," she replies with a groan. "That's embarrassing."

"It really was. I think he was too, since my parents conveniently forgot to mention it to me. So there we both were, sitting there in awkward silence, trying to figure out what to say."

"Did you tell your parents not to do that again?"

"I still have to make that call. I've been avoiding it."

"Well, you better unavoid it, or they'll send bachelor number two down to your bakery."

"That's not a word."

"Bakery? Of course it is," she states.

"Unavoid. It's not a word."

"Well, it should be," she insists with a huff. "And quit deflecting. Call them and tell them to stop it. If my parents did that, I...well, I don't know what I'd do. I mean, my parents *did* help Marcus get to LA and surprise me at my party."

"That's because he was in love with you. It wasn't some random dude they were trying to set you up with."

"Yeah, you're right. Still, you need to tell them to stop."

I exhale and close my eyes, picturing that awkward conversation. "You're right."

"Of course I am." I hear Buddy bark, his nails hitting the floor as he takes off running. "Marcus is home, so I'll let you go. Oh, before I forget, I'm coming by tomorrow morning. I'm doing a video for my YouTube channel, and I want to get an iced coffee drink. I'll have it on my desk, logo to the camera. It's visual advertising, my friend."

My eyes fill with tears at what she's doing for me. "You don't have to do that."

"Yes, I do. I mean, all these people are flocking to town because of me, so they might as well stop by and support you while they're here."

"Thank you," I whisper, overcome with emotions.

"Hey, princess," I hear as the screened door opens and closes through the phone line.

"Welcome home," she greets, the happiness evident in her voice. It's followed by the sound of a kiss, one that goes on longer than it should in the presence of a phone friend.

"Excuse me, stop making out while you're on the phone!" I holler, earning a chuckle and a giggle.

"Then, get off the phone," Marcus retorts good-heartedly.

"Uhh, done, because now I have to go shove Q-tips in my eardrums to try to strip away your little make-out session," I grumble, just giving them a hard time. Not that I want to listen to my friend and her boyfriend welcome each other home with some tongue action, but I am happy for her, so my complaints are more for show.

"See you tomorrow, Jillian. Oh, and call your parents."

"I will. See you tomorrow," I reply, hanging up the phone and dropping it onto the couch cushion beside me.

I don't bother turning on the TV. I rarely watch it, and since it's already pushing seven, it won't be long before I'm heading off to bed. Four a.m. comes awfully early, even when you're used to it. That's probably why sleeping in for me is pushing it until five.

My parents are also early risers, which means it won't be long and they'll be preparing for bed too. They don't quite get up as early as me, but they both enjoy their first cup of coffee around six.

I delay the inevitable for a few more minutes and get up to refill my water. I have several of those fancy tumblers that keep your water cold all day. They come in a variety of colors and designs, and when I have pretty cups, I'm more apt to use them. These fancy cups keep my kidneys flushed and me from drinking iced coffee all day.

Which is a shame, because iced coffee is so damn good.

Once my tumbler is full, I take a few long drinks and return to the couch. I grab my phone, but I don't sit. Instead, I stand in the middle of the room and move. I don't pace—at least not yet—but I always have all this extra energy when I'm nervous. I shift from side to side, tap my feet, and, if I'm sitting, bounce my leg uncontrollably. I can practically feel the jitters coming on.

I grab my phone and press the first number in my favorites. It rings twice before my mom answers.

"Well, good evening, Jillian."

"Hi, Mom. How's it going?"

She sighs. "We were watching television."

"Sorry to interrupt," I reply, the weight of this conversation sitting firmly on my chest. "Listen, I won't take much of your time, but there's something I need to discuss with you."

"Oh? Does it have to do with George and the fact you practically ran him out of the bakery yesterday?"

I close my eyes and count to three. "Mom, I didn't run him out. Our conversation was brief, but over. You shouldn't have sent him there without telling me."

"Well, I knew what you'd say if I mentioned it."

"You're right, I would have declined the offer. Just like I did at dinner on Sunday," I tell her, starting to pace.

"You never date, Jillian. All we were doing was—"

"I know what you were doing, and I appreciate it," I state, interrupting her. I'm not usually so rude, but I have things to say, and I need to get them out. "I love you guys, but my life is just that. Mine. I don't need dating advice or random men sent to my place of business. I'm perfectly capable of finding my own dates, ones I'm actually attracted to and want to spend time with."

"Well, of course you're capable, but you don't seem to be in any hurry."

"No, Mom, I'm not. I've spent the past five years working my tail off and building a storefront business in town. It takes a lot of hard work, long hours, and patience to do this. My dating life has been put on the back burner, because I've needed to focus on making sure Flour Power is successful."

"And you've done a wonderful job of that, honey," she assures me. Even though they're both pushing for me to marry and have kids, my parents have always supported me. Especially when it came to the bakery. Mom is the one who helped me figure out my business plan and what I'd need for my start-up loan. As a legal secretary, she and her boss have provided valuable resources throughout the entire process.

"Thank you. All I'm saying is I can find my own dates. Please don't send any more bachelors to meet me, especially at work. It was so embarrassing," I grumble.

"We certainly didn't mean to embarrass you. We just wanted to help. You never know when you'll meet the right man. It might be a chance encounter, like your dad and me," she encourages, always trying to be positive. "I just want you to be happy."

"I know you do, Mom."

"I'm glad that's settled," she says, clearly happy with the conversation, even though I'm not sure my point was completely made. "Since I have you on the phone, I was talking to Ellie at the diner the other day, and she told me about the new assistant football coach in town."

"Mom," I start, but she keeps going.

"Hear me out. Anyway, he's from Hudson and works as a police officer over there."

"Mom, stop," I reply with a groan.

"That's how TD knows him, and—"

"Mom!" I holler, shocking even myself. When I'm met with silence, I add, "I'm sorry to yell, but you have to stop."

"But it sounds like he's single," she counters.

"Yes, but maybe I'm not!"

My outburst stuns even me, mostly because I wasn't planning to tell her that. At least not yet.

"What does that mean?" Her question holds a mixture of shock and excitement.

"Maybe I'm seeing someone, Mom," I grumble, flopping onto the couch and closing my eyes.

"Are you?"

I think about Kameron and the tale we're about to spin in a few short days. "Yes."

She woops through the phone line and hollers, "Dennis, Dennis! She really is dating someone." To me she asks, "Who is it?"

"Wait, what do you mean by that? I really am dating someone."

"Well, George told us you mentioned to him you were seeing someone, but I just assumed you made that up, since we hadn't heard hide nor hair of this mystery man. But now, well, now you've confirmed it to be true. When can we meet him?"

I exhale slowly, the weight of the lie starting to press down on my chest. "Not yet, Mom. It's still pretty new."

Isn't that the truth...

"I can respect that," she states eagerly. I can feel her excitement pulsating through the phone line. "Will you share his name?"

"I know you're excited, but I'd rather keep this low-key for just a little bit longer. When the time is right, I promise I'll share more."

She sighs, clearly not happy she's not getting the dirt she wants. "I suppose," she mumbles.

"Thanks, Mom. Listen, I'll let you get back to your television program."

"Yes, well, do keep me updated on the status of your relationship. When you're ready, we'd love to meet him." I can tell it's a big step for her not to be overly pushy.

"I will. Bye, Mom. Love you."

"Love you too, sweetheart."

Hanging up, I toss the phone onto the couch cushion and close my eyes. What a mess. I'm finally getting my parents off my back about dating, but only because my so-called new beau is fake. He's not entirely made up, but the entire relationship is a lie. A mutual one, but a big fat fib, nonetheless.

I'm a decent looking woman, who owns her own house and a successful business. I have great friends, think I have a fun personality, and can bake like no other. Yet, I'm participating in a bogus relationship because it's mutually beneficial to myself and the man I'm fake dating.

How desperate am I?

CHAPTER
six

KAMERON

"You okay?" I ask, noticing how fidgety Jillian is. When she doesn't respond, I ask, "Jillian?"

"Huh?" Her green eyes widen as she stares up at me.

"Are you okay? You seem...nervous."

She huffs out a long breath. "Yeah, no, I'm okay," she reassures me, but I'm not certain I believe her. If she's about to back out, I'm screwed. We are ten minutes away from meeting Mrs. Krokus, and if the old woman shows up and I no longer have a girlfriend—fake or otherwise—I'm in a world of trouble.

We're standing in my office, ready to go into the dining room to meet Mrs. Krokus, but I can tell something's bothering her. Taking her hands in mine; I shift our positions so we're facing each other. "Talk to me, Jilly."

"Well, I had to tell my parents about us, but I left out your name."

Confused, I ask, "Okay, but that's ultimately what we're going to have to do, so I don't see the issue."

She shifts from side to side, those green eyes dancing with worry. "I told them I was dating someone, because they sent their accountant to the bakery to meet me."

Okay, now that *has my attention.*

Holding her hands, I work at keeping my voice even and my heart rate down. This wild feeling creeps into my chest, one I refuse to acknowledge, even though I'm very much aware of what it is. "They sent someone to your bakery? Why?"

She nods. "Like a date or something, but they didn't tell me. So this poor guy—George—shows up to have coffee with me, and I have no idea what to say or do. We sat at the table, and when I tell you it was awkward, it was *awkward.* I was so embarrassed."

I can't help but crack a little smile. She's adorable as hell when she's flustered and rambling. "What did you tell him?"

"That I was dating someone," she informs me, pulling her hands from my gentle grip and throwing them in the air. "What else was I supposed to say?"

I go ahead and grab her hands once more and bring them to my lips. "You did the right thing, Jilly. I'm sorry your parents sent someone to your business and made you uncomfortable." And I don't know why I add a second kiss to her knuckles. Her skin is soft and smells like sugar, and I'm enjoying this way too much for someone in a fake relationship.

A throat clears at the doorway of my office. "Excuse me, Kameron, but the rest of your party is here."

I nod without looking at Veronica. I'm certain she witnessed the kiss to Jillian's knuckles, but she'd never comment on it now. Instead, she'll wait until we're alone and ask me what it was all about. "We're on our way." I hear Veronica step away and keep my focus on the beautiful woman in front of me. "You good?"

She exhales slowly and nods. "Yes. Sorry. I'm not usually this dramatic."

"It's fine, and I want you to tell me if something has you rattled, okay?" When she nods, I continue, "Now, let's not keep Mrs.

Krokus waiting. The future of my potential expansion rests in her hands."

I place my palm against her lower back and gently guide her out of my office, pulling the door closed behind me. We walk down the hallway toward the table where we'll be having dinner. "Don't be nervous," I whisper just as we reach the dining room.

"Right," she replies with an uncomfortable chuckle.

As soon as we step into the dining room, my eyes scan the room before landing on the small table in the back. It's the same one Jillian and I used on Wednesday, the one that offers the most privacy in the room.

Leaving my hand on her back, I escort Jillian to the table, where a beaming Mrs. Krokus waits. "Well, look at you two," she greets.

"Mrs. Krokus, it's lovely to see you again," I reply, bending down and placing a kiss on her cheek.

"Dorothy, please."

I nod. "Dorothy, this beautiful creature, I'm sure you know, is Jillian Kirby."

"Good afternoon, Ms. Dorothy," Jillian greets, stepping forward and shaking the woman's aged hand.

"Well, Kameron is quite the charmer, but he's also correct. You are beautiful, Jillian. Please, won't you both join me?"

I pull out Jillian's chair, seating her directly to Dorothy's right, and then I take the seat directly across from the woman I'm hoping to charm into selling me her building. "Have you heard about today's specials?" I ask, hoping Veronica took good care of my guest when she seated her.

"I have," she confirms, reaching for her water glass to take a drink. "They all sound delicious, but I think I'll go with the crab cakes. They're my favorite."

I nod proudly. "An excellent choice," I assure her, knowing Marlin will take great care of our food. "How about you, love?" I ask Jillian, the term of endearment rolling easily off my tongue.

Jillian smiles and I give her credit, she doesn't so much as flinch at my question. Though, I suppose it would be more about the word I used than the question itself. "The crab cakes sound amazing. I think I'll have that too."

"We'll make it three," I reply, gathering the menus that weren't used and setting them aside.

"I brought the plans with me," I tell Mrs. Krokus as I reach for my phone. I have a digital version, as well as paper copies in my office. I don't know why I didn't think to bring those.

Dorothy holds up her hand. "Business can wait, can't it?" she practically beams at the two of us. "I'd love to hear about your love story first."

I'm silent as the server, Della, arrives to ask us for our drink orders. We all decide to stick with water, even though I'd rather have a shot of something hard and very strong right about now. "I believe we'll all have the crab cakes," I tell the server when she completes our drink requests.

"That comes with our homemade macaroni salad and roasted corn on the cob, and either a garden salad or bowl of soup. Today's soup is clam chowder, which you already know," Della replies with a chuckle.

I glance at the two ladies at the table. "Clam chowder is one of our specialties," I inform with a wink.

"I'll have the chowder," Dorothy requests.

"Salad for me," Jillian orders, "with ranch dressing."

"I'll also take the chowder," I state, handing the menus over before she walks away. "Now, where were we?"

"You two were just about to tell me all about falling in love." The old woman is practically batting her eyelashes in anticipation.

"Oh, yes," I reply with a chuckle. "Jilly, why don't you share that one?"

She looks at me, and without batting an eye, jumps into the story. "Well, we've known each other practically our whole lives, thanks to growing up in this town. We had mutual friends, but I would probably consider us more acquaintances than friends ourselves," she says, glancing my way.

"I'd agree with that. I've been friends with Gabe Rhodes my entire life, and Jillian was friends with Blair O'Connor. Their relationship brought us together, really," I add, offering her a warm smile.

"Oh, I love a good friends-to-lovers tale," Dorothy coos.

I can't help but wonder what the hell that means, but I don't ask.

"So, one day, out of the blue, this guy comes over and asks me to be his girlfriend," Jillian states, a wide smile stretched across her lips. "How could I refuse?"

Realizing she's sticking to as close to the truth as possible, I add, "It was one of those moments I decided just to take the leap, and fortunately, it worked out for me."

"You two are adorable," Dorothy states. "So, how long have you two been dating? Kameron said you've kept it quiet."

Jillian nods. "It hasn't been too long, but I admit, sometimes it feels like we just started," she says with a chuckle that borders on uncomfortable.

Reaching over, I place my hand on top of hers. "I think what she means is every day feels brand new." With a cheeky smile of my own, I bring her hand to my mouth and place a kiss on top of her knuckles. I can practically feel the eyes of the room zero in on my action, and if there was any question as to the status of our relationship moments ago, I think the question is answered now.

We've gone public—as public as you can in a town like Pine Village.

There's no going back now.

Mrs. Krokus claps happily. "This makes me so happy. I adore new love. It's so fresh and fun, not that it can't be that way after years together," she says sternly. "That love grows so strong over the years, and eventually, the bond is unbreakable. That's what I had with my Louie."

Jillian reaches over and places her other hand on top of Dorothy's. "I remember Louis from when I was younger. He was always such a happy, caring man. Always had a smile on his face."

Dorothy nods and smiles fondly. "He was, dear. Such a classy, hardworking man. He valued his family and respected my desire to work outside of the home early on. It was one of the key ingredients to our successful marriage. I'm sure it's far too early for you two to start planning a trip down the aisle, but I see a lot of the same qualities in both of you. It's important for you two to spend time together outside of work."

Jillian and I glance at each other. "We try, Mrs. Krokus—Dorothy."

"Good," she states with a decisive nod. "It's not easy, I know. And you two have extra challenges in front of you, because you both own businesses that hold different hours."

"We do," Jillian confirms. "Kameron has stopped by for coffee in the mornings, and I've enjoyed dinner here a few evenings."

"Perfect," she says before leaning in, her eyes bouncing between Jillian and me. "And be sure you make time for *other* things, if you know what I mean. That's an incredibly important part of any relationship."

Oh, I know instantly what she means.

Jillian must too because she blushes a deep shade of red. "Thank you for the advice," Jillian chimes in, clearing her throat. "There's tremendous value in talking to people who have worldly experience and success, such as yourself."

That seems to make Dorothy happy, because she preens like a peacock at such flattery. "Well, I have plenty of experiences and successes, much like you two will by the time you reach my age. But with each success there was a failure along the way too. You can't have one without the other, and while it's nice to listen to those around you, don't forget, opinions are like assholes. Everyone has one."

I'm barely able to keep my shock off my face, as Jilian seems to choke on air. I reach over and gently pat her back as she sputters and coughs. "Here," I murmur, barely keeping my laughter at bay, as I hand Jillian her glass of water.

"Thank you," she whispers, taking small sips as she regains her composure. I can tell she's trying to hide her own smile.

Just then, Della delivers our salad and soups to the table. She also tops off our waters before asking, "Can I get you anything else?"

When everyone agrees we're set for now, I say, "We're good, Della. Thank you."

She turns and walks away, stopping by another table to check on them. I want to glance around the room, to see who is dining this evening, but I don't. I keep my focus on my own table, on the two women I'm sharing a meal with.

"This smells amazing," Dorothy announces, leaning in and taking a whiff of her clam chowder. "Let's eat."

"I tell you, Kameron, every time I eat here, the food is simply marvelous," Dorothy announces, leaning back in her seat as she places her used napkin on the table.

"I'm glad you enjoyed it." And I am. Watching a customer appreciate the food we prepared is one of life's greatest joys.

"And I have plenty of leftovers for tomorrow," she adds with a wink.

Chuckling, I reply, "Sometimes food is even better the second time around."

"Well, they're not quite as good as fresh, unless we're talking about pizza. Cold, leftover pizza. It's almost better than hot, am I right?" Dorothy asks, giving her attention to Jillian.

"You're very right," the woman to my left confirms. "Especially when the diner does their thin crust pizza. It's the best the next day."

Dorothy smiles. "I couldn't agree with you more. Now that we've enjoyed our meal, let's get down to business. I'm sure Kameron needs to get back to work at some point."

I worked the lunch hour, so even though I'm not expected back in the kitchen, I'll use the rest of my evening to catch up on office work before helping close. "I have plenty of time," I assure her.

"Well, still. I'm an old lady, and my bedtime is much sooner than yours," she announces with a pleasant smile. "Tell me your plan."

I pull out my phone and tap on the plans I had drawn up. "These measurements are taken from an old appraisal the county had on file," I tell her as I slip my phone across the table.

Dorothy looks down at the drawing, which includes both my current building and the one I hope to purchase from her. I can tell she's studying the rendering, but I can't tell what she's thinking.

Leaning over the table, I point to the space between the buildings. "I want to open up the wall here. I picture a large arched entryway, keeping the exposed brick look. I appreciate the old, warm feel it provides, giving ode to the building itself and the history it possesses."

She nods, not even looking down at the rendering. "What else?"

"The back of your building would be opened up to create a bigger kitchen. Some of your existing storage space can still be used, but the biggest transformation would be the kitchen area. I've started to secure quotes from different vendors. Kitchen equipment and the construction remodel costs will be the biggest expenses. Plumbing and heating and electrical, not to mention the additional tables and chairs needed."

Dorothy smiles in agreement and turns to Jillian. "And where will your influence be, dear?"

Jillian seems surprised by the question. "My influence?"

"Yes. I understand this is Kameron's business, but a man always includes the woman he loves in his decision-making process."

Jillian glances my way, her eyes hinting at the uneasiness she feels. I also notice her foot starts to tap on the floor as she leans toward Dorothy a bit and glances down at the phone screen. "Well, I personally love the open brick look. The high ceilings with the exposed rafters bring a sort of old-style feel. Like you're dining in one of the best restaurants in the twenties or thirties," she says. "But I don't think it feels industrial. In fact, splashes of color will bring the atmosphere to life."

"What sort of life?" Dorothy asks, hanging on Jillian's every word.

"Well, flowers, for one. Real flowers. And not the simple carnations you see at other restaurants. Beautiful, elegant roses, lilies, peonies, and hydrangeas. Splashes of reds, pinks, blues, and whites will complement the overall vibe Kameron is going for, without making it look overdone."

"I love that," Dorothy coos. "Hydrangeas are some of my favorite flowers."

"Me too," Jillian confesses. "I once saw a bouquet of pink peonies with purple and white hydrangeas, and it was the most stunning vase of flowers I've ever seen."

"Oh, that sounds lovely," Dorothy agrees, leaning in and continuing her conversation with Jillian.

All I can do is sit back and watch.

"Lighting. Low lighting is essential, but I think he can get away from these classic overhead lights. There are so many pendant lighting options out there that would bathe the tables in essential lighting. Maybe a gold fixture that's open around the bulb. It would match the ambiance with the open brick and wood floors."

"Yes, new lighting, and if you could keep the original hardwood floors, that would be divine!" she proclaims with a clap. "My Louie redid those floors back when we purchased the building.

They're a bit dirty, but still in excellent shape. I'm sure with a little elbow grease and some sanding, you could have them good as new in no time

"Maybe stained a dark color, to match the open rafters," Jillian agrees, sipping her water.

"Oh, I love that. It would be dark, but with the ample natural light from the windows and the gold fixtures you suggested, it would all tie in beautifully. Don't you think, Kameron?"

The smile on my lips is easy, light, and natural. "I do."

"Then, it's settled," Dorothy announces, causing my breath to catch. "Kameron, I'd love to sell my building to you and Jillian."

My heart stops beating. It literally just stops in my chest, refusing to pump blood through my veins. "Excuse me?"

"This vision is both of yours, correct?"

Jillian and I both just sit here, staring at each other like a deer in the headlights. I have no idea what to do or say, no idea how to stop this freight train from running off the tracks, because that's how this moment feels. Like all I can do is stand back and watch the destruction unfold around me.

"You two make a beautiful couple, and I think this place will be just as lovely with your combined expertise."

"Oh, but, Mrs. Krokus, I don't have any expertise here. This is Kameron's restaurant. I have my own bakery, and that's where my focus is."

She reaches over and pats Jillian's hand. "Your expertise is being right by your man's side. He may not put your name down on the mortgage papers, but I have no doubt you will take your rightful position beside him through not only this expansion endeavor, but the beautiful journey through life as well." She pauses and smiles at me.

"I will sell to you," she announces confidently, "because what you and Jillian represent is just what this building needs. Life, love, and family. Thank you for continuing the legacy my Louie started."

My throat is tight. "Thank you, Mrs. Krokus."

I almost call the whole thing off.

"You're most welcome, Kameron. Now, what do you have on your menu for dessert?"

CHAPTER
seven

Jillian

"I hate this," I say the moment we step inside the privacy of his office.

Kameron exhales. "Me too. I'm sorry to be putting you in this position."

I can tell by the look in his eyes he means it. He doesn't like this any more than I do, but now we're stuck. Sure, we could probably call the whole thing off, but I doubt he would. Especially not after verbally agreeing to the terms set at the end of our dinner meeting.

Mrs. Krokus is excited. She's ready to see new life breathed into her old building, and after they discussed the terms of the sale, she told us all about the history of the building over tiramisu. The sparkle in her eyes and the joy in her voice was evident, and I think that's the only reason I didn't run screaming from the room.

The weight of this lie is heavy.

Swallowing over the lump in my throat, I say, "Closing in a month, huh?"

He nods and the faintest smile stretches across his lips. "I've been wanting this for so long, it's hard to believe it might actually be coming true."

"So, what are you thinking? A month until you close, and then we break up...in a few weeks? Another month?" Not that Kameron isn't a great fake boyfriend, but knowing my luck Mr. Right really will appear out of nowhere, and I'll miss him because I'm fake dating my friend for business.

"I'd say a month? Four weeks feels like a good timeline, though I've never actually had a fake girlfriend, so I have no idea what's deemed the appropriate length of time for this."

"I'll agree to four weeks," I tell him, shifting my weight from side to side as my brain spins.

"Why do you do that?" he asks, stepping toward me.

"What?" I ask, noticing how very close he's standing.

"That. You shift, like you're nervous." He's directly in front of me now, and I have to look up to keep eye contact. "Are you nervous?"

Clearing my throat over the instant dryness, I reply, "I'm nervous about the situation."

"But not about me?" he confirms, reaching out and resting his hand on my hip. It's warm and big and very much wanted right now.

"No, not about you."

His eyes drop to my lips, and I can't help but wonder what he's thinking about. Is he going to kiss me? Do I want him to kiss me? Ummm, hell to the yeah I want him to kiss me again, but that doesn't mean he's going to. "Good. I'd hate if I were the cause of your nervousness."

I lick my lips. "You're not."

He's still staring at my mouth, neither of us moving. "Jillian?"

"Hmm?"

"Are you thinking about the kiss?" He finally looks up and meets my eyes. "Because I am."

"Me too," I murmur.

He clears his throat, his Adam's apple bobbing. "Can I kiss you again?"

"Okay." My answer is quick and honest and probably comes out way too eager.

His mouth descends, his lips pressing firmly against mine. I feel his hand tighten around my hip as he gently draws me into his body. My arms wrap around his shoulders as I lean my body into his. As his tongue dances across the seam of my lips, coaxing them open, his other hand shifts to my lower back before angling down. I feel his fingers flex against the globe of my ass. My entire body is alive, craving more.

Going up on my tiptoes, I practically glue my chest to his. He's tall enough I have to work to get up to his height, but I don't mind. Not when we're pressed together the way we are. His other hand joins the one on my ass, and with one swift action, I'm spun around, being lifted into the air at the same time. My legs wrap around his waist as I'm crowded against the back of his office door. His tongue delves deeper, his hands flexing against my backside, and all I can do is hang on and enjoy the ride.

Now this is a kiss...

My hips rock, completely on their own, as I take notice of his erection between my legs for the first time. I gasp, sucking in a greedy gulp of oxygen as pleasure races through my veins. It's too much, and not enough, all at the same time.

"Jesus," Kameron mutters against my lips, breathing hard.

He meets my gaze, his eyes dark with desire and wicked intent, and even though there are probably a dozen reasons why this is a bad idea, I can't seem to think of a single one. Not when he kisses like a dream, all possessive and raw, and I am here for it.

Here. For. It.

"Chemistry," he murmurs, leaning forward and running his nose along my jaw. I hear him lightly inhale, as if he's committing the scent of my hair or skin to memory. Hell, he can probably smell my pheromones. They're pouring from my body, practically holding up signs, directing him to the place I ache for him most.

"Chemistry," I confirm, recalling how he used that word on Sunday night after we shared our first kiss.

There's no doubt, Kameron and I have it in spades.

"I'm sorry for mauling you," he adds, but I notice he doesn't release his hold. He's still very much there, pressing me into the door, his body between my legs.

"Don't be." I'm ready to beg but somehow keep my clit and incredibly wet core from making all my decisions.

Kameron sighs, his warm breath tickling my cheek. "I should apologize," he starts, looking up and holding my eyes, "but I won't. No, I can't. If I should apologize, I will, but dammit, I'm not sorry for kissing you like this, Jilly."

My heart beats wildly, both in desperation and happiness. "I'm not sorry either, Kam."

The corner of his lips curls up into a small smile, and as handsome as I thought he was before, that slight gesture seems to add a thousand percent to his hotness scale. Something as simple as a little grin transforms his entire face, brightening his dark eyes.

Carefully, he slowly helps me down. "Well, I'm glad we have that settled."

I nod, even though I'm not sure what he means. Yes, it's settled in the regard we have chemistry and both enjoyed the kiss. But then what? I don't know about him, but I'm sexually charged right now, and that's most definitely not settled. The only thing that is certain is I'll be busting out my trusty vibrator again when I get home, just to take the edge off.

Even then, I'm not sure it'll help much.

"What are your plans for the rest of this Sunday evening?" he asks, stepping back so he's not overcrowding me.

"Umm, probably just go home and get ready for bed. Maybe stop by Molly's Ice Cream Parlor and grab a caramel crunch dish on my way." I'm hoping it'll help cool me off.

"Mmm," he practically purrs, causing a fresh wave of wetness to flood my panties. "I'm a cherry chip guy myself."

Saliva gathers in my mouth as I picture Kameron licking ice cream off a spoon. Of course, then I start thinking about him licking *other* things...

Clearing my throat again, I give my head a gentle shake, trying to dislodge all the dirty thoughts that seem to be front and center. "That's a good one too," I reply lamely.

He gives me a panty-melting smile. "Maybe we'll share a bowl soon."

"Sure," I reply, standing up straight. "Thank you for dinner."

"You're welcome." I can't help but notice how close he still is. "I enjoy sharing my love for food with people, especially when they appreciate it."

"I understand that. That's why I bake."

"Food is about an experience," he murmurs, the room starting to close in on me.

"I agree," I whisper, my lips suddenly feeling too dry, the room too hot.

He gives me a slow nod. "I like sharing meals with you, Jillian. Let's do it again soon."

"Okay," I agree easily.

"I have tomorrow night off. How about I cook for you at my place?"

His offer surprises me a bit, and I find myself adjusting my foot a bit and tapping it. "What can I bring?"

Kameron finally moves, stepping back and sitting on the corner of his desk. He crosses his arms, his crisp button-down with the restaurant logo embroidered over his left pec stretched tightly across his chest. "Just yourself."

"How about I bring dessert?" I suggest.

His eyes drop, taking a slow perusal of my body, and I swear I can feel the dirty thoughts parading through his mind. "Perfect."

I nod. "What time?"

"How about six?" he suggests.

"All right."

"You know where I live?" he asks.

It's a small town. I know where Kameron lives, even though I've never physically been to his address. "I do."

"See you tomorrow, Jilly," he replies, standing up and walking to the door. Since I'm standing directly in front of it, he brushes against me as he reaches for the knob and gives it a turn.

"Good night, Kameron," I whisper, stepping out of the small room and into the hallway. With my head held high, I exit the restaurant, refusing to glance around to see who's in the dining room. I can feel their eyes on me and know people are speculating about what I was doing there. I was seen having dinner with Kameron—twice now—and just exiting the hallway that leads to the bathrooms. But just past that, the office of the owner.

I push out of the restaurant, offering Veronica a pleasant goodnight as I pass. She does the same, and I don't miss the knowing smile stretched across her pink lips.

It's a beautiful night as I head home, having walked to the restaurant for our dinner meeting. There's a light breeze that holds a hint of the cooler temperatures on the horizon. It won't be long, and I won't be able to walk as much as I do during the summer months. The snow will be flying and winter coats, gloves, hats, and boots will be necessary to step outside.

But that's not for me to think about tonight. I let the breeze cool my flushed skin as I walk, a little extra spring in my step, accompanied by the memories of more amazing kisses. Not to mention the feel of his erection pressed very firmly against my body.

I have plans with him again tomorrow evening.

Dinner.

At his house.

I can't help but wonder what might be on the menu.

Is it wrong to hope it's me?

I'm startled by a knock at the back door. I glance at the clock, noting it's just after five thirty. I don't have too long before I need to be at Kameron's house for dinner, and since I'm not expecting a delivery at this point of the day, I'm not sure who it could be.

Looking through the peephole on the door, I shake my head when I see a familiar face. No, not just one face, but several. I release the lock, knowing this moment was coming. My friends have been too quiet, and I have a hard time believing they haven't heard about my dinner last night with Kameron and Mrs. Krokus. Which means they're here—and all together—for one reason.

They want dirt.

"Hey," I greet when I open the door, a friendly smile on my face.

"Start talking," Hallie demands as she pushes through the doorway, Blair, Ava, Ellie, and Ryan hot on her heels.

"Well, hello to you too," I say, closing the door behind them. When I turn and face my friends, I ask, "Is this an intervention?" There's humor in my question, but I can't help but wonder if it isn't somewhat true.

"No, of course not," Blair replies.

"We didn't mean to bombard you," Ava says.

"But we were all just curious as to what's going on with you and Kameron," Ellie adds. "Not that it's any of our business."

"Oh, it's definitely our business," Hallie states with a giggle. "I knew something was up all those months ago when he provided the tacos for our girls' night."

"That was just friends helping each other out," I insist, even though I still didn't necessarily clarify us as friends. "I made him some cheesecakes for his restaurant when his regular dessert maker had to cancel last minute, so in return, he offered to help me with a meal of my choice in the future."

"So...what is going on now? Are you two dating?" Blair asks, her eyes sparkling with excitement.

"Yes."

All five of them hoot and holler, all equally as excited for me and my new relationship status.

"Yay! You two make the cutest couple. Not to mention the food," Blair says, causing everyone to agree.

"Truth! I bet you two could seriously heat up a kitchen," Ellie adds, before blushing. "I didn't mean it like that. Wait, maybe I did."

I can't help but think about the kisses and being pressed against the door last night, and I'd be lying if I said I wasn't hoping for a little more of that tonight.

"She's blushing," Ryan says, a big grin on her gorgeous face.

"Of course she's blushing. You've seen the man," Hallie chimes in.

"Anyway," I reply, drawing out that word. "Is that what brought you all here? To get the dirt on Kameron and me?"

"Yes," they all reply in unison.

"Well," I start, my throat thick and dry. "We're dating. It's pretty new and low-key, and we're not making a big deal of it."

"Not making a big deal? Of course it's a big deal," Blair insists. "You two are both great people, and it's exciting. Since I've been back here, I don't think I've known either one of you to date."

"That's true," I agree, trying to recall the last guy I actually dated. And not just went out for a date or two. I mean had the whole boyfriend/girlfriend titles and whatnot. It's been a really long time.

"And besides, you totally blushed and were probably thinking about sex when we walked in," Hallie informs me, causing my face to blush even more. "See? That right there. That tells me this is a bigger deal than you're letting on, and that's okay."

I shrug. "We're taking it slow."

"Nothing wrong with that," Ellie replies.

"You'd say that because it took you and TD like seventeen years," Blair teases, making all of us laugh. "But all joking aside, we're all really excited and happy for you."

The others all nod eagerly.

"We really are. I know I'm the newest one to the group, but I think you're amazing and I'm so glad someone else is seeing it too," Ryan states, reaching out and taking my hand.

I tear up, but not for the reason they're thinking. I want to tell them it's all fake—that Kameron doesn't think I'm amazing. I'm convenient, at best. I'm one of the only single ladies in his age demographic that could help him pull this off.

But I can't help but think about that kiss—kisses.

There's no denying the chemistry we share. I felt it pressed against my center. But that doesn't mean anything more than attraction. We're not dating for the right reasons, and I need to remember that. This is fake, and at the end of our two-month arrangement, we'll both be walking away after we get what we want.

For him, it's the building to expand his restaurant.

For me, it's the added security to my business of selling my baked goods to his restaurant year-round.

That's why we're dating, and I need to remember that.

Not the way he kissed me or pressed me against the door.

"You look nice," Ava says, having noticed my small attempt at making myself presentable for this evening.

"Oh," I reply, glancing down at my capris and fitted blue top. "Thanks."

I'm usually wearing a T-shirt with my bakery logo on the front, leggings, and flour and icing.

"Date?" Hallie asks, a mischievous grin on her face.

"It's just dinner."

"The restaurant is closed," Blair replies with a knowing smile.

"At his house. I'm bringing dessert," I add lamely, pointing to the fresh angel food cake with strawberries and homemade whipped cream.

Ryan steps forward and gives me a hug. "You two are so adorable. We won't keep you, since you have plans. We just wanted you to know we all love and support you."

"And we're all really happy for you," Ellie adds, giving me a hug too.

"Totally agree," Blair states.

I hug each of my friends before they move to the door to leave.

"Let's do a big date night soon. All of us together. I know Kameron's schedule is difficult, because of his restaurant, but maybe with some notice, he can take a Friday or Saturday night off," Hallie suggests.

"I'll ask," I reply, wishing they wouldn't have suggested it. It's one thing to play a fake girlfriend while we're both working, but it's an entirely different scenario when you're surrounded by your closest friends.

"All right, have a good night," Ava says as they take their exit.

"And by that she means have all the sex," Hallie hollers before I can shut the door.

Sex.

Would I like to have it with Kameron?

Ummm, any red-blooded woman who has a pulse would say yes. But I don't think it would be wise. Talk about muddying the waters.

Yes, sex would definitely add a layer of complication I don't want.

Yet, I hope it's not off the table...

CHAPTER eight

KAMERON

I just put the finishing touches on tonight's meal when there's a knock at the door. My heart leaps in my chest, beating a little harder now that she's here.

It's been like this since she left the restaurant last night. The thought of seeing her again makes me...happy. Eager. Grateful. Because, while I have friends, it feels different with Jillian. Maybe it's because we're both business owners, and we understand exactly what it takes to make it succeed. Not that any of the others don't, because they do. Logan owns the hardware store and Marcus owns the auto repair shop. Gabe is a doctor, owning half of the practice. But it still feels different.

Better.

It's hard to explain, really. I've spent the last twenty-four hours trying to figure out why I'm drawn to her so much, but I really haven't figured anything out. I'm attracted to her. I don't know when it happened, but it did. Jillian went from another business owner I know in town to someone who makes my heart race and my dick hard. As juvenile as that sounds, it's true. I'm a forty-year-old man, and yet my body reacts like I'm seventeen again.

I clear my throat and adjust my pants, trying to do anything I can not to pop an erection right about now. But the moment I open the door, all thoughts of keeping calm fly straight out the window. She's wearing a pair of blue jean capris and a pretty blue top, both pieces of material conforming to her delectable curves. Her hair is down, and all I want to do is slide my fingers through those soft locks as I kiss her.

"Hi."

"Hi," she repeats, still standing on my porch. After a few seconds, she holds up a cake carrier. "I brought dessert."

I would rather eat you...

Shaking my head to clear that thought from my brain, I push open the screened door. "Come in," I insist, stepping back.

As she passes, entering my living room, I catch the clean scent of her detergent, the fruitiness of her lotion, and the sugar that seems to always be hanging on her skin. "Thank you." She glances around and adds, "You have a lovely home."

"Thanks," I reply, clearing my throat once more. Things always seem a little drier when she's around. "Dinner's ready."

She smiles brightly, her green eyes sparkling with anticipation. "I'm starving."

"It's nothing special," I tell her as we enter my kitchen. "Just chicken with sides."

"Well, it smells amazing, and I never consider anything you make nothing special. Everything I've had has been excellent," she states, placing the cake carrier on the counter and pulling two small containers out of her bag. "Can I put these in the fridge?"

"Of course. Do you want wine?" I offer, not knowing what she'd like to drink. "Or I have water, Coke, or lemonade."

"Actually, lemonade would be perfect. I drove tonight, so I probably shouldn't drink."

I nod, walking over to the fridge and retrieving the pitcher of lemonade. I pour two glasses and take them to the table. "Have a seat."

She smiles and slides into one of the chairs. "Freshly squeezed?" she asks, a hint of humor in her eyes as she reaches for the glass I place in front of her.

I snort a laugh. "Hardly."

"I just figured since you do everything else from scratch, maybe you squeeze your own lemons for lemonade."

"Nope, never have tried it," I reply, taking the lids off the dishes on the table. "This lemonade comes from a can that was in the frozen section," I confess, earning a laugh. "It was how I grew up drinking it, so that's how I've continued to make it."

She shrugs and takes a second sip. "It's good, so it doesn't matter where it comes from." She looks at the casserole dish in the middle of the table. "What's this?"

"It's my take on Million Dollar Chicken," I inform her, scooping up the first smothered chicken breast and slipping it on her plate. "There's also buttery mashed potatoes and roasted carrots."

Jillian's eyes are wide. "A girl could get used to this," she murmurs as she takes a scoop of both the potatoes and the carrots. I wait, watching as she cuts into her chicken, making sure she scoops a bit of the baked topping with her bite. "Oh my God," she practically groans, slowly chewing her food. She closes her eyes and appears to be savoring her first bite, and I can't help but smile.

"I'm glad you like it."

"Soooo delicious," she says as she cuts a second bite. "So, what's Million Dollar Chicken, and how is yours different?"

"Well, the traditional Million Dollar Chicken is a chicken breast, coated in a cream cheese mixture, crumbled bacon, green onion, and Colby Jack cheese. I alter my recipe with a little extra flavor, as well as stuffing the chicken with a creamy spinach, bacon, and Monterey Jack cheese spread."

"Well, it's amazing," she says before switching to eating her potatoes and carrots.

"Do you like mushrooms?"

"Love them. Mushrooms, green peppers, and sausage on my pizza," she confirms between bites.

I keep my facial expressions neutral, but barely. Why, you ask? Because that's exactly how I order my pizza on nights I don't want to cook anything for myself. "I, uh, make this mushroom and cranberry stuffed pork tenderloin that's one of my favorites."

Her eyes dance with excitement. "I would definitely try that."

I nod, digging into my own food. "Good. Maybe I'll make that soon."

A light blush creeps up her neck. "I'd like that."

Spending time with Jillian isn't a hardship, that's for sure. Our entire meal is both relaxing and enjoyable. She's engaging and witty and doesn't seem to be bothered by any probing questions. Really, I want to get to know her better, because with each passing minute, I like what I see, and I'm not just referring to her gorgeous good looks.

After dinner, she helps me clean up the leftover food and place it in the fridge. Once the dishes are in the sink, I ask, "Would you like a tour before we have dessert?"

"Absolutely," she replies eagerly. "Your home is beautiful," she adds as we head into the living room.

"It's more space than I need," I confess. "When I made the decision to return to Pine Village and start my restaurant, I jumped at one of the first available places on the market that didn't require much work. I was going to be putting so much into my business, the last thing I wanted to do was come home and have to work here too."

"Makes sense," she replies, following me toward the opposite end of the house.

"Three bedrooms," I tell her, noting the two doors toward the front of the house. "One is my home office, and the other a guest room. Honestly, no one has ever used it, but I didn't want it to just sit empty, so I threw an extra bedroom set in there and called it a day."

She smiles, taking in the plain, basic bedroom. "This is better than I have. My place is only two bedrooms, and the second is a storage room/guest bedroom/home office/workout room. And by workout room, I mean I have an old treadmill there where I throw my off-season clothes since the closets are full."

I can't help but smile at the description.

"In my defense, since my family lives here, the only person to use my guest room is my friend, Olivia, when she comes to visit. Though, she got married last year, and I don't see them both crashing in my twin-sized daybed anytime soon," she says with a cute little nose-crinkling grin.

"I don't know, her husband might enjoy sharing a small bed with her," I find myself saying, the innuendo heavy.

She shrugs. "Maybe, but I need space. That's why I have a king-sized bed. I like to spread out, and often, I sleep on the hot side, so I don't want someone all up in my business."

Images of Jillian spread out in bed—naked—plague my brain. Her brown hair feathered across the pillow, her smooth leg hanging out of the blanket. I can picture it so clearly, despite the fact we've never shared a bed, and I have no clue how she actually sleeps. But in my dirty mind, it's naked.

With me beside her.

We step out of the guest room and cross the hall. There are two doors on this side too, one for the bathroom and the other for my bedroom. I start to feel a little hot under the collar at the thought of her being in my private space. This is where I sleep, read late at night when I try to unwind from a long, hectic day, and dress. I rarely invite people in here, especially since I haven't dated much in recent years, but here I am, wanting to have her in my bedroom.

"Wow," she says as we cross the threshold. "This is gorgeous."

"I admit, I didn't do much to the room. The couple who lived here before me had it remodeled, and I left it."

"Do you use the fireplace?" she inquires, walking over to the whitewashed brick fireplace and running her hand across the dark wood mantel.

"Actually, yes. During the winter, I do. I read to unwind, so I'll use it to warm up the room while I read and relax."

She nods, taking in the space. "I would too," she says, walking over to my reading nook. There's an oversized chair there, as well as a small table. The previous owners built bookshelves, and while I don't have them filled, I do have a decent selection of historical nonfiction books, as well as biographies. "I like to read, but since I go to bed so early, I don't have a lot of time to indulge."

"Well, I'm usually so wired at the end of a long day, I have to do something to calm my mind. I usually read after taking a dip in my hot tub and then showering."

Her eyes widen. "You have a hot tub?"

With just a smile on my lips, I walk over to the French doors and release the lock. She follows as I open the door, stepping out onto the back patio area where my hot tub is housed.

"Oh my gosh, I have total porch envy right now. My backyard looks nothing like this," she says, taking in the yard.

"Again, the previous owners did a big part of it. I did add the hot tub though. When I worked in Chicago, my apartment building had one for tenants, and I figured out really quick that they work wonders on tired muscles after a long day. I ended up using it every night after work and knew it was one purchase I'd make when I moved here."

"I can only imagine," she says, walking over to the tub. The cover is on, but you can hear the soft hum of the pump. "Have you used it? Today?"

"Not yet," I reply.

"Will you after I leave?"

I shrug my shoulders. "Possibly. Since I didn't work today, I don't require a dip."

She runs her hands over the top. "I bet it's amazing. The only time I was in a hot tub was when I stayed in a hotel with my family for vacation back when I was thirteen or fourteen."

"You're welcome to give it a try," I tell her, already imagining her in a little bikini, her curves on full display.

She meets my gaze, her eyes dancing with humor. "But I don't have a suit."

I couldn't stop my wicked grin if you paid me a million bucks. "You don't necessarily need one. In fact, I'd be fine if you went without."

She barks out a laugh. "I bet you would."

I shrug, noticing the hint of a chill hanging in the air. "Well, the offer stands anytime you want to use it. Suit or no suit." After a moment, I add, "Ready to head back inside? You can tell fall is around the corner. Not too many warm days left."

Jillian walks toward my door and enters my bedroom. "I don't mind cool evenings. I'd rather have that than sweltering heat."

Locking the door behind us, I face her and agree. "I've never been a big outdoorsy guy. I don't mind cookouts or bonfires, but I'm not a boat in the middle of the lake kind of guy."

"I understand that. I'm the same. I love hanging with my friends, but definitely prefer the evenings where we're at a cabin or just enjoying each other's company in someone's kitchen."

She's fucking perfect.

We enjoy many of the same things, and for the first time in my life, I feel a connection stronger and deeper than what's on the surface. Considering my past, that's saying a lot. And I'm not trying to minimize what I had with Lilly. I loved her all those years ago, but this feels...different.

The air seems to thicken around us. I take notice of the casual way she stands in the middle of my bedroom. Her brown hair has a fresh curl, begging for my fingers. Her chest rises and falls with each breath she takes. She licks her lips, maybe in anticipation. And her eyes are a darker shade of green, as if she's possibly thinking about the same things as me.

My legs move before my brain gives them the cue. I stalk toward her, memorizing the way she looks, and also giving her ample time to tell me no. She can clearly see my intent, as her eyes sparkle with desire, her body humming with need. It's pulsating between us, this draw.

This craving.

When I reach where she stands, I lazily move my hands to her neck, letting my fingers slide into her hair. It smells amazing, so soft and hypnotic. I've never been so damn attracted to hair before, but I can't seem to stop wanting to touch it.

"Jillian?" I ask, my voice hoarse.

"Yes?" Her eyes are full of hope and anticipation.

My heart is trying to beat out of my chest. "I want to kiss you."

"Yes, please," she replies instantly, lifting her chin and waiting.

I don't delay.

I *can't*.

It's as if the very air I need for survival lies solely in the taste and feel of her lips.

I need them that badly.

Her hands grip the sides of my shirt as she angles her head for me to deepen the kiss. I get lost in her, wishing there were some magical way to kiss her until the end of time. We both turn, as if knowing exactly what the other is thinking and needing. I slowly back her against the wall, and within seconds, she's climbing me like a tree. Her arms wrap around my neck at the same time I hoist her up. Her legs are around my waist, and she's pinned right where we both want her to be.

My erection is there, hard and ready. She shifts her core against it, grinding down on me in a way that makes my brain explode. It feels too fucking good, too fucking right. Her hands slide into my hair, bringing her body even closer. We're pressed tightly together, her nipples hard and begging for my mouth.

Ripping my mouth from hers, we both suck in greedy gulps of air. My lips trail down her neck, my tongue slipping out and tasting her skin. "Jilly," I whisper, not really sure what to do.

I want this woman, but I'm afraid sex would further muddle an already complicated situation.

"My answer is yes, Kameron."

A faint smile crosses my lips as I move to look into her eyes. "I haven't asked a question."

She swallows hard, her lips swollen and wet. "You didn't have to. The question is written all over your face. So, to answer it, yes. I want this."

My brain feels foggy, like I'm intoxicated or something. Drunk on Jillian. "You do?"

"Yes."

I clear my throat, my cock pulsing with need and anticipation. "I, uh, should confess. It's been a while for me. Since I had a woman with me here, but also since...you know." I feel like the world's biggest loser, but I won't lie to her. It's been almost a year since I had sex, and much longer since I had a relationship.

She cups my jaw in her palm. "Well, since we're confessing stuff, I haven't had sex in a while either."

"Like how long?" Not that it matters. I'm just curious.

Her throat bobs. "Almost two years."

"Really? How is that possible? You're..." I glance down to where her chest is pressed up and out of the top of her shirt, "fucking gorgeous."

She smiles. "Like you, I've been a little busy running a business."

I nod, spinning her around and setting her down on the floor. "You can say no. At any time," I reassure her.

Reaching down, she quickly lifts her shirt up and over her head, dropping it on the floor. Just as fast, she toes off her shoes and releases the button and zipper on her pants. With a few shimmies, they're around her ankles in seconds, leaving her standing in just a pale pink bra and panty set. "I'm not saying no, Kameron. In fact, I'm wondering why you still have your clothes on."

Me too, Jillian. Me too.

CHAPTER
nine

Jillian

Who is the bold, brave woman?

No one—me included—would ever think it was me, standing in front of Kameron in my underwear, waiting on him to catch up. Definitely not my ex-husband, Davis. Not that I want to think about him right now, but I never felt this bold with him, and we were married. I let him lead. Not to mention, he would have already had the lights out by now. Lights out and socks still on because his feet were always cold every time we had sex.

But not Kameron.

His eyes are devouring me like I'm a prime piece of steak and he hasn't eaten in days. He runs his hand over his mouth as he continues to stare at me. His eyes are so intense, it's a little unnerving. "I'm afraid to look away."

I glance down, taking in my less than perfect stomach and my curvy hips. You can definitely tell I own a bakery, even though I try to eat healthy and work out when I can. "Why?"

"I'm terrified you might disappear. Like this was all a dream. No, a fantasy."

Feeling that bravado return, I step forward and place my hands on his chest. "I'm not going anywhere, Kam. Promise."

He swallows hard, his Adam's apple bobbing. His palm is warm as he brushes it against my hip, sliding along my skin and resting on my lower back. I move closer, wrapping my arms around his neck and pressing my chest to his. He claims my mouth once more, the kiss instantly turning ravenous.

When he rips his mouth from mine and sucks in a greedy gulp of air, he murmurs, "I'm going to touch you, Jillian."

"Yes, please," I practically beg, the words coming out in a pant.

His hand slips between my legs, brushing against the apex of my thighs. Pleasure zings through my veins as his fingers connect with the spot I ache. He gently pushes my panties to the side, and then he's finally there. *There.* His long, very deft fingers glide easily over my clit, causing my hips to buck forward from the contact.

I lean against the wall and let his masterful fingers explore. He slips one inside my body, quickly followed by a second. The stretch is intense, but the pleasure is unparallel to anything else. He places gentle kisses against my neck, his tongue dancing against my skin and driving me absolutely crazy.

Then, his palm makes contact with my clit, and I see stars. It's hard to breathe, hard to think, his touch is all-consuming. "Are you going to come, Jilly?"

My eyes are closed, and all I can do is think about how amazing this feels. It's been so long since something other than my vibrator has touched me down there. "I think I just might."

I can feel his lips curl upward in a smile as they kiss just below my ear. Knowing I'm close, he seems to double down on his efforts. His thumb circles my clit, applying the perfect amount of pressure, while his fingers move, gently pumping inside of me. My orgasm builds, and all I can do is enjoy the climb and fall.

And fall I do.

The moment my climax hits, I feel like I'm flying, floating in a sea of clouds and bliss. That's the only way to describe it. I cry out and the waves wash over me. He doesn't stop either. Kameron draws out every ounce of release I possess until I'm all but boneless and sated against the wall.

"I want to do that again," he murmurs. "Feeling you come on my fingers was the highlight of my night."

I clear my throat, trying to find the strength to talk. "Well, I definitely give you a gold star."

He snorts. "Perfect. I do love earning stars." He places another kiss against my lips. "Wonder what else I can earn a gold star on."

"I have ideas," I tell him, hoping sex with Kameron is just as spectacular. Reaching out, I cup his erection through his jeans. "It involves this."

He hisses as I apply a little more pressure with my hand. I run my palm against the length of him, feeling the moisture from his precum seep through the denim. "You keep doing that, darlin', and this will be over before it gets good."

I release my hold on him and take a step back to give him a little space. He toes off his own shoes and tosses his socks off to the side. Then, he releases the button on his jeans and lowers the zipper. I swear that noise echoes louder than ever before. It's the only sound in the room. Before he can slide them off, I step forward and grab his shirt. I lift, watching as his muscular, tanned skin comes into full view. He helps remove the shirt the rest of the way, and my fingers are drawn to his chest like a magnet.

He's hard and soft at the same time. Kameron doesn't have a six-pack, but I can see definition, feel his abs beneath my touch. He takes care of his body when he can, considering he has a pretty demanding job.

I take a step back as he removes his jeans, and I'm left dumbstruck by the sight of him. He's wearing boxer briefs that leave little to the imagination. His cock is hard, long, and ready.

And so am I.

Kameron walks over to his nightstand and pulls a condom from the drawer. He tosses it on the bed before turning his intense gaze back to me. With his blue eyes glued to me, he slips his boxer briefs down his legs and grabs the condom. My mouth waters at the sight of him. I've never wanted to take someone in my mouth more than I want him, but I can't seem to make my legs work. Instead, I just stand here and stare, watching as he rips open the condom and covers his erection.

Then, he's slowly making his way to where I stand. With each step he takes, I grow wetter with need, my body flushed and humming with anticipation. "Let's get you the rest of the way naked," he suggests, reaching for the waistband of my panties. Before he removes them, however, he meets my gaze and asks, "Yes?"

"Yes," I quickly blurt out, praying he doesn't back out now.

He gives me a wink and slides my panties down to my ankles. As I step out of them, he reaches back and releases the clasp for my bra, causing it to drop around my elbows. When that too is on the floor, he pulls my naked body against his and kisses me. It's a deep, all-consuming kiss, one that promises good things yet to come.

His hands are everywhere I need them to be, yet I still crave more. They work their way around to my backside, cupping and drawing me closer. With one swift lift, I'm being hoisted in the air, pressed firmly against the wall of his bedroom. My legs snake around his waist, his erection trapped between our bodies. I grind against it, the pleasure flooding my body.

"Ever been fucked against the wall?" he murmurs, those penetrating orbs of his holding me hostage.

Every sexual encounter I've ever had flashes before my eyes. Sadly, there's not an incredibly high number, the number of guys I've been with can be counted on one hand. And Davis wasn't one to lift me up and fuck me against a wall. No, he was a missionary position guy, maybe the occasional flip where I was on top. But the times I suggested doggy-style I got a look that suggested I need to head straight to church and repent for my sins.

With a quick clear of my throat, I confirm, "No. No, I haven't."

He grins mischievously as he pulls back enough to put a little space between us. "I'll hold you up," he says, using his arms to lift me.

I reach between us, which isn't as easy to do as I expected, since he can't move his arms, but I eventually get him lined up at my opening. Then, in unison, he gently lowers me down while I angle my hips. I feel every inch of his cock slowly start to fill me. "Oh, fuck," I groan.

It's a tight fit—an incredibly, amazing tight fit. He takes my lips with his and slides his tongue along mine. The distraction allows my body to relax and his cock to move a little deeper until he's completely seated inside me. He stops, holding completely still, while he gives me a few moments to adjust to the invasion.

When I open my eyes, I can tell he's struggling. A sweat has broken out on his forehead and his jaw is tight. His entire body is rigid, like he's afraid to move. I run my hand up his cheek. "I'm okay, Kam."

"You sure?" he asks, his eyes full of concern. "I don't want to move until you're ready."

"Oh, I'm ready. *Very* ready," I assure him, rolling my hips. My clit brushes against his pubis, sending a shockwave of desire through me. "Move."

And he does.

Kameron carefully lifts me up without dislodging himself and brings me back down. His pace starts to increase, my back pushes into the wall for leverage. All I can do is hang on and enjoy the ride. He thrusts hard as I roll my hips. I can feel another orgasm brewing. I can feel the head of his cock brushing against my G-spot. My limbs start to shake as we move together, both chasing a common goal.

"Let go, Jilly," he whispers, brushing his lips against my shoulder. It's a featherlight touch but causes an eruption.

I feel myself tighten as I come hard. Kameron groans in my ear, his body thrusting up as he brings me down on him. He stills before pumping a few times, short, measured movements as our releases start to subside. My entire body is floating, even though I'm sure I must be nothing but dead weight.

Before he puts me down, I relax the back of my head against the wall, and he kisses me once more. This one is much more leisurely, as if we have all the time in the world to make out like teenagers.

"Gold star," I murmur when we both come up for air.

He chuckles, a low, gravelly sound that makes his cock flex inside me. "The highest honor," he replies, careful to slowly lower me down to the floor.

My legs are a bit wobbly as he pulls out and steps back. I take a few moments to catch my breath, leaning against the wall. I notice Kameron still standing in front of me, reaching down for the condom. Except, he doesn't pull it off. He's examining it.

"Fuck," he mutters, pulling the tip out.

"What's wrong?"

His eyes are wide with panic as he gazes up at me. "Uhh, the condom broke."

I look down, noticing the lack of anything inside the condom. That might explain why I suddenly feel a rush of moisture on my thighs.

"Stay right here. Don't move," he says, turning and heading for the en suite bathroom.

He's gone less than a minute and returns with a wet washcloth. "Here," he says, handing over the warm rag so I can clean myself up. After I run the wet cloth over my thighs, he adds, "I don't know what to do. This has never happened to me before."

I glance at the bathroom, the euphoric glow of what just happened suddenly gone. "Give me one second, okay?" I say, heading for his bathroom.

Closing the door, I quickly take care of business and clean myself up. When I step up to the sink to wash my hands, I can't help but notice the rosy hue to my cheeks and my swollen lips. A small smile spreads across my face, despite the rather unexpected ending to the sex we just had. It was…amazing. Earth-shattering. And whatever equally explosive adjectives I could come up with here.

But now we have to discuss the post-orgasmic issue.

I've never experienced a condom break. Not that I have a ton of experience, but I've heard of it happening, of course. I remember them talking about it during health class back in high school. Our teacher had always suggested two forms of birth control for this exact reason. No single form is one-hundred-percent foolproof. Pregnancy can happen even when using contraceptives.

When I was dating and married Davis, I was on birth control. I was anxiously waiting for the discussion when we'd decide for me to go off it. I wanted a baby. That was the ultimate dream. The end goal, you could say. And not just one baby, I wanted a few. Three was what I envisioned for myself, but I wasn't going to be picky. If I only had one, I'd take that child and love it to the max.

But that dream didn't happen. Davis decided parenthood wasn't for him, despite telling me throughout our time dating that it was. He changed his mind, as he said.

And because of that, I couldn't stay married to him.

Instead, I returned to the dating scene, only to find it not what I expected. Every first date I had was just that. A once and done. I didn't connect with any of them, not the way I thought I had with Davis. That's the number one reason why I put so much of myself into starting my own bakery. It was a distraction from my dream being dangled in front of my face all those years ago and then ripped away.

As I stare at my reflection, trying to push those darker thoughts from my mind, something hits me. A quick run of the math lets me know it's not the right time of the month for me to potentially get pregnant. Another bit of info they taught in health class is that a woman's most fertile right before or after ovulation, which happens around day fourteen in a woman's cycle. I'm a week past that, closing in on the last week before Aunt Flo comes for her monthly visit.

It's the wrong time.

I need to go back out there but need a little protection. Not from Kameron, I realize, but from the words I have to speak. They're incredibly personal, and I can't go out there and have this conversation without a shield.

Instantly, I spot what I'm looking for. I grab the white button-down shirt hanging on the back of the door, probably his work shirt from the night before. As I bring the material to my nose, I inhale his masculine scent mixed with the kitchen, and even though they're two totally different things, I don't hate it. In fact, I like it. Probably too much. It's the perfect representation of Kameron.

Once I've donned the shirt and have most of the buttons secured, I step out into his room. Kameron is sitting on the bed wearing a pair of shorts, his hands in his hair. "Hey," he says, jumping up and looking a bit stressed. It's in the moment he realizes what I'm wearing. His eyes devour, taking in my bare legs and the shirt that's way too big. It hits just above my knees and the cuffs well past my hands.

Approaching where he stands, I say, "So, I did some math. We're okay."

"Okay?" He wrinkles up his nose and forehead, clearly not understanding.

"It's the wrong time. Of the month."

Realization hits him hard, and he visibly relaxes. "Oh? Okay. You, uh, can tell that?" he asks sheepishly.

A little grin spreads across my lips. "We can, generally speaking. Well, based on where it falls in our monthly cycle."

He makes a little face, as if the thought of talking about my cycle makes him a touch uncomfortable. "Okay."

I walk to where he's standing and place my hands on his hard chest. He positions his hands on my lower back, drawing me to his body. His cock starts to get hard again. "I should probably head home."

"Probably," he murmurs, running his lips across my jaw.

My nipples get hard beneath his shirt. "I have to get up early in the morning."

He nods, sliding his tongue up my neck and across the lobe of my ear, making me shiver. "You *do* have to get up early."

I throw my arms around his neck and slam my lips to his, while his hands shift to my ass, and he maneuvers me toward his bed. "Maybe just once more before I go."

CHAPTER Ten

KAMERON

"Glad you had some time to join me," Gabe says when he slides into the booth across from me.

"You're the one who's incredibly busy, Dr. Rhodes," I tease. I've never faulted my friend for his career choice. In fact, I admire his dedication to healthcare and the community. He's a great doctor, and I'm honored to call him my friend.

"Blair took the afternoon off to take Wrenlee to the pediatrician for a checkup, so our patient load isn't too heavy," he informs me.

"You don't go?"

"I did for the first couple, but Blair told me I asked too many questions," he replies with a snort.

I can't help but chuckle. "Why doesn't that surprise me?"

"I just wanted to make sure my daughter was being checked out properly."

"And I'm sure it has nothing to do with you being a doctor yourself."

He pins me with a look. "Blair's a doctor too—a pediatrician at that—and told me I stressed out the doc."

I can't help but laugh a little harder than before.

"Stop it, it's not funny. The one we chose is a young doc, only thirty-one. I just wanted to make sure she was overseeing every aspect of my daughter's medical needs."

"And questioning her every move?" I deduce, reading between the lines.

"It's fine," he waves off the comment. "Blair does the doctor thing, and I get to do the bath thing."

"Yeah?" I ask, smiling at how excited my friend seems just by mentioning giving his baby a bath.

"Yep. Way better anyway. There're no shots at bathtime," he states with a grin.

"True."

"Hey, guys. Good to see you both," Ellie greets when she reaches our table. "What can I get you?"

"Ice water for me," Gabe answers.

"Same."

She nods. "Do you know what you want to eat?"

"I'll have the Cobb salad with Italian dressing," I request.

"You know what, I'll do the same, but with ranch."

"Coming right up," she replies cheerfully before stepping away to retrieve our drinks.

"So, you're the talk of the town," Gabe announces.

I snort in disgust. "When am I not?"

"Stop it. The only time I ever hear someone say your name is when they're referring to how amazing their meal was at your restaurant."

I do admit I like to hear that. I'm about to say more, but Ellie returns with two glasses of water. "Salads will be up in a few."

"Thanks, Ellie," I reply, taking a drink of my water.

"Anyway, you and Jillian are all they're talking about." Gabe just confirms exactly what I expected to hear.

"Don't people have anything better to do than concern themselves in others' lives?" I ask, already knowing the answer to that too.

He laughs. "Sure. Right. It's Pine Village, my friend."

I give my eyes a playful roll. "I know, but there's nothing for them to gossip about."

He leans forward a bit. "How about the fact you've barely dated since you moved home about ten years ago?"

"I've been busy," I retort.

"I know, and I get that. On a personal note, I'm happy for you."

I fidget in my seat, starting to feel a little hot around the collar. "Thanks," I mumble.

"Seriously, not only am I happy you're finally dating, but everyone likes Jillian."

I think back to having her naked in my bed last night, to seeing her come. It was a pretty amazing night; one I wouldn't mind repeating again soon.

Of course, maybe without the condom mishap. The second time we had sex was fine, no breakage in the protective barrier, but I still went out and purchased a brand-new box before I met Gabe here at the diner. Honestly, I'm not sure when I purchased the ones in my drawer, but if I had to guess it was a while ago.

How embarrassing is that?

"We're taking things slow," I tell him, despite the fact last night was anything but slow. In fact, it's been a little more than a week since we entered this weird agreement we share, and I've never slept with someone so fast. Not that I have a set number of dates to go on before we wind up in bed, but I've never felt this sort of connection before.

Ever.

"That's all right," he confirms, taking a drink. "But don't take it too slow. You're forty," he states with a smirk.

"My lower back reminds me every single morning when I get up." I chuckle and shake my head. It was like flipping a switch when I turned forty. Everything started to ache and shutdown. That's why I make sure to stay moving, running a couple times a week, as well as doing some weight training.

"Don't I know it. Being a first-time dad at forty is rough," he confesses. "But I wouldn't trade it for anything. In fact, I think we'll be adding to our family sooner rather than later."

"Yeah?" I ask, doing the math quick and realizing Wrenlee's already about six months old.

He shrugs. "We're not expecting—*yet*—but we're not preventing."

"Good for you. You're a great dad," I tell my oldest friend. Even though we lost touch for a while when we were both incredibly busy with our lives—he was in med school and I had finished culinary school and was working at a fast-paced restaurant in Chicago—we reconnected the moment I returned back home a decade ago.

Of course, a lot can happen in about ten years, and for me, it did. He doesn't know about my biggest secret, the one I haven't told a single soul in Pine Village. Not because I didn't want to, but simply for the fact it's no one's business. It happened a long time ago, and I hate dredging up the past.

"Thanks," he replies with a sheepish grin. "How about you? Any plans for fatherhood?"

I open my mouth to reply, but Ellie returns with our food. "Here you guys go. Do you need anything else?"

"Nope, I think we're good, El," Gabe replies, unrolling his napkin and pulling out his fork. "Thank you."

"You're both welcome. I'll check on you shortly." And with that, she's gone, moving down the line to help other customers.

He stabs a bite of his salad with his fork, but before he eats it, he adds, "You'd make a great dad too."

I shift in my seat, hating this conversation. Distracting myself by adding dressing to my salad, I reply, "I don't think so. I'm too old."

His eyebrows arch. "You're the same age as me."

I shrug. "Yeah, but you've already got a wife. That helps," I add with a chuckle.

"True, but that doesn't mean it's out of the question. Do you remember Jack Singleton? He and his wife just had a baby, and he's pushing fifty."

Shaking my head, I reply, "First off, his second wife is almost twenty years younger than he is. And can you imagine having a baby at fifty?"

Gabe shrugs and takes another bite. "It wouldn't be ideal, but I wouldn't be heartbroken if it happened. I love Wrenlee, and I'd take a dozen more just like her."

My heart is happy for my friend. He finally found his forever love, and even though they're getting a slightly later start, they're wildly compatible from what I've seen. They're both doctors, though Gabe is a general practitioner and Blair a pediatrician, and they get along well. They fit, and I'm glad he has Blair.

"I hear ya," I reply, shoveling more salad into my mouth. The last thing I want to do is think about babies. I had come to terms with the fact I was probably never going to be a father, and I'm okay with it, but this touchy subject is full of many emotions, including regret.

Coulda, shoulda, woulda.

"Anyway, back to you and Jillian. Blair was wondering if you two wanted to join us for dinner one night. Talk it over with Jillian and let one of us know."

I nod, feeling a bit excited to spend a little more time with her in the company of my friends. "Yeah, I can talk to her, but it might have to be a weeknight."

"That's fine. I already mentioned that to Blair," he says, attacking his salad like he hasn't eaten all day. "Mondays and Tuesdays are best for you, right?"

"Yeah, but I can make Sundays work too. Jilly is off, and I'll just work the lunch shift and have Marlin work dinner." I glance up and he's smiling at me. "What?"

"You called her Jilly. That's cute."

I roll my eyes, wanting to punch myself in the face for the slip of the tongue. Jilly is the nickname I only use in private, because it's more personal. Intimate.

"Anyway, moving on. There's something else I wanted to tell you, but you have to keep it close to your vest."

Gabe smirks. "I'm not wearing a vest."

I sigh, waiting on him to stop being an ass. "Never mind, I'm not going to tell you."

He barks out a laugh. "You're too easy to get worked up. Tell me."

I wait a few seconds, drawing out the suspense. I want him to wonder if I'm going to tell him or not. Of course I am, since he's my closest friend, but I don't want him to know that. "I got a deal for the building next to mine."

His eyes widen and a huge smile breaks out across his face. "Yeah? That's frickin' amazing, man. Congratulations."

"Frickin'?" I ask, teasing.

"Trying not to say it now that I have Wren. She hangs on my every word, and the last thing I want is her first word to be fuck."

I snort a laugh. "Would serve you right."

His mouth falls open. "What? I was an angel. My sister was the hellion," he says, referring to his younger sister, Hallie, who is married to another friend, Logan. "But in all seriousness, congratulations. You've wanted to expand next door for years. You've earned this."

My stomach drops to my shoes. I might have earned it in everyone's eyes, but I can't help but feel a ball of dread in the pit of my stomach, thanks to the lie. I can't deny the hard work and dedication it took to get to this point, but I also can't ignore the one big, fabricated detail that pushed the deal over the edge.

"Thanks," I mutter, picking at the rest of my salad. "Jillian's going to make the baked goods for me. I've already contacted my supplier, and the contract will terminate at the end of the month."

"That's good news for Jillian. I'm sure she'll appreciate the extra exposure."

I toss my napkin onto the table and move my salad plate to the side. "I wish I would have thought of it sooner, honestly. She has a solid business, but I know how hard it can be during the non-tourist seasons."

"Very true," Gabe agrees, finishing off his salad and checking his watch. "I hate to eat and run, but I have patients scheduled to start soon.

I wave him off. "You're fine. I'm just glad I got to see you for a bit." He pulls his wallet out as he climbs from the booth, but I wave it off. "I got it."

He drops a few bills on the table. "I'll at least cover the tip."

I nod. "I'll let you know about dinner."

"Sounds good. Say hello to Jillian for me."

"I will."

And then he's off, walking back to the clinic to see more patients.

I slip from the booth and head for the front counter where the register is. "Sorry, I didn't get back over there. Was everything all right?" Ellie asks, setting our bill down in front of me.

"It was perfect, thank you. Gabe had to get back to the clinic." I pull enough cash from my own wallet to cover our lunches.

She nods, tapping on the register until it opens to make change. "Usually, they don't even have time to sit and eat. They always take it to go and eat together at the clinic."

"I believe Blair has the afternoon off today," I confirm, taking the change Ellie hands over. "Thanks for lunch. It was delicious."

"You're welcome. Thanks for stopping by. Oh, and can I just say I'm loving you and Jillian together? She's the sweetest."

I can't help but smile. "She is."

Ellie stands up straight and leans in, hands firmly on her hips. "You better treat her right or else you'll deal with all of us."

"I will. Promise." With that, I head out of the diner, waving to a few patrons I know as I go.

The moment I hit the sidewalk I know exactly where I'm going. The restaurant is closed again today, and while there's always something I can do there, I don't have anything pressing that needs my attention.

The walk to the bakery is short, and the moment I pull open the door, I'm hit with the scent of sugar and cinnamon, two things I will forever associate with Jillian. She's behind her display case, moving pastries around on the trays and pulling out the empty ones. She glances up and smiles. "Hi."

"Hey," I say, making my way toward her. I've made several visits to her place, grabbing a cup of coffee on my way to the restaurant, but this is the first time I've arrived in the afternoon. It's quiet, only one table occupied by a couple of older ladies. They appear to be enjoying coffee or tea and a sweet treat as they visit.

"What brings you in? On your way to the restaurant?"

"No, I just had lunch with Gabe. He invited me to meet him for a quick bite while he took lunch."

She sets the empty trays on the back counter and gives me her full attention. "Blair didn't join you?"

"No, Wrenlee had a doctor's appointment, so it was just Gabe."

"Isn't it funny they're both doctors and they take their daughter to a different doctor?" she asks with a giggle.

"Yeah, I assume they didn't want to treat their own child, which I don't blame them."

"Oh, me either," she quickly adds, waving her hand. "It's just comical to me. I'm weird like that."

I look around once more, noting the calm and quiet. Even with the group of ladies enjoying an afternoon treat, there's a relaxed, peaceful vibe. "What do you have that's good?" I ask, taking in her display case.

"Everything." She flashes me a smile, one that I return. "It's pretty picked over by this point in the day, but the good news is afternoon pastries are half price."

I glance up, giving her a quizzical look. "They are? Why?"

"Well, I don't want leftovers in my line of work. Pastries aren't as good the next day, and they don't sell well. So, I bake what I think I can sell that day. My breakfast pastries are a huge hit. There are always people who stop by in the mid-morning or early afternoon for a sweet treat to get them through the day, so I offer anything left in the case after twelve at half price. Sometimes it's completely gone by twelve thirty and other times, it takes until closer to two."

"Huh," I reply, giving her business model some consideration. I can understand why she does it, but I can't help but wonder how much revenue she's losing by offering it at half price.

"I'd rather recoup some of the money than just completely throw it away, which is what I would end up doing if it didn't sell by the time I lock the door," she adds, as if reading my mind.

"Makes sense." Scanning the case, I take note of what's left. A few dozen cookies in a variety of flavors, a couple slices of cake, and some jumbo cupcakes. "I'll take a cupcake, please," I say, pointing to the one with fresh blueberries on top.

"That's lemon," she informs me. "With a vanilla buttercream and fresh blueberries."

"Sounds good," I reply. I'm not usually much of a sweets guy, but I do admit her offerings always sound so damn delicious.

She places the cupcake on a small ceramic plate and asks, "Would you like something to drink?"

I look up at the menu on the wall. "How about one of those fancy teas."

She nods. "Any particular flavor?"

"You choose. I'm not picky," I tell her, reaching into my wallet and pulling out some cash.

She makes me tea with blueberry and sets it on the counter. "This will enhance the blueberry flavoring in the cupcake."

I nod, taking the drink. "How much?"

She waves off my question. "On the house."

My eyes narrow. "How much?"

Jillian crosses her arms and lifts her chin. "I got it."

Sighing, I take the cash I was about to give her for my purchases and slip it into the tip jar.

"You don't have to do that," she insists.

"Yes, I do," I tell her, taking my cup and my plate and heading toward a table as far away from the older ladies as I can get.

So I can enjoy my dessert in peace.

And appreciate one hell of a view.

CHAPTER *eleven*

Jillian

I make myself a decaf caramel iced coffee and head toward his table. "Ladies, holler if you need me," I say to the quad group of regular customers. They come in every Tuesday afternoon and enjoy a drink and pastry together.

"Take a break, dear. We'll be fine," one of them replies.

Kameron is taking his first bite of his cupcake when I reach him. "Mind if I join you?"

He swallows his cake and nods. "Please do. This is fantastic. It's not overly sweet or zesty. Sometimes you get a lemon dessert, and it's too much."

I take a sip of my iced coffee and set it on the table. "Thank you. I think there's more flavor when you don't overdo it, if you know what I mean."

"I do," he says, taking a second bite. "And the blueberry is nothing but complementary."

"I usually do vanilla buttercream instead of a lemon flavored so it's not too strong."

"Well done. I might even take one to go before I leave," he replies with a wink.

Grinning, I add, "If there's any left."

I watch as he enjoys his cupcake. When he's down to the last bite, he asks, "Are you the only one here?"

I nod. "In the afternoons, yes. Lisa is one of my part-timers, and she's here six to twelve, four days a week. Helen works one day a week and fills in when Lisa needs time off, and then there's Emmalynn, who's a senior in high school. She works with me on Saturdays and helps do cake deliveries when needed."

"I know Helen," he replies, taking his final bite of his cupcake. "She was friends with my mom, even though she was a bit older."

I nod, realizing this was the first time he's mentioned either of his parents. I know the story—bad news travels fast in a small town—and remember them from when I was growing up. "Helen is a godsend and doesn't seem to mind being called last minute. She retired a few years back and just wanted to be out of the house a little bit. She agreed to one day a week, but since Lisa is a young mom, sometimes she is needed to fill in when one of Lisa's boys is sick or has a field trip or something."

"She comes into the restaurant with her husband from time to time, but it's...hard. She gets emotional when she sees me. I definitely caught her by surprise when I stopped in last Friday for coffee. She wasn't expecting me."

My throat is thick with emotion and my eyes fill with tears. "I can imagine."

He gives me a soft smile. "Not that I blame her. She was a good friend. My mom loved her."

I nod, recalling hearing the news more than a decade ago about the untimely passing of both Sidney and Peter Markley. They were in a car accident outside of town on an icy road. They slid through a T-intersection, breaking through an already-damaged guardrail from a previous accident two days prior, falling into a ravine below. Because of the weather, no one was out and about, and unfortunately, they weren't discovered until it was too late. Both passed from injuries sustained in the accident, and the town was left reeling from the loss.

He clears his throat and looks down at his empty plate. "It's why I moved home. I was already starting to miss the small-town lifestyle I grew up in, but I needed that connection to them, even though they were both gone. I had been thinking about starting my own restaurant, but it was when I came home for their funeral and to get their affairs in order I realized what my next step was going to be."

A sad smile stretches across my face as I reach out and place my hand on top of his. "They'd be very proud of you."

"Thank you," he replies, his words heavy with emotion. "I'm certain they would have been my first customers in the door on opening night."

I remember seeing the photos in the local newspaper of his opening and how he dedicated that night to his parents. In fact, now that I think of it, a photograph of them hangs inside the door at the hostess stand. "I'm sure they would have."

"Were your parents your first customers?" he asks curiously.

I nod. "They were. They insisted on standing out on the sidewalk on that cold December morning and watch me flip the sign to open."

He smiles. "I'm glad."

"They took me to a celebratory dinner later in the week to your restaurant."

Kameron seems genuinely surprised by that. "They did?"

"Of course. Your place is the nicest restaurant we have, and sometimes the occasion calls for a step up over the diner and Mexican restaurant in town."

"It does. That's why I chose that avenue. I didn't want to directly compete with another local staple in town. My previous experience was high-end steak houses, so that's the route I continued on. But there's also a difference between a Chicago steak house and Pine Village steak house, so I had to take the location into consideration from the start."

"You've done well, Kam."

He blushes a bit at the compliment. "Thanks."

The ladies across the room stand up, scooting in their chairs and picking up their trash. "The cake was delicious, Jillian," one of them says.

"See you next Tuesday," another adds as they all head for the door.

"Enjoy your afternoon, ladies. See you next week."

The air surrounding us thickens as we're left alone. He looks so casual, so relaxed as he stares at me. "So, now what?"

Clearing the dryness from my throat, I answer, "Well, now I would go in back and do some dishes. I'd clean the table that was just vacated, and then I'd prepare to decorate the cakes for tomorrow morning's pickup."

"Cakes?" he asks, his eyes full of excitement.

"Yes. That's a big part of my business and usually what I do in the afternoons and evenings after I close."

"Interesting," he replies, leaning back and taking a drink of his tea. "How many cakes do you make?"

"In a week? Gosh, some weeks it's only one or two, but others, it might be ten to fifteen."

His eyes widen comically. "Fifteen cakes? A week?"

I shrug. "Fall is a busy birthday season. Apparently, a lot of people make babies during the winter."

He chuckles at my comment. "I can see that. Not much to do in the dead of winter when you're stuck inside but...make babies." His eyes dance with anticipation and desire, and I have to squeeze my thighs together to ward off the onslaught of need it provokes.

Suddenly, he stands up. "How about I help you?"

His abrupt movement catches me off guard. "Help?"

"Yeah. I'll go clean the table and help you prepare to close, and you can do your cake prep stuff."

My legs seem a little unsteady as I stand up and face him. He's so damn beautiful, he's like the sun. You don't want to look directly at him because it'll hurt your eyes. "You want to help?"

"Of course," he says with a casual shrug. "Unless you don't want the help. I know what it's like having someone underfoot and messing up your rhythm. Just say the word and I'll leave."

"No," I blurt out, unnaturally fast.

He cracks a smile. "Okay, but if you ever want me to go, just say the word. You can tell me you have to wash your hair or something, and I will leave without asking questions."

"Like a code phrase?" My lips flicker upward in a hint of a smile.

"Yes, exactly."

"All right. How are you at dishes?"

He pretends to push up imaginary sleeves on his shirt. "Are you kidding? I'm great at them. In fact, that's how I got my start in culinary excellence. I used to wash dishes at Frannie's Diner."

I turn to head toward the kitchen area. "Really? I didn't know that."

"Yep. Saul taught me some of my early tricks and tips in the kitchen," he confirms, following me behind the counter. "He was a great mentor."

"That's cool. I bet he's super proud of you too."

He slowly nods his head, running his hands through his hair. "I think so. He stops by for dinner once or twice a month. He always brings his sister, Frannie, and treats her. I give them the best table in the house."

"Which one is that?" I find myself asking.

"The one I use with you."

My heart is doing this happy little jig in my chest, and I want to throw in some hand motions, like raise the roof. That's how much of a weirdo I am. "That's nice of you," I tell him, reaching into the sanitation bucket and removing the warm cloth.

"I got this," he says, taking the cloth from my hand and wringing it out.

I can't help but stand here and watch as he walks to the table my customers had vacated and starts wiping it down. You can tell he's in the food industry, because he carefully moves the napkin holder in the middle and wipes beneath it. Then, he wipes down the holder before replacing it in the center of the table. He even goes as far as to wipe the chairs down, including the backrest and the seat before pushing them beneath the table.

My eyes go ahead and take a leisurely stroll down his backside, memorizing the way his ass looks in a pair of blue jeans. They fit well too, like they were custom-made to accentuate everything God gave him, including an impressive bulge in the front.

"Quit staring at me, perv," he quips, offering me a wink and a grin when my eyes finally meet his.

"I can if I want," I insist, grabbing the small stack of dirty trays I pulled from the display case. "It's one of the perks of being your girlfriend."

He laughs hard. "I guess that's true. Lord knows I've been doing my fair share of perving." He looks down, clearly gawking at my chest before his eyes drop to below my waist. If only I could read his thoughts, because I'm certain they're in the gutter, and frankly, I wouldn't mind hearing them. Like a detailed list of everything he'd do to me the moment he got me naked.

Is it suddenly hot in here?

I head to the kitchen and start filling up one of the sink basins with hot, soapy water. When I turn off the water, Kameron is there. "Go get your cake work ready. I got this."

He doesn't push me out of the way, but he definitely lets me know he's there to help. To wash dishes. What man willingly volunteers to wash dishes? My ex-husband hated it. He would rather have left a pile beside the sink than take a few minutes to wash them.

But Kameron understands that dishes are a part of owning a food-based business. To be completely transparent, that alone boosts his hotness by a million percent. Why? Because any man who helps with any of those pesky "woman's" household chores is a man to marry.

Not that I'm thinking of marrying him.

I'm not.

Why would I?

Our relationship is fake, even if the orgasms weren't.

But a real relationship isn't built on orgasms, and while we have chemistry, that still doesn't scream long-term relationship.

It screams fun while it lasts.

Ignoring my Debbie Downer moment and the way my heart sinks at the thought, I head to the freezer to retrieve my cake rounds. I pull all three out and place them on my workstation.

"You froze your cakes?"

I glance over at Kameron, who's watching me intently, and nod. "It makes it easier to decorate."

After a couple of seconds, he offers a simple, "Huh."

I retrieve my ingredients for the vanilla buttercream and set them aside. The butter was already pulled from the refrigerator and should be room temperature soon, which is the one step you don't want to forget. Anytime I'm prepping to decorate, if I'm making buttercream frosting, the butter must be warmed to room temperature. Otherwise, it doesn't blend well and doesn't give the best results.

Just as I start adding the ingredients to my mixing bowl, I hear the bell chime over the door. Kameron is just finishing drying the second pan, setting them aside on the counter, and turns to me. "I'll get it."

Surprise must transform my face. "You'll get it?"

He shrugs. "Yep. I'll holler if I need anything."

I should continue to prepare the icing, but I can't. I want to witness the moment Kameron goes up front to help the customer. Plus, I'm sure he's going to need help. Whether it be for a coffee or blended drink or using the register, I know he'll have a question or two.

"Kameron! What in the world are you doing here?"

I push through the swinging café doors that separate the front serving area and counter from the kitchen and find one of my favorite customers at the counter, having recognized her voice.

"Hi, Mrs. Rhodes," he replies to Gabe and Hallie's mom.

"Oh, stop that. Call me Debbie." She looks over at me and smiles. "I heard there was a new budding relationship in town, and I'm so happy to see it's true. Two of my favorite people," the woman proclaims. To Kameron, she adds, "It's been a while since you've come over for dinner. Now I see why." She adds a wink with her smile.

Kameron chuckles. "It's new. We've been taking it slow," he says to her, glancing over his shoulder and meeting my gaze.

"Well, I admit, this is a pleasant surprise. When I decided to stop by and see what sweet treats were left for the day, I wasn't expecting to find you here."

"Jillian is preparing to decorate a cake, so I offered to help her out. What can I get you?" he asks, lifting his chin and clearly falling into his self-proclaimed job easily.

"I'm happy to see cookies. I'd like a half-dozen," she informs Kameron.

When he looks my way, I point to the middle-sized white box on the shelf. It'll hold six cookies perfectly and make transportation easier.

Kameron grabs the top box and opens it up. Before I can say a word, he grabs one of the clear serving gloves from the box and slips it on his hand. Both Debbie and I laugh when we notice the tight fit. I stock the medium size since everyone who works here has smaller hands, but it's clear Kameron could use a larger size.

You know what they say about big hands, right?

It's true.

I fight the blush and turn my attention to watching him open the case. "What flavors would you like?"

"I'm not picky. Surprise me," she tells him.

Kameron pulls out two chocolate chunk cookies, one frosted sugar cookie, a chocolate drizzled peanut butter cup cookie, and two strawberry shortcake cookies. "Is that all?" he asks, closing the box.

"That is," she confirms, retrieving cash from her purse.

Kameron turns and grabs a small square box, one that fits a cupcake or piece of cake. He slips a lemon cupcake from the case and sets it inside. "My treat," he tells her as he places the small box on the counter.

"Oh, you don't have to do that," she insists.

"Yes, I do. I had one earlier, and it was amazing. So I'm buying one for the woman I've always considered a second mom," he tells her. There's a heaviness in his words, in the insinuation.

I can't help but notice Debbie tear up, seeming to struggle to swallow over an onslaught of emotions. "Well, I'll think of you the entire time I enjoy my afternoon treat."

He rips off the glove and tosses it in the trash can before moving to the cash register. It's an electronic device, with a touchscreen and easy to find categories. I don't have any specifics on the screen, just a generalized listing like cupcake, slice of cake, cookies, and more. So it's not hard for him to figure out how to use it, and he's able to add a half-dozen cookies to the order quickly.

Only when he goes to total it do I step forward and help. "Since it's after noon, everything from the case is half price," I remind him. He watches as I tap on the discount button and indicate it's a fifty percent off item. My cookies are two dollars each, and a dozen receives a free thirteenth one. The baker's dozen special, as I call it.

"Six forty-two," Kameron tells Debbie, who hands over a ten-dollar bill.

He easily makes change and slides her treats toward her as she adds her change to the tip jar. "Thanks for visiting Flour Power Bakery. Come back soon," he says, making me smile.

"Oh, you know I will. And Roger and I will be by the restaurant this weekend. Our anniversary is coming up, and I can't think of a better way to celebrate than with a wonderful meal made by my son's best friend. The one who helped eat me out of house and home during those horrible growing pain years of high school."

Kameron chuckles. "I think I owe you more than just a cupcake," he says with a wink. "I probably owe you a few dinners too."

"Don't you even think about it." She gives him a stern look before abandoning her purse beside her pastry boxes and walking around the counter. She throws her arms up, indicating she's expecting a hug from Kameron.

He obliges, stepping into her embrace and giving her a hard squeeze. She's so much smaller than he is, but neither seems to mind. Their embrace lasts several long seconds, and I feel my own emotions lodging in my throat. I know I should look away, to let them have their private moment, but I can't.

Finally, they pull away and she offers me a hug as well. "Be good to my boy. He has a tough exterior, but his heart is pure gold."

I nod, not able to find words all of a sudden.

"I'll leave you two to get back to work," she says, retrieving her purse and boxes. "Thank you for this. You've both made my entire day."

"See you this weekend," Kameron says. "I'll save you the best seat in the house."

She offers another motherly smile, full of fondness and adoration, before heading for the door. With one final wave, she exits the bakery, leaving us alone once more.

He taps on the screen, ringing up a cupcake—the one he gifted Debbie. I can't help but notice he doesn't add the fifty percent off discount, and before I can say a word about it, he hits total and pulls money from his wallet. Not only does he pay full price for the treat, but he also puts the change in the tip jar.

Turning back to me, I can't help but notice how utterly perfect this man is. From his handsome, rugged good looks to his willingness to help and learn. Plus, he knows his way around a kitchen.

And a female body.

I need to remember this is fake.

Clapping his hands together, he offers me a big grin. "Let's decorate a cake."

Yeah, I'm toast.

CHAPTER
Twelve

KAMERON

Like the creeper I apparently am, I've spent the last hour watching Jillian decorate a three-layered blueberry lemon cake with vanilla buttercream frosting. Apparently, the cupcakes she's selling today were made from the leftover batter last night. She let the cupcakes cool before placing them in an air-tight container. Then, decorated them first thing this morning. The mixture of flavors was so exquisite, I'm hoping she adds thick slices of the cake to the dessert menu for my restaurant.

Maybe a summertime treat.

"What are you thinking about over there?" she asks, adding the finishing touches to the decorated cake.

"We should discuss the menu for desserts at the restaurant. I'd love to see this lemon blueberry cake on the list."

She nods, setting the piping bag down on the counter and brushing a wayward strand of hair off her forehead with the back of her gloved hand.

I reach over and swipe away the hair, taking it between my fingers and gently moving it behind her ear. The gesture has a romantic feel, the room sexually charged. I like her hair, plain and simple. Like the way it smells, the way it feels between my fingers, the way it frames her heart-shaped face.

Her green eyes hold mine; her lips are parted just a touch. Her mouth looks completely kissable, and I find myself leaning in and doing just that. The kiss is light but still packs a punch. It makes my entire body flush with need; my cock starts to thicken in my pants. And that's just from a simple kiss.

Before it can go anywhere—like bending her over the workstation and messing up the cake she's spent the last hour perfecting—I pull back and smile. "Tell me what you're thinking." When I register confusion on her pretty face, I add, "For the dessert menu."

"Oh," she replies, standing up straight and clearing her throat. She takes a couple seconds to collect herself before telling me her plan. "I know your current baker does two different desserts weekly, refrigerated to help keep them fresh, but I was thinking of trying something new."

I give her a quizzical look. "How do you know that?"

She shrugs her petite shoulders. "I know desserts. I've learned a lot over the last few years of owning this place, and the best way to keep baked goods fresh is in the refrigerator in an air-tight container."

"Fair enough. Yes, that's exactly what she does. She delivers on Wednesdays before I open for dinner." I prop my hip against her workstation and watch as she completes her cake, placing it gingerly inside a white box and closing the lid. Then, she wraps the top in plastic wrap to help seal it.

"I was thinking, since I'm here—in town," she clarifies, "I can make them fresh sooner. So the chocolate cake is truly fresh and not refrigerated, and the peach cobbler is still warm from the oven."

Her suggestion shocks me. "Jillian, that seems like a lot of extra work. You'd be making desserts every day," I counter, knowing how busy she can get, especially during high-tourist season.

She turns and meets my penetrating gaze. "But it's not work when you're doing what you love."

My respect—the huge amount I already had for her—just skyrockets once more. She's truly a remarkable creature, and I don't understand why someone hasn't claimed her as his own yet. Or why someone would let her go, because I'm definitely thinking her ex-husband is the dumbest asshole this side of the Mississippi. Maybe even the entire continent. But it also seems like a big ask. Not that I'm asking—she's offering—but still. I do understand her, maybe even better than anyone else. "How about this. We'll give it a try that way and see how it goes, but if it's too much for you, I want to know. We can adjust the delivery schedule so you're not making fresh desserts every day."

A faint smile crests her lips. "I'll be fine, Kameron, promise. This is what I do."

And making sure I take care of you is what I do.

Except, that's not exactly true.

Our relationship isn't real, even if it's starting to feel like it is.

I push that thought from my head. "Still, let's do a trial run."

She shrugs and moves the decorated cake to the fridge for tomorrow's pickup. "That's fine." Turning to me, she hops up on the corner of the counter. "So, this is what I've been thinking," she starts, and then proceeds to tell me all about the menu options she's been working on.

My mouth waters at all the delicious options she's come up with, but mostly, I can't get over her enthusiasm. The excitement that transforms her face as she tells me about her ideas. One chocolate and one non-chocolate, mostly a fruit option, each week. Honestly, I want to try them all. Many have been featured at my restaurant before from the other baker, but there's something so different about hearing about them from Jillian's lips. I know she'll make each dessert as unique as possible and the best she possibly can.

I'm excited for this partnership.

"Let's plan to finalize the details at the end of the month," I suggest.

"Sounds good."

"Now, are you done for the day?"

She gives me a slow grin and shakes her head. "I still have to prep for tomorrow."

My heart sinks a little, only because I was hoping to steal her away for a bit right now, but what I have planned can wait. "Okay, I'll help. Then, I'm taking you to dinner."

"Dinner?" she asks, her eyes brightening a bit.

"Yeah, unless you already have plans?" The thought of her going to dinner with someone else doesn't sit well in my gut.

"No plans. I was just going to make a salad or something when I got home."

"How about a taco salad? We can walk down to the Mexican restaurant after we're done here."

She nods. "Sounds great, though I don't get a taco salad." She moves over to the shelf and retrieves a new mixing bowl.

"No?" I ask, watching as she sets the dirty, used utensils and bowls on the small counter beside the sink basin.

"Nope. I can eat my weight in chips and salsa, and then still consume an entire steak burrito with queso on top."

Fuck, she's perfect.

"Yeah? It's a date."

Best. Date. Ever.

"Oh! Let's get ice cream!" she proclaims as we walk back to her bakery from the Mexican restaurant.

"You're still hungry?" I tease, even though I'm honestly a little impressed. Jillian was absolutely right about eating her weight in chips and salsa and then wolfed down a big steak burrito with queso. How in the world she has room for ice cream right now is beyond my comprehension.

"See, here's the beauty about ice cream. It melts in your mouth, so when it reaches your stomach, it just slides into the cracks and crevasses around the other food. Ice cream is a filler, if you will."

I can't help it; I bark out a laugh. "Makes total sense," I assure her with a smile, turning a bit so we can cross the street and hit Miss Molly's Ice Cream Parlor. We do have to walk a little farther down the street, past Jillian's bakery, to the next block.

When we reach the door, there aren't too many customers hanging around. The outside picnic tables are empty, since the evenings are starting to cool off now, but there are a few customers sitting at the little bistro tables inside. It's a small place, similar in size to the bakery down the street and is a popular place for the kids, especially after football games.

"Hi, Jillian, Kameron," Molly greets with a smile.

"Hey, Molly. How's it going?" Jillian asks pleasantly.

"Not too bad," she says with a little shrug. "Always gets a little slower after Labor Day, but fortunately, we have a great community who supports us and keeps us hopping."

Jillian nods in agreement, and I imagine they're both in the same boat. They rely heavily on the busy tourist seasons to help create enough revenue to help sustain them during the slower months. "So, what do you have on special this week?"

Molly's eyes brighten. "I have cotton candy ice cream and a lemon sherbet with raspberry swirl."

"Oh, the sherbet sounds amazing. I'll have a single scoop cup of that, please."

Molly looks at me expectantly. Usually, I get the mint chocolate chip ice cream, but the sherbert does sound good. "I'll have the same."

She moves quickly, grabbing two paper bowls and placing a hearty scoop of the sherbet in each. She slips a little wooden spoon inside and sets them on the counter. "Six forty-two," she says, taking off her plastic serving gloves and tapping on the register screen.

Jillian goes to retrieve money, but I wave her off and hand over a ten-dollar bill. When Molly grabs my change, I put it directly into the tip jar. "Thank you," she states with a grin. "Enjoy your sherbet."

We take our bowls over to one of the bistro tables and have a seat. Upbeat pop music pipes through the speakers in the corners of the room, just loud enough to hear, but not so loud you have to raise your voice to talk.

I take my first bite of the lemony, raspberry goodness, happy with my choice. "This is good," I confirm, earning a nod of agreement from Jillian.

"It really is. Very summery."

We sit in comfortable silence for a few minutes, enjoying our treat and taking in the décor and ambiance. A couple of teenagers arrive, walking to the counter and placing their orders for double scoop waffle cones. "You know, I don't think I've ever been here on a weeknight."

"No?" she asks, licking the sherbet off her little wooden spoon. My dick definitely takes notice.

"Nope," I reiterate. "The restaurant is open Wednesday through Sunday, and the other two days are spent doing housework and prepping at the restaurant."

She meets my gaze, her green eyes reflective pools of curiosity. "You've never brought a date here?" Her cheeks turn a light shade of pink.

"Uhh, no. You're my first," I reply with a wink.

"Oh." She blushes even darker, and I can hear her foot starting to tap beneath the table. She shifts in her seat before adding, "You're kinda missing out, my friend. Ice cream dates are the best."

I can't help but smile. "I'm realizing that." After a beat, I ask, "Been on a lot of ice cream dates before?"

She shrugs. "Not a lot, honestly, but there were a few. Ice cream is the new coffee date. I'd suggest we meet here and have ice cream. Then, if it went well, a dinner date."

I nod, considering her suggestion. "Makes sense. This way, if you weren't feeling it, you could thank them for their time and leave. And if it was going well, then dinner is the likely next step."

She nods.

"How many made it to the dinner part of the night?" I ask, wanting to know, yet not wanting to. I know Jillian has dated before—hell, she was married—but I don't want to think about it. Jealousy burns in the pit of my stomach, making my sherbet sit funny.

"None," she replies with a chuckle.

"None?"

She shakes her head, averting her gaze. "Pathetic, huh?"

"Absolutely not," I insist. "You just hadn't found the right guy to share sherbet with."

I don't know why I say that, honestly. This agreement is fake, our relationship built on a ruse. But while the relationship might be fake, these budding feelings aren't. I *like* Jillian. A lot. And not just the sex we had last night either, though that was pretty fucking amazing. I enjoy spending time with her, even doing the most mundane tasks like washing dishes and decorating cakes.

"I think, technically, we did it backward, considering we just ate dinner," she says matter-of-factly.

"True, but we've kinda been a bit unconventional from the start, right?" I ask with a playful wink.

She giggles the sweetest sound, and I have this overwhelming urge to make her do it over and over again. "That's the understatement of the year."

And we leave it at that.

I feel giddy as we enjoy the rest of our treat, both of us stealing glances at the other and not being shy about it when busted. By the time our bowls are empty, I know it's time to head out. As much as I'd love to sit and talk with her until Molly flips the closed sign, Jillian gets up incredibly early in the morning, and it's nearing the time she goes to bed.

"The chariot is going to turn into a pumpkin, Jilly," I state, checking the time on my watch for verification.

"Yeah." That one word holds so much disappointment.

Before I can, she picks up our empty bowls and carries them to the trash bin. We both wave at Molly and offer thank yous before stepping through the door and onto the sidewalk. It's a bit chillier than it was earlier, but I'm not sure if the temperature actually dropped that much in the last thirty minutes, or if it's simply because we just ate frozen sherbet.

Probably the latter.

Fortunately, we don't have far to go. We start to cross the street to return to the bakery, where we left our vehicles, when she stops me dead in my tracks.

"Oh my God! It's a dick!"

I scan the roadway in front of me, trying to figure out what in the world she's talking about. When I look her way, concerned I'm not getting some sort of joke, she's blushing a dark shade of red. Even under the falling night sky and the dimly lit streetlights, I can see the color of her skin. Her green eyes are wide with embarrassment and humor, while she tries to cover her face with her hands.

"I can tell what's on your mind," I mutter, humorously.

"No! Oh my God," she bellows, dropping her head into her hands and laughing. "I can't believe I said that out loud."

"I'll be honest, Jilly, I'm just glad there wasn't a real dick out here somewhere. You know, like someone lost theirs?"

She barks out a laugh. "Does that happen? Guys just randomly lose their dicks?"

I shrug. "As a teenager, I thought if I didn't use it, it'd fall off."

She laughs hard, tears forming in the corners of her pretty eyes. "Stop it!"

"No, it's true. Though, when I was a little boy, my grandma told me the opposite. She told me and my brother if we played with it before marriage, it would fall off."

The memory hits me hard. I can see the scene as if it happened just yesterday. My grandma sitting in her favorite easy chair and my younger brother, Kelvin, on the floor beside me. I was nine, wishing I could go outside and play with neighborhood kids and not have to be inside playing with my little brother, especially one who was only four years old.

We were playing with Matchbox cars, most of them left from when our dad was a kid. I can somewhat remember how the conversation got started too. I recall Kelvin laughing because someone on TV mentioned their wiener getting hard, in so many words, during one of Grandma's daytime TV shows. Kelvin giggled uncontrollably and proclaimed his own wiener gets hard too. That's when Grandma made us promise not to play with them before marriage.

That particular recollection is like a punch to the gut.

Even though I think about my brother often, it hurts.

Bad.

Just like the memory does right now.

Jillian's hand wraps around my arm and gives a gentle squeeze. "I'm sorry," she whispers.

I clear my throat and look around, realizing we're still standing in the middle of the roadway. Fortunately, downtown Pine Village isn't too busy right now, but that doesn't mean we should continue to stand where we can get hit by a car.

Reaching down, I take her hand in mine and lead us the rest of the way across the street to the sidewalk. "You're fine. It wasn't anything you said or did."

She drops her gaze before looking up at me. "I'm sorry, but I don't really remember him. He was two years younger than me in school, I think."

I nod. "He was. He had just started kindergarten when he was diagnosed."

Her eyes hold sadness, and maybe a touch of pity. Who doesn't pity the guy who lost his little brother to childhood cancer and then his parents when he was thirty?

She offers me a gentle, warm grin before looking up. With her hand firmly in mine, she lifts them and points. "Do you see that?"

I look up, staring at the clouded night sky. "What?"

"That cloud," she informs me. "It's long and has that little puff on the bottom? It looks like—"

"A dick," I finish her sentence, shaking my head and chuckling.

She nods. "Yeah. So, when I was a little girl, my dad and I would play this game when we were outside. We would find shapes in the clouds and try to outdo each other. Of course, most of them were animals or general shapes. I think this is my first dick."

I bring her hand to my lips and murmur, "I'm glad I could be here for your first dick find."

She giggles naturally, and we start to walk toward the bakery. "This is a big moment. I'm glad too." After a moment she adds, "Sorry I just blurted it out. Not very appropriate for the middle of Main Street."

I shrug. "If you can't talk about cloud dicks with your boyfriend, then who can you talk about them with?" I ask. Immediately, I realized I didn't use the term fake. Why? Because it doesn't feel fake anymore.

"Good point."

When we reach the bakery, we walk around the back alleyway, where her car is parked. I'm on the street, but there's no way I wouldn't escort her to her vehicle, especially at night. Yes, this is Pine Village, but shit can happen anywhere.

"Thank you. For everything," she says after unlocking her door.

I pull open her driver's door and wait while she slips inside. "You're welcome. I'll, uh, be pretty busy over the next few days, but

I was wondering if maybe you wanted to stop by and have dinner with me one night."

She gives me an eager grin. "I'd like that."

"Good. Just text me what night works best for you, and I'll save us a table."

She nods and starts her car. "Sounds good, Kameron."

"Be safe, Jilly. Let me know when you make it home," I tell her. I don't know if I've ever done that before, requested a woman I'm seeing tell me when she's home, but it seems natural and appropriate, even if our relationship is slightly unconventional.

"I will."

I close her door and step back, giving her a wave as she pulls out of her parking spot and prepares to head home. It isn't until she's exiting the alley that I finally make my way around to the front of the building and climb into my own vehicle. As I start my SUV, I glance in the rearview mirror. There's no missing the smile on my face.

Jillian does that.

She makes me smile for the first time in...a long time.

A real one.

And I don't hate it.

In fact, it's quite the opposite.

I'm enjoying the hell out of spending time with Jillian Kirby.

CHAPTER Thirteen

Jillian

"Welcome to Prime Steak House," Veronica says politely as I step inside on Friday.

"Hi, Veronica," I reply as the door closes behind me.

"I have your table ready," she informs me, grabbing a stack of menus and leading the way. We head to the same table we've used the last couple of times we've dined together, but it catches my attention it's set for four.

"Is this the right one?" I ask, not wanting to take a table from another party.

She nods and gives me a polite smile. "It is. Kameron asked me to prep it for four."

"Oh. Okay." I slip into a chair toward the wall, so I'm out of the way for whoever else is joining us. I pull out my phone and check for messages. Surely Kameron would have sent me a quick note to let me know if someone was joining us, right?

But I don't see a text message, which is strange.

The server approaches and fills my water glass. "Can I get you anything else to drink while you wait for your party?" she asks politely.

"No, this is perfect, thank you."

She nods and fills up the other three glasses at the table before turning and moving to another table. I glance around once more, wondering who's joining us for dinner. Fortunately, my question is answered a few minutes later when I spot familiar faces entering the restaurant and are led my way.

"What are you two doing here?" I ask Blair and Gabe, who are smiling widely as they join me.

"Well, I called Kameron to see if I could still get a table tonight before the game, and he mentioned you two were having dinner and invited us to join you," Gabe says after holding Blair's seat before taking his own.

"I'm so glad," I tell him, taking a sip of my water. "What about Wrenlee?"

"My dad and Patience offered to keep her earlier than planned so we could have dinner before the football game," Blair informs me as the server returns to take their drink orders. They both decide to drink water, and the server promises to be back in a moment with fresh bread.

"Actually, I think it was more Aggie's insistence that they called," Gabe adds once the server has stepped away.

Blair chuckles. "True. She loves spending time with Wren," his wife confirms. Aggie is her younger sister, the product of her dad's second marriage to a much younger woman. For many years they were estranged, until Blair came back to help run her father's medical practice. That one decision changed her life. She reconciled with her dad and young stepmom and also fell in love with Gabe.

"She's a great aunt," I add.

"I see I'm late to the party."

I glance up and see Kameron approaching the table, a warm smile on his face and holding a basket. He places it in the middle of the table and takes the last available chair. "Sorry I'm late, but I don't come empty-handed."

"Oh, yum," Blair sings, diving right into the fresh, warm bread and butter.

I do the same when she has her slice on a small plate, followed by Gabe and Kameron. "I hear it should be a good game tonight," Kameron says.

Gabe nods. "It is always a good game when we battle Westwood."

"I remember that rivalry from when I was in school," Kameron adds.

"We always looked forward to kicking Westwood's ass," Gabe confirms with a big grin, making Blair chuckle.

"Hey, boss, can I get you something to drink?" the server asks Kameron when she arrives at the table.

"No, I'm good with water, but thanks, Stacia." To us, he asks, "Did you guys get a chance to look at the menu or hear the specials? I have a roasted red pepper chicken with creamy Tuscan sauce served with asparagus and mashed potatoes or a honey-glazed bacon-wrapped pork chop with roasted potatoes and carrots."

My mouth waters, as it seems to always do anytime Kameron talks about food.

"Ohhh, the roasted chicken for me, please," Blair requests.

Kameron looks to me, waiting for me to make my choice. "What do you recommend?"

His eyes soften and hold a hint of a smile as he gazes back at me. "The pork chop. It won't be quite as mouthwatering as when I make it, but Marlin will still do the recipe justice," he quips with a teasing grin and a wink.

"I'm telling him you said that," Veronica states as she happens to be walking near our table to overhear the comment.

"You would," Kameron jokes back as he turns to Gabe.

"I'll have the pork chop special too," Gabe confirms.

"And I'll have the chicken but tell Marlin to put part of mine on Jillian's plate so she can try it," Kameron says to Stacia, who makes a note on her pad and nods.

"I'll get these put right in for you," she announces, scurrying off toward the kitchen.

"Awww, that's so sweet," Blair says, smiling over her water glass as she sips.

My foot starts to tap on the floor as my cheeks burn.

Kameron shrugs and takes his own drink of water. "I wanted her to try it, and this way she can without having to reach across the table."

"You two are the cutest," Blair adds, making my face flame even warmer. "You're, like, the best boyfriend."

"Hey!" Gabe proclaims, giving his wife a look.

"Oh, knock it off, Gabriel. You easily transitioned from amazing boyfriend to perfect husband."

"Yeah, Gabriel, don't be jealous because I'm the best," Kameron teases his friend.

"Did you hear her? I'm the perfect husband," Gabe proclaims, patting his flat stomach before reaching over and taking his wife's hand, placing a gentle kiss on her knuckles.

"I heard her use your full first name," he replies with a smug smile.

"She can call me Gabriel all she wants. That usually means I'm gonna get lucky." Gabe wiggles his eyebrows and shoots his wife a wolfish grin.

"Oh my God, stop it," Blair sings through her laughter.

"Gotta keep working on baby number two."

A longing I wasn't expecting hits hard.

My heart starts to beat a sad little number in my chest as I think about the children I always wanted but will likely never have. Funny how life works, isn't it? One minute you think you have everything, and the next you're having to reevaluate goals and give up on the things you wanted most.

But I refuse to wallow in the sadness. I may not have a baby—or the family I thought I'd have by age thirty-seven—but I have a great life. A bakery I love and amazing friends. I even have Kameron, despite the circumstances surrounding our relationship. Fake or otherwise. I'm content, even if I feel like a piece of myself is still missing.

I take a quick drink of water to give my hands something to do, swallowing the cold liquid over the lump in my throat. I feel Kameron's eyes on me, and though I know I should just paste a bright smile on my lips, that's not what happens. I turn my uneasy gaze his way and am rewarded with a small smile. One that tells me he's with me, understanding the pain. I'm sure that's not true, but whatever. I still appreciate the support.

Kameron reaches over and takes my hand, lowering it beneath the table and resting them jointly on his knee. It feels...right.

We make more small talk until our food is delivered, and the moment our plates arrive, the aroma is sinful.

"Holy moly, I can't wait to dive into this," Blair murmurs when her plate is set in front of her.

"Me either," I whisper, taking in the oversized entrée. Thanks to them adding some of Kameron's meal to mine, I look like I'm eating for two. Or three. Heck, this plate could feed the golf team at the high school.

I don't know which to try first, they both look so delicious, but I opt to slice into my pork chop. I could cut it with a butter knife, it's so tender and juicy, and the moment it hits my tongue, I groan in appreciation.

"Good?" Kameron asks, watching me intently.

"Unbelievable. I think I'm going to stop cooking and just eat here every night," I tell him, joking.

He shrugs and slices into his chicken, and I can tell by watching it's just as tender. "I'd do that for you," he replies with a wink.

Deciding to try the chicken next, I cut a piece off the small helping added to my plate and say, "But you're only open five days a week. I suppose I could eat cereal the other two."

He pins me with a look full of intensity. It makes my clit throb as desire sweeps through my veins. "First off, Jilly, I would cook for you every night, whether my restaurant is open or not, and second, cereal isn't an appropriate dinner substitute." He takes a sharp bite of his chicken all while holding my gaze.

"What do you have against cereal?" I find myself asking, refusing to crack a smile.

"Nothing, if it's seven in the morning."

I shrug. "I actually don't mind a bowl of Cinnamon Toast Crunch for dinner," I state with a shrug. "It's my go-to."

His mouth gapes open as he watches me. "You're serious?"

I nod, taking a drink of water to keep myself busy so I don't burst into a fit of laughter, but the problem is drinking liquid isn't helping. I almost choke on water, which isn't funny or attractive.

He places his fork on his plate, continuing to stare at me. "You're fucking with me right now, aren't you."

It's not a question.

"Maybe," I sing with a smirk.

He narrows his eyes, and I can't help but let the giggles I've been holding fly. "Just for that, I'm not sharing any more of my chicken with you," he grumbles.

I can't help but laugh more. "It's been a long time since I've eaten cereal for dinner, Kameron. Now, cupcakes on the other hand, I've had plenty of cupcake dinners in the last couple of years. That's why my ass is twice the size as it used to be."

He narrows his eyes at me, as if he didn't like what I said. "Your ass is perfect."

The heat in his statement causes my cheeks to flush and dampness to flood my panties.

"I used to eat breakfast a lot for dinner myself," Blair chimes in, breaking the thick sexual tension suddenly accompanying us to dinner.

I blink a few times before feeling the rush of embarrassment. I turn to face her, trying to put thoughts of Kameron and what he's doing to my *panties* out of my mind. "I bet. Your hours are probably crazy."

She nods between bites of her food. "It can get a little hectic every now and again," she starts, glancing to her right to where her husband sits, "especially with us both being physicians, but it's so much better than when I was in Chicago. I can breathe here."

"I get that," Kameron replies.

"Did you two ever run into each other?" I find myself asking, since they were both living in Chicago at the same time, even if it was a very short time period.

They both shake their heads. "No, but I'll be honest, I didn't know he was there. I barely kept up with anyone from here after I moved away senior year. Well, except Hallie, but even then, it wasn't very regular. Med school was intense, and the first few years afterward were a blur," Blair states.

"Same. I didn't keep track of many people when I went away to culinary school," Kameron says, "and when I started working after school, I dove headfirst into the frying pan. I barely slept those early years, so keeping up with relationships wasn't something I was good at."

Gabe looks at Kameron, and I swear something passes between them. It reminds me of a private conversation, one only the two of them know about.

"I bet it's good to be back," I say to both of them, and they both nod in agreement.

"Very much so. I never realized how much I loved the slower pace of small-town life until I came home to help with Dad's practice. Now, I don't think I could ever go back to a bigger city. I love it here," Blair says, looking over at Gabe, who clearly agrees and is happy to hear her say that. They're both established physicians in Pine Village, and I know the entire town would take a huge hit if they left.

"I agree wholeheartedly. I could never go back to a place like Chicago, and even while I was away, I missed this place. I just wish it wouldn't have taken me so long to get back here," Kameron adds, a far-off, sad look in his eyes.

I know what he's thinking—hell, the other two at the table probably know too. He wishes he would have come back sooner and gotten to spend time with his parents before their unexpected deaths.

"You're here now," Gabe says, lifting his water glass. "A toast." When we all do the same, he continues, "To friendship, being home, and to new relationships."

He winks at Kameron before moving his glass to clink against ours. I follow suit, but my stomach feels heavy. I take a small sip of water, wishing my heart wasn't beating out of my chest.

I don't like deceiving our friends.

Especially when my heart is starting to get the wrong idea about my time with Kameron.

The rest of dinner goes well, and when Gabe goes to pay, he's informed by the server there is no bill. Kameron just smirks and takes a drink of his water. "One of the perks of owning the restaurant."

"Well, that's bullshit, but I do appreciate it. We'll have you over for dinner soon. You and Jillian. But you can't bitch that my burgers aren't as good as yours," Gabe says, placing a very healthy tip on the table.

Kameron laughs. "I'd bitch even if they were the best burgers I'd ever eaten," he teases his friend.

"I wouldn't expect anything less," he replies as he stands up and turns to Blair. "Ready to head to the field?"

"I am," she replies before turning her attention my way. "We'll see you there?"

I nod. "I'll be there."

Before I can gather up dirty dishes, the waitstaff is there, collecting our used dishes and cutlery and preparing to ready the table for the next guests. I've noticed it has picked up quite a bit, the Friday evening diners ready to enjoy their own meals before heading off to their next destination. I know I should go. Kameron will need to get back to work. It's a busy night.

"Come with me," he says, gently taking my hand and guiding me toward the back area where his office is located. As soon as we step inside the room, he spins me around and presses me against the door. His lips find mine, softly at first, but then more insistent as the kiss deepens.

I whimper against his mouth, desperate for more as he glides his lips down my neck. "I like kissing you, Jilly."

I feel breathless and a little lightheaded. "I like it when you kiss me, Kam."

He sighs deeply, his warm breath fanning across my flushed skin. "I wish I could go with you to the game. I don't even know when the last time I went to a Friday night football game was."

I clear my throat, trying to push all thoughts of kissing him out of my head. "TD is a great coach. He makes it fun to watch, even though I don't necessarily know what's happening."

He chuckles and straightens to his full height, leaving his hand wrapped around my hip. "Will you tell everyone I said hello?"

"I will," I confirm, wishing I didn't have to leave.

"Good. Maybe I can figure something out and go to a game before the season ends."

"If you do, hit up the first half of the season. Those games in October are too cold for my blood," I state, hating bundling up in fourteen layers of clothing just to go sit on a freezing bleacher to watch a game. I do it, of course, but it's not my favorite.

"Noted." There's a promise in his eyes, a hint of conviction, as if he's vowing to attend a game soon.

Maybe even with me.

"You better get going, Jilly," he says, taking a step back and putting some distance between us.

"Okay," I say, holding his gaze.

After a few seconds, he adds, "If you don't go, I'm liable to kiss you again."

My body heats instantly. "That doesn't sound like a threat."

The corner of his mouth curls up in a wicked grin. "It's a promise, Jilly, so go. Before they fire me from work for making out with my girlfriend in my office instead of cooking food like I'm supposed to."

I can't help but grin. "They can do that?" I ask, skeptically.

"No," he replies with a chuckle. "But it shows you where my head is at, because I'd rather stay in here and kiss you instead of going to where I'm needed." He takes a deep breath and holds my gaze as he adds, "That's a first for me."

Like a peacock, I practically preen with giddiness.

"Well, I wouldn't want to continue causing you duress while at work," I say.

"You're very duress invoking," he informs me.

I step forward and go up on my tiptoes, pressing a light kiss to his lips. "Thank you for dinner, Kameron."

"You're most welcome, Jillian."

I step back and grab the doorknob. "I'll talk to you soon."

He nods. "I hope so."

As if I were floating on clouds, I exit his office and head for the front door. I wave at a handful of patrons I know, and offer a friendly, "Good evening," to Veronica as I leave the restaurant, all while wishing I could stay.

Because of Kameron.

He makes me want to be where he's at, plain and simple.

He puts the smile on my face just by being near.

He stirs up feelings I have no business entertaining.

It's the last one I should be most worried about.

CHAPTER *fourteen*

KAMERON

I'm startled by the loud knock on the back door. Looking up, I take a quick count of the staff left, closing down the kitchen. The front staff just left, having cleaned up and prepped the dining room for the next day, so I'm not sure who it can be. Unless someone forgot something, which is a possibility.

Setting down my cleaning cloth, I head for the door and release the lock. I'm shocked when I find the prettiest girl in town standing there, a wide, excited grin on her face. "I'm so sorry to just drop by like this," she starts.

"Is everything all right?" I ask, reaching for her hand and practically dragging her inside.

"Yes," she replies quickly. "I just heard the best news, and I wanted to share it with...someone." A look flashes in her eyes, but it's quickly masked by her anticipation.

"Come on, let's head to my office," I suggest, taking her hand and leading the way. Even though she said it was good news, I can't help this little bubble of uncertainty that erupts in my chest.

As soon as we cross the threshold, I spin around and give her my full attention. "TD and Ellie are pregnant!" she declares, beaming from ear to ear.

I can't help but smile myself. "Yeah? That's great."

She nods. "It really is. They've been trying for a while," she adds, dropping her voice, as if sharing a secret. "Pretty much since they got married." There are tears in her eyes as she gazes up at me.

"I'm happy for them," I tell her, reaching out and resting my hand on her upper left arm.

"Me too." But mixed in the depth of her green eyes swirls heartache, and something tells me it isn't because TD and Ellie are finally expecting.

She refuses to acknowledge whatever else is bothering her, but I could wager a guess easily. Instead of bringing it up, I notice the way she's swaying back and forth. This movement is different than her normal nervous energy. This almost looks like an ache.

"What's up?" I ask.

Jillian must catch my eyes watching her shift, perhaps trying to adjust her back.

"Oh," she replies, waving off my concern. "Just my back. The bleachers were uncomfortable as hell, and I think I slept funny last night."

An idea instantly pops in my head. "You should go sit in my hot tub."

Her eyes widen a bit. "What?"

Shrugging, I reply, "It would help. I know it's late, but even just for a little bit. It'll help relax your muscles and soothe the achy ones." Placing my hands on her shoulders, I gently start to knead.

"Oh, my God, that feels amazing," she replies with a groan. My cock notices, recalling the sounds she makes when she was about to come.

"Just think, relaxing in the hot tub while I massage your shoulders," I whisper, unable to keep my dick from joining the conversation. He's hard and eager for some action.

Her eyes narrow just a bit. "I don't have a suit."

I lift my shoulders. "There're privacy shades. I rarely wear trunks," I confess with a wink.

She looks confused. "I didn't notice shades."

"They drop from the ceiling. There's a button just inside the door."

I can tell she's considering it, but then she mumbles, "I have to work tomorrow." I think she's trying to talk herself out of it, and if that's the case, I'll support whichever way she decides.

"Well, the offer stands tomorrow night too. Or even Sunday." I dig my thumbs into the tight knots around her neck. "But...you *could* just stay at my place. It might actually be a little closer to the bakery, you know? I mean, that would save time in the morning so you could stay up just a few extra minutes tonight and soak in the hot tub."

Her eyes sparkle, and I can tell she's considering my offer. "I don't have clothes."

"That does bode a problem," I reason, continuing to rub her shoulders. "Of course, you won't need them until the morning."

She chuckles, holding my gaze. "You seem to have all the answers."

"Just helpful little suggestions." I offer a cheeky grin.

"Helpful little suggestions. You sound like Bob Ross."

A gravelly chuckle slides from my mouth. "That's me. Bob Ross." Sobering, I add, "I'm not trying to push you. I thought a dip in the hot tub might help you, but I know it's late and you're usually in bed by now."

She stares up at me, and I wish I knew what she was thinking. Did I go too far by suggesting she come over? Was it the part about spending the night? That was a pretty bold statement to make, especially in light of our...situation, but I don't regret it.

"I have a confession to make," she whispers, leaning a little closer. Her lips are just within reach, and even though I long to kiss her, I hold back. "I kinda want to try out that hot tub."

My lips curl up in a wolfish grin. "Your wish is my command."

"I think," she starts, clearing her throat, "I may run home and grab some clothes. It would be easier to just...get up and go to work."

My heart is pounding in my chest at the idea of waking up with her beside me in the morning. "Makes sense. I'll give you my door code so you can go in. I shouldn't be too much longer here, but I do probably have another thirty minutes or so."

Of course, if I don't get back in there and help tear down the kitchen, my staff will revolt and leave me with all of it to do.

She nods in agreement, and I don't miss the light blush covering her cheeks. I quickly write down my six-digit code to the door and tell her how to turn on the jets on the hot tub and lower the privacy shades.

"I got it," she replies, gazing up at me with those damn hypnotic green eyes. "I'll see you soon?"

"As soon as I can get out of here. You can count on it." I don't think I've ever been this anxious to go home before.

With a smile, she exits my office, my eyes glued to the sway of her hips with every step she takes. When she reaches the back door, I help her open it and lean in. I can't help but brush my lips against hers in a soft kiss. Yet, it still packs a punch to the gut like Mike Tyson. "See you in a bit," I whisper.

"Uhh huh," she murmurs, sending bolts of desire straight to my groin.

I watch her go, making sure she gets to her vehicle okay. The moment she starts to back out of the parking spot behind the restaurant, I close and relock the door. Catcalls fill the kitchen, making me grin with pride. I've never—and I do mean never—brought a woman to my place of business the way I've invited Jillian into it. From the multiple dinners throughout the week to taking her into my office to steal a kiss or two, this is a new side my employees are seeing.

Considering I've always been an incredibly private man, I don't hate it.

Not at all.

Even their teasing, like now.

Shaking my head, I return my attention to the task I was completing before Jillian's surprise visit.

"All right, everyone. Get back to work."

I do the same.

With a smile on my face.

The moment I step inside my house, I feel her presence. Sure, her car parked in my driveway the moment I pulled in was a pretty big indication she's here, but there's something different that hangs in the air, not to mention the vanilla and sugar scent that seems to follow her wherever she goes.

There's life within these walls, something I don't think I've felt at all since I purchased this place.

Making sure the door is secured behind me, I take off in search of the woman I can't seem to get off my mind lately. And knowing she's here—in my house—is doing a number on me. My heart is pounding in my chest, and my cock is already hard in anticipation. Where will she be? In the hot tub, waiting? Will she be in a suit or naked? I'm not sure I'd care either way, honestly. She could be already naked or wearing a wetsuit that covers her from head to toe, and I'd still be just as eager to see her.

I make it to my bedroom and find the room dark—and empty. But I can hear it. My hot tub jets are running, and my blood starts to heat even more. Probably not a good idea for me to get in the hot tub, if I'm being honest. I'm liable to stroke out from overheating if I'm not careful.

The door to the back porch is open, so I move to the doorway and take a look outside. Even though the party lights are off, I can see her in the water. She's resting on the side, her head lying on her arm.

She looks so peaceful, and I worry she's fallen asleep with the faintest smile on her face, but I can hear her humming faintly over the sound of the jets.

Leaning against the doorjamb, I listen to her hum a classic country tune. I recognize it right away, recalling the late-nineties power ballad by one of country's biggest names. I stand here for a few before the desire to be closer to her becomes too great. I walk over to my closet and strip out of my clothes. I noticed a bright pink strap around her neck, indicating she's wearing a bathing suit, so I quickly grab a pair of trunks off my shelf and slip them on. I head for the bathroom next and grab two towels, just in case, before making my way to the door. It's the first time I spot her overnight bag sitting off to the side, and this overwhelming wave of happiness washes through me.

Having her here, in my space, feels better than anything else I've ever experienced, and I just don't want to wait a second longer to be with her.

As I step outside, she lifts her head and smiles. "Hi." There's a touch of shyness to her greeting that makes me grin.

"What do you think?" I ask as I hang the towels on the hooks attached to my house, noting she did bring a towel out with her.

"It's heaven," she practically sings, closing her eyes and letting the warm jetted water massage her back.

Climbing inside, I slowly lower myself into the water, taking a seat directly beside Jillian. Our legs brush against each other, and even the faintest touch does a number on my libido.

But getting my hands all over her—or specifically, getting my cock *in* her—isn't what I'm here to do. She does have to work tomorrow and is probably looking forward to going to bed soon. I'd be content to just falling asleep with her in my arms.

At least for tonight.

"Come're," I insist, turning slightly so I'm facing her.

Jillian looks my way with a questioning look, but when she sees me lift my hands from the water, she understands. She shifts, angling her back toward me, but the positioning is awkward.

"Between my legs," I tell her, knowing she needs to be directly in front of me. Her wide eyes glance back at me over my shoulder, and I add, "No funny business, I promise."

She snorts, clearly not believing me—I'm not sure I believe myself either—but she moves. Jillian shifts closer, placing her hands on my thighs and slips between my legs. I do everything I can to keep myself from getting hard, but it's no use. There's also no concealing it. It's practically pounding against her lower back, begging for a little attention.

I place my hands on her shoulders and start to knead, just like I did earlier in my office. Her head falls forward and a groan slips from her mouth. I work over her knotted muscles, slowly making my way down her back. She relaxes, letting my hands do all the work. It's erotic as fuck, even if not particularly sexual. There's something about having her here, sitting between my legs, while I give a massage. It just does something to me.

She just does something to me.

As I work out the knots and kinks in her back, shoulders, and upper arms, she starts to get a little wiggly. She shifts back, pressing her ass against my cock and making it damn-near impossible to think straight. I dig deep, drawing out every ounce of gentlemanly politeness I possess. She doesn't need me to maul her right here and now in the middle of my hot tub, even if that's exactly what I want to do.

"Kameron?" she whispers as I run my wet hand up the column of her neck and gently massage where it meets her head.

"Hmm?" It comes out more a grunt, since her ass is rocking against me.

"I think you missed your calling."

"Yeah? Maybe I should have become a masseuse instead of a chef?"

She giggles and rolls her head. "You could do both," she whispers. "Your food is out of this world, but your hands...they're simply amazing."

Before I can say a word, she moves, easily spinning around and straddling my waist. I shift to my left a little to give her knees more room on the seat and wrap my hands around her waist. "What are you doing?" I mutter, my cock hard and ready between us. Fortunately for him, I can feel just about everything through the thin layers of her swim bottoms and my trunks.

"Taking the bull by the horns, so to speak," she informs me, rocking her hips against my erection.

"I see," I reply, letting my hands trail down her back to cup her ass. "What would you like to do with the horn, now that you've caught the bull?"

She snickers at my question and grinds herself on my cock. "I have a few ideas. Ever have sex in a hot tub?"

A smile spreads across my lips as they angle down to claim her lips in a brief kiss. "No, can't say I have, but it's been a bucket list item of mine for a while now."

"Yeah?" She meets my gaze with a devilish glint. "Wanna cross it off the list?"

I claim her lips in a searing kiss, letting my tongue delve deep inside as my left hand moves up to her head. My fingers slide into the strands of her ponytail as I anchor her against me.

Jillian starts to wiggle, slipping back just enough to reach between us and grab hold of my cock through my trunks. A groan of pure pleasure erupts from my mouth as my hips automatically buck. "Christ," I mutter, my body moving against the friction of her hand.

Ripping my mouth from hers, I suck in a greedy breath of air and murmur, "You know, this probably isn't going to work."

She tenses against me, so I quickly add, "Because hot water, it doesn't make the best lubricant. Plus, I don't have a condom."

Jillian relaxes a bit, appeased by my words and seems lost in concentration. "I have an idea."

"Tell me," I insist, anxious to hear all about it.

"Go grab a condom and come right back." She scoots off my lap, leaving me and my hard dick missing her contact.

I practically vault out of the hot tub, skipping the steps and towel. I hurry into my bedroom, not even caring I'm soaking wet and leaving puddles of water with each step I take. I practically dive into my nightstand and pull out a condom.

Then, I quickly grab a second, just in case.

When I get back outside, I notice Jillian checking out the shades. "No one can see through them," I tell her, dropping the two condoms onto the chair.

She turns hesitant eyes my way. "You're sure?"

I nod. "Positive, Jilly. No one can see you," I say, taking a few steps toward her and wrapping my hand around her waist. "Now, hearing you is a totally different thing. You're going to have to be quiet."

Her eyes widen with a mixture of humor and determination. "I can be quiet."

I run my finger down her lips, chin, and between her breasts. "You sure? You weren't very *quiet* the last time."

She flushes a dark shade of red. "We weren't outside."

"Good point," I tell her, reaching for the right cup holding her breast and giving it a tug. "You gonna be quiet, Jilly?"

"Yes, I'll be quiet."

Bending down, I latch on to her exposed nipple and suck it greedily into my mouth. "Good girl. Now, let's cross hot tub sex off my list."

CHAPTER fifteen

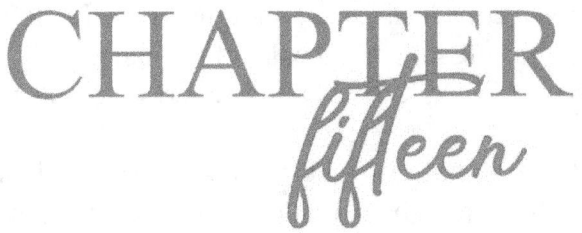

Jillian

I have no idea what has come over me.

Sex outside?

On a hot tub?

Me??

But that's exactly what I'm about to do, and besides the initial worry or fear that someone might see or overhear, I'm all in, without a care in the world.

Hell, it was my idea!

I reach for his trunks and start pulling them down. They don't seem to have any netting inside, just a pair of basic swim shorts, so they slide down his legs easily. His cock springs free, and all I want to do is get my mouth on it.

I drop to my knees, grab his cock around the base, and slide my tongue across the head. A strangled groan erupts from his mouth as I slowly draw it into my mouth. His hands move to my head. He's holding, but not tightly. He doesn't force me to move but seems to be using me as an anchor, needing the contact to keep him grounded.

I take him in as far as I can without choking. I've never been a big fan of blow jobs, but I've also never felt this powerful before. Like I hold the key to the kingdom in the palm of my hand.

Or at least the key to his ability to come in the next few minutes…

But that's not what we're here for. At least not right now. I release his cock, even though I'd much rather keep going, and stand up. Grabbing a condom from the chair, I rip open the package and point to the tub. "Sit."

He practically bolts over to the hot tub, stumbling on the step outside as he tries to climb in. With a smile, I move to the hot tub and follow. His legs are spread, his cock jetting straight up from his groin, and as tempting as it is to take it in my mouth once more, I opt to get to the good part.

Carefully, I roll the protection into place and stand up on the seat. He reaches for my bikini bottoms and helps me shimmy them down my legs. They land somewhere in the water behind me, but I have no time to think about it. His mouth settles on mine as he draws me in, deepening the kiss with his magical tongue. I feel him release the clasp on the back of my top moments before the cool air kisses my skin and pebbles my nipples.

When I open my eyes, his are full of that familiar intensity I crave. "I have an idea, but I don't know if it'll work," I tell him, shifting from side to side.

"Oh, believe me, gorgeous. It'll work," he replies with a wicked smirk on his handsome face.

I spin around and he places his hands on my hips. Gingerly moving myself over him, he reaches down and grabs his cock, holding it in place while I lower myself onto it. I bite back my groan, but it's difficult. As I take every glorious inch of him, I feel fuller than ever before, tighter than I ever imagined.

He returns both hands to my hips and guides me as I move. My back arches as I place my hands on his thighs for leverage. Kameron reaches around and grabs my breasts, pinching and rolling the nipples between his fingers. I bite back another moan, but as I start to bounce against him a little faster, it's getting hard to keep quiet.

I want to unleash it.

He seems to know when I need help too. My thighs are burning, and it's getting hard to move the way I want to. Kameron shifts forward, holding me tightly against his chest. The new position gives my feet more real estate on the seat so I'm not on my tiptoes. It also gives him a better position to thrust.

And thrust he does.

Up—hard and fast.

He fills me completely, setting a reckless pace. He hits me so deep, stroking my G-spot and making me see stars. I come quickly; he's in total control of my release. I bite my lip, trying to keep my cries of pleasure silent, but the moment he thrusts up and stills, coming himself, I just can't be silent anymore. His name slips from my mouth and echoes off the still night surrounding us.

He shivers and starts to pump again, drawing every last ounce of release he can from both of us. When he stops moving, my legs give out as he slides back a bit and gets comfortable. With his arms wrapped around me, he presses his lips to my bare shoulder and breathes heavily.

"That was...wow," he murmurs against my skin.

"Worth crossing off the list?" I ask, a soft smile on my lips.

"Oh, sweetheart. So worth it. Even worth having the neighbors hear you come on my cock," he teases with a brush of his lips against my neck, sending shivers through my entire body.

"I tried to be quiet," I insist, slightly embarrassed by crying out his name.

"Don't apologize. I will wear the sweet noises you made like a badge of honor."

My giggle turns into a yawn, and thanks to the epic orgasm I just had, and the fact it's more than two hours past my normal bedtime, I suddenly feel incredibly exhausted.

"Come on, Jilly. Let's get you to bed," he whispers, hugging me tightly before carefully helping me stand.

I'm so tired, I don't even care I'm standing naked or climbing from his hot tub as bare as the day I was born. Carefully, I step on the concrete patio, and as soon as my feet are planted, I feel a towel being wrapped around me. I don't know how he got out of the hot tub so fast, but he did, taking care of covering me first. Then, he reaches down and slides the used condom off him and reaches for another towel.

My eyes are glued to him as he wraps it around his hips and tucks one end behind the material. I can still see the bulge between his legs, which sends this new wave of desire sweeping through my veins.

I have no idea what's come over me.

Yes, you do.

Good sex with Kameron.

"Go inside. I'll take care of buttoning up out here," he says.

I take him up on his offer, needing to use the bathroom and get ready for bed. Slipping inside the house, I go straight to his bathroom and shut the door. The reflection staring back at me in the mirror is almost unrecognizable. Not because of a big change in appearance, but simply because the woman in the mirror looks...content and very satisfied.

And frankly, I'm not used to seeing her so confident.

Fearless.

Happy.

I use the bathroom and wash my hands, hanging the wet towel on one of the bars on the wall. I probably should grab something to sleep in, but honestly, I didn't bring anything. I debated for what felt like several minutes back at my house while I packed a bag, but ultimately, decided to just wing it. I figured Kameron would have plenty of T-shirts I could borrow for the night if I needed one, but deep down, I've been hoping it wouldn't be necessary. The thought of sleeping beside Kameron—naked—is too tempting.

Even when I tell myself repeatedly it's not real.

Well, the sex is real, but the relationship isn't.

Yet, despite that, I still want to stay. To sleep naked in his bed. To wake beside him in the morning.

Is it a bad idea? Most definitely. Why? Because he's an addiction I can't seem to overcome, even when I know this has bad idea written all over it.

I move to the door and gently pull it open, flipping off the light as I step out. Kameron is there, still naked, and watching me intently. I feel his gaze roam over my body from head to toe like a soft caress, and my brain just sort of shuts down. In fact, I blurt out, "I didn't bring pajamas."

I'm such a dork.

Embarrassment burns my cheeks as he gives me a little grin and takes a few steps toward me. "Well, I personally prefer you this way, but if you'd feel more comfortable, you can borrow a shirt and pair of shorts or something from me," he says, waiting for my reply.

I shake my head. "No, I'm okay like this."

"Good. I'm gonna use the bathroom, and then I'll join you. Go ahead and get comfortable."

He steps inside the bathroom, leaving me standing in the middle of his bedroom, staring at his bed. I walk around to the right side, since his phone charger, TV remote, and a book are sitting on the nightstand on the left.

I grab my phone and set the alarm, placing it on the nightstand. It'll be an early morning for sure, but I don't regret it. Not for a second. Pulling back the blankets, his scent wafting from the bedding as I slip inside. It's warm, comfortable, and smells just like him. I can't help but snuggle a little deeper into the pillow and inhale. Call me crazy, but this may be my new favorite scent.

Eau de Sexy Man.

I'd buy a thousand bottles of it.

The door opens and the light is flipped off, bathing the room in darkness. The blinds are closed across the French doors, so moonlight doesn't filter into the room. As my eyes finish adjusting to the darkness, I feel the bed dip and the blankets pull back. Kameron climbs beneath the covers and reaches for me. I move into his arms willingly.

We lie together, skin on skin, for several minutes before either of us speaks. "I like this, Jilly," he whispers.

My throat is thick with a rush of emotion as I reply, "Me too."

He shifts to his side and adjusts his arms. His index finger glides down the side of my face, and now that I've had time to adjust to the lighting, I can see him clearly. "I'm glad you're here. Thank you for staying."

A grin slides easily across my lips. "I'm glad I'm here too."

"Night, Jilly," he murmurs, resting his chin against my forehead.

My breathing evens out quickly as I'm drawn toward sleep. My body relaxes, and I'm not worried about where I am or who I'm with. I don't care I'm getting less sleep than normal, or I'll be a zombie in the morning at work.

Because this?

This is the best feeling in the world, and falling asleep in Kameron's strong arms is exactly where I want to be.

Even if it's just for a short period of time.

This feels right.

I glance down at my ringing cell phone and cringe. I know what this call is about, and even though I don't want to deal with it now, I can't avoid it forever. If I do, they're liable just to show up when I least expect it and demand answers.

Looking over at Emmalynn, my Saturday employee, who is reorganizing the pastry case from this morning's breakfast rush, I hold up my phone and say, "My mom. I need to take this real quick."

She waves off my comment. "Go talk to your mom. I've got this," she says before returning her attention to the cinnamon rolls.

"Hey, Mom," I greet, heading toward my small office off the kitchen and close the door.

"Kameron Markley?" she practically bellows into the phone. "You're dating Kameron Markley?"

I close my eyes for a brief moment and take a deep breath. This level of excitement is exactly what I expected. "Yes."

"That's...so wonderful! He's such a nice young man," she starts, barely taking a breath as she continues, "I know he's had a lot of tragedy in his life, and that's exactly why he needs you. You're a ray of sunshine. And his restaurant? Well, when Dad took me last month for our anniversary, it was simply amazing. He's done so much for this town, that's for sure. And to know he's dating my daughter?"

She squeals.

Like actually squeals in exhilaration.

"I still can't believe this," she says, a bit calmer than a few seconds ago. "I wish I wouldn't have had to find out while at the grocery store though. You know, everyone is talking about the two of you."

"I'm sure they are," I reply with a yawn, knowing exactly how this town operates. We're surely some of the biggest news right now. The only thing I can hope is last night's public announcement of TD and Ellie having a baby will quickly replace Kameron and I dating as top chatter.

"Tired, huh? You probably had a late night," she states with a giggle.

The hairs on the back of my neck stand up, and I push thoughts of spending the night at Kameron's from my brain. That's the last thing I need to imagine while on the phone with my mother.

"I didn't get to bed at my normal time," I start. "I went to the football game."

"And then stayed at Kameron's."

My heart falls into my shoes.

"It's okay, you don't have to tell me all the dirty details," Mom says, making me cringe, because telling her the *details* is the last thing I want to do. "I ran into Lucy this morning, and she said your car was parked in his driveway all night, and then Harry was up to use the bathroom because his high blood pressure pills cause frequent urination and saw you leave."

I don't need to know about Harry's overactive bladder...

"Anyway, I'm glad you're having fun. You've worked so hard over the last few years, and I love the fact you're finally putting yourself out there. Who knows, maybe he's *the one*!" she proclaims, sending my heart rate into overdrive.

"Mom," I warn, trying to come up with the right words. "It's new."

It is.

It's also fake, but she doesn't need to know that.

"Yes, I know, but still, a woman can hope, right? All I want is for my daughter to find forever love, and maybe give me a grandchild or two along the way."

I close my eyes, my gut churning and the lie we're telling like a bitter taste on my tongue. "Mom," I mutter, tears filling my eyes.

She's so excited.

"I know, I know, honey. I promise not to push you, I mean, it's not like I've pulled your grandmother's wedding ring out of the safe yet," she states with a laugh.

My heart races.

"There's time for that, but not much. You're thirty-seven already, Jillian, and he's what...forty?" Before I can mutter a reply, she adds, "Oh, Dad and I want to officially meet him. Soon."

"Okay," I whisper.

"Maybe we can all get together for dinner? I know he's busy at the restaurant, but perhaps he can join us for a quick meal, like he's done with you a few times over the last week or so."

Of course she'd hear about that too. This town loves to talk.

"I'll ask," I repy.

"Great, just let me know. I can always cook dinner one night too, if he'd rather come here for a more intimate get-to-know-you type of gathering. I'll cook pot roast, but I'm sure it's not as good as his," she says, referring to her go-to dish when she's entertaining.

"I'm sure he'll love it," I state.

"Hmm, maybe I need a new dish? Try something different for a change?"

"Whatever you'd want to make would be perfect," I assure her.

"Well, just let me know what works best for you two." Again, she squeals. "I'm just so dang happy right now. My daughter and Kameron Markley. He's such a catch, Jillian. I can't believe no one has snatched him up yet."

Me either, if I'm being honest, but I do understand his commitment to building his restaurant. I've felt the same drive and determination over the last five years too.

"Anyway, I'll let you go. I know you're at work. Keep me posted on dinner with Kameron," she sings into the phone.

"I will."

"Great, love you, sweetie."

"Love you too," I mutter, hanging up after telling her goodbye.

I drop my phone onto my desk and close my eyes.

I hate this.

I hate lying.

I thought fake dating Kameron would help get my parents off my back, but now that we're involved, it seems to help fuel her desire even more. Sure, she *said* she wasn't pushing, but she still stuck plenty of digs in there. Not to mention her bringing up my grandma's engagement ring. She wanted me to have it when I was dating Davis, but he insisted on me having something new.

Fat good that did for either of us...

Just goes to show how much he really knew me. I would have loved to receive my grandmother's engagement ring. We were so close when I was growing up, and I was left completely heartbroken the day she passed away when I was about to turn twenty.

A knock sounds on my door, and I look up with a start. I get up and move to open it, expecting to find Emmalynn standing there, but when I pull open the door, that's not who's waiting on the other side.

It's Kameron.

And he's holding a bouquet of flowers.

Not just any flowers either.

Hydrangeas.

My favorite.

He remembered.

"What are you doing here?" I ask, my eyes bouncing between the beautiful blooms and the gorgeous man holding them.

"Well, I know you've had a long week, and you're a little short on sleep," he starts, flashing me a wicked grin, "so I thought I'd just swing by with a surprise."

"They're beautiful," I say, taking the vase of flowers and inhaling.

"Almost as beautiful as you," he says, swiping a strand of hair off my cheek and brushing my cheek with his thumb.

My heart leaps and pirouettes in my chest. Little butterflies take flight in my stomach. And my mind? It pictures the happily ever after I've always wanted.

Yeah, I'm in deep shit.

I'm falling for my fake boyfriend.

CHAPTER
sixteen

KAMERON

"What's wrong?" I ask, noticing the slightly distressed look in her emerald eyes.

She flashes a quick grin. "Oh, nothing. My mom called," she replies. I know her parents and the fact they're pushing for grandkids weighs heavily on her mind. That's a big part of the reason she agreed to this farce.

"Everything okay?" I ask cautiously.

"Yeah," she replies, turning and setting the bouquet on the corner of her desk. I don't miss the grin she gives the blooms once more before turning back to me. "They, uh, want to have dinner soon. With us." She shifts back and forth, one of her nervous tics.

"Okay," I reply easily.

"Yeah? I mean, they're gonna bombard us with questions, I'm sure."

I shrug and lean against the doorframe. "It's fine. Honestly, it comes with the territory, right? Having dinner with your parents seems like part of the gig."

She gives me a slow nod, her cheeks flushing a bit. "I know, but, well, they'll likely embarrass me or you or both. They can be intrusive and persistent."

"I can handle your parents," I assure her. I've known them my whole life, even if not on a very personal level. Everyone knows everyone in this town. "It'll be fine. How soon?"

"Soon," she replies, repeating what her mom said.

"All right, I should be able to make it work any day this week. Well, except Friday. Marlin is taking the night off, so I'll be down one in the kitchen. I won't be able to slip out for a quick dinner break."

"That's no problem," she states. "What about Thursday?"

I do a quick mental check of who's working Thursday before agreeing. "That should work."

"Okay, I'll call my mom and let her know. She did offer to cook for us, but I think dinner at the restaurant is better. This way, it has a deadline. If we go to their house, she'll end up pulling out the photo albums and wanting to grill you all night about recipes or your dating history."

I snort a laugh. "Well, first off, she'd be sadly disappointed in my past. It's not very interesting."

Lies.

"And second, I'd be fine with dinner at their house, if that's what you prefer," I reason, trying to ignore the quick beat of my heart at my omission.

"No," she blurts out. "I think I prefer the restaurant."

"Okay then. We'll plan on Thursday, but if that doesn't work for them, we can figure something else out."

She nods, seeming relieved to have that conversation out of the way. "Yeah, that works. Thank you."

Reaching out, I move that sprig of hair once more, needing to touch her. "You're welcome." Knowing I'm about out of time, I add, "I need to get back. I had to run to the bank to get some change and saw the gift shop open. I got lucky she had some of your favorite flower in stock."

Jillian smiles. "You did. They bloom throughout the summer and are usually done by early fall."

I can't help but wink. "Lady luck is on my side then. I got the gorgeous girl *and* the flowers."

I don't miss the blush explode up her neck and stain her cheeks. "Thank you."

I step forward, prepared to give her a kiss goodbye—because even if this relationship started off fake, it feels too right to kiss her—but we're interrupted before I can.

"Umm, Jillian, I'm sorry to interrupt. There's someone here to pick up their cake order," the high school girl working the counter says from behind me.

"Okay, thank you, Emmalynn. I'll be right up with it," Jillian says, glancing around my body to her employee.

I hear the girl walk away, my eyes still glued on Jillian. "I'll let you get to it." I take a step back, even though I don't want to. "Oh, I almost forgot. My hot tub is open tonight too. You know, if your back is still bothering you."

Cue the cute-as-shit blush.

"Umm, yeah. I think I could use another soak." She fights a smile, but I can see the naughty thought reflecting in her eyes.

"You know the code," I tell her.

"I do."

"See you later, Jilly," I state, turning and walking away before I say the hell with it and throw her down on top of her desk to have my wicked way with her.

Something to look forward to...

It's Thursday night.

Jillian is nervous as hell to have dinner with her parents and has been fretting about it for the last few days. In fact, the closer it gets, the more anxious she becomes.

Last night, she stayed late at the bakery to work on a couple of cake orders. I delivered her a quick meal before the after-work crowd picked up at the restaurant and found her flustered and worked up. She had messed up the design on the top of the cake and had to scrape it off and start over, so I did the only thing I could think of to take her mind off everything.

I kissed her.

A lot.

To the point it was damn near impossible for me to leave and return to the restaurant. All I wanted to do was stay, to hold her and kiss her, to help relieve the extra stress she was feeling.

I know a big part of that stress is the fact our relationship is a lie.

Even if it doesn't feel like it anymore.

It feels more real than any I've ever had, and that's both sad and thrilling.

I glance at the clock and make sure I'm on time. "I'm taking a dinner break," I tell Marlin, who offers me a grin.

"Meeting the parents tonight, huh?"

"I've already met them, but this is the official introduction since we started dating," I tell him, pulling my apron off and hanging it on my hook.

"Everything will be fine," he assures me. "You're a great guy, and they'll see that right away. Just don't mention the fact you're banging their daughter."

My eyes widen as he barks out a laugh. "Jesus, Marlin. I'd never say that."

"That's good, because dads hate that shit."

"I can imagine," I deadpan before walking over to the warming tray and grabbing a fresh basket of rolls and butter. "I'll be back in a bit, but holler if you need me."

"I got this, boss," he states before returning his attention to the new order that just came in.

My plan is to arrive a few minutes early, hoping to steal a little time with Jillian before her parents arrive. I texted her earlier, reminding her it would all work out fine and to not worry, but I'm not sure my words really worked. Even if she replied with a thumbs-up emoji, I can picture her fretting and worrying.

Stepping into the dining room, I'm surprised to see her parents already there, waiting. What's more surprising is the fact Jillian isn't. Lydia spots me first, offering a warm smile that reminds me of her daughter's. "Kameron," she greets.

"Hello, and welcome to Prime," I reply, approaching the table and setting the bread in the center. "Happy to have you."

"This place is just beautiful," she replies warmly.

I turn my attention to Dennis, Jillian's father. "Good evening, sir," I state, holding out my hand to shake.

"Kameron," he replies with a curt nod as he reaches for my hand and gives it a firm shake.

"I'm surprised Jillian isn't here yet," I say, taking a seat in one of the empty chairs.

"Me too," Lydia replies, pulling her phone out of her purse and checking it.

I do the same, retrieving my device from my pocket and I'm a little surprised when I don't find a message. I know she still has a few minutes, but one thing I've noticed about Jillian is the fact she's always early.

Until today.

I contemplate firing off a message to her when I see the door fly open and the woman herself bursts through the doorway. I quickly stand, taking in her frazzled appearance and slightly gray complexion. She says hello to Veronica before making her way toward our table. I can tell by the look on her face she isn't having a good day.

"Hey, sorry I'm late," she says, plastering on a big smile I can tell doesn't reach her eyes.

"You're not late," I reassure her, giving her a kiss on her cheek. "You okay?" I whisper so only she can hear.

She blinks away tears and nods before turning to her parents. "Hi," she blurts out, moving to her mom and giving her a quick hug.

"We just ordered a few drinks, and Kameron brought bread," Lydia informs her daughter with a pleasant smile.

"Oh, bread," Jillian practically moans out. "G'me." She reaches for the breadbasket after flopping onto her chair and dives in.

"Can I get you something to drink?" Nicholas asks when he approaches the table, delivering drinks to Lydia and Dennis.

"Yes, strawberry margarita, please," Jillian blurts out. It surprises me, but I don't let it show. Mostly because in the short amount of time I've known Jillian, she rarely drinks, and when she does, she prefers red wine.

"Of course, and for you, boss?"

"I'll stick with the water tonight," I tell him.

"Busy day?" Lydia asks her daughter, who takes a hesitant sip of water.

"Busy *and* exhausting *and* expensive," she mutters.

"What happened?" I ask, focusing my attention on the latter part of her list. I already know why she was busy—because she's fucking amazing and everyone wants her sweet treats. I also know why she would be exhausted, and I don't like it. After working later than normal at the bakery yesterday, she found it hard to sleep. I'm hoping tonight, after the completion of dinner with her parents, she'll finally be able to relax.

She sighs and closes her eyes for a few seconds. "I dropped a cake."

"Oh no," her mom replies, reaching over and giving her daughter a supportive squeeze of the hand.

I extend my hand too, linking my fingers with hers and bringing our joined hands to rest on my thigh. She turns and offers me a small smile. "I have to go back to work. I got a new cake baked, but I have to decorate it yet."

"I'm sorry, Jilly," I find myself murmuring softly. I take quick stock of her features. There are lines around her eyes, confirming the fact she didn't sleep well. Her lips are dry and her skin a bit chalky. She looks like she's coming down with something, and I don't like it.

Not one bit.

All I want to do is make her smile.

"That's not like you, honey. What happened? Did you bump into something?" Lydia asks, pulling my attention away from the woman beside me and across the table.

She drops her eyes for a second before responding. "I don't know. I got a little lightheaded, but it passed quickly. I'm fine," she assures her parents before taking a sip of water and giving them a smile. But her smile seems off. Forced. Fake.

"Well, I'm sure the new cake will be better than the first. You're the best baker in the state," Dennis boasts to his daughter proudly.

"Thanks, Dad," she replies as the margarita is delivered to our table.

I want to ask her about her dizzy spell, but don't want to make a big deal of it either. At least not in front of her parents. Instead, I let Nicholas do his thing and take our orders. "This week, we have a slow roasted prime rib on special, as well as crab au Gratin with a homemade creamy cheese sauce, and our side is a baked potato or horseradish smashed potatoes. You also get to choose between a side salad or cup of soup, which is creamy asparagus this evening."

I've heard the specials before—obviously, since I set them— but I've rarely been rewarded with watching the excitement pass through the eyes of those about to enjoy them. And Jillian? She seems downright ravenous now that she's heard the list, which makes me both excited and worried. When was the last time she ate? Has she eaten at all today? She seemed to inhale what I brought her last night, but perhaps she hasn't gotten the proper nourishment today, which is why she's felt dizzy? I had a roommate in culinary school who would get sick when he had low blood sugar. Maybe that's what's going on with Jillian, and if it is, I can definitely fix that.

She will eat until she's ready to burst.

We all place our orders and dive into easy conversation. Jillian drinks her margarita and even when talk is turned toward me, I can't seem to take my eyes off her. She seems to relax a little, probably thanks to the tequila, and engages effortlessly in discussions about her bakery, her parents' work, and some chores they still need to do around the house before the cold winter sets in.

Conversation turns to me, just as our meals are delivered. "So, what made you choose the route you took, Kameron?" Lydia asks with interest as she uses her fork to cut a piece of her crab dish.

"Well, believe it or not, I have always loved cooking. I used to help my mom in the kitchen a lot when I was growing up," I tell her, my throat starting to clog with emotion. "It became our thing, something we'd do together often." It helped us heal, I want to say but keep that nugget to myself. I rarely talk about my brother and what life was like after he passed away.

"That's wonderful, not only because you learned such a difficult craft, but that you have memories to carry with you throughout the rest of your life." Lydia gives me a knowing smile, clearly understanding the deep meaning of why I chose the path I did.

I flash her a small smile before glancing over to Jillian. She's having the prime rib, and I remember a conversation we had very early on in our...relationship. She doesn't like fish but doesn't seem to mind shrimp. "Would you like to try some of my crab au Gratin?"

She glances down at it and wrinkles her nose. "It doesn't look very appetizing," she murmurs.

Taking a small bite with my fork, I make sure there's a taste of the creamy cheese sauce on top and hold it out toward her. "Try it."

Her green eyes bounce between the food on my fork and my own eyes eagerly watching, waiting. Holding my gaze, she leans my way and wraps her lips around my fork. If her parents weren't sitting at the table, I might picture those very lips wrapping around something else, but I push all thoughts of that out of my head right now.

"Well?" I ask when she swallows.

"It's good," she replies, seeming surprised.

"Of course it is," I tell her with a wink, undeniably cocky when it comes to my food. "Here." I carefully scoop some of the food off my plate and set it on hers.

"I can't take your food," she insists.

"Sure you can," I reply, recalling how she got lightheaded earlier. She can have all my food if it means she's healthy and well again.

"Thank you," she mutters, her leg bouncing a little under the table.

"You're welcome." Feeling two sets of eyes on me, I look up and give her parents a quick smile. "How's your food?"

"The crab au Gratin is delicious," Lydia insists, already halfway through her first one. "And the smashed potatoes are so tangy and perfect."

I nod before turning my gaze to Dennis. "How's your steak, sir?"

"Very good, Kameron," he replies, taking only his second bite of meat. He chose to pair his steak with a baked potato, loaded with butter, sour cream, and fresh chives. After he chews and swallows, he asks, "I hear you're buying the building next door."

The hairs on the back of my neck stand up and I sense Jillian's tension escalate. "Yes, sir. Mrs. Krokus has decided to sell her building to me for a restaurant expansion."

He nods. "That's exciting. Do you think you have enough business for that?" he asks, watching me intently.

"Dad," Jillian chastises, as if his question isn't a valid one.

I glance her way and smile, letting her know it's okay. "Actually, sir, yes. The last three years have seen a steady growth, despite the season. Obviously, the heavy tourist season will see a greater need for the space, but we often fill up on Saturday nights and Sunday afternoons. Plus, we've had more inquiries for small dinner parties or gatherings, and with the current space we have, it can be difficult to meet their needs."

"But surely, it'll take more of your time and energy to expand and renovate." He glances at his daughter, and I catch his meaning loud and clear.

Taking Jillian's hand in mine, I give it a gentle squeeze as an easy smile crests my lips. "I'm sure it will be, sir, but I'll always make time for your daughter. Spending time with her isn't a hardship or a chore. In fact," I turn to look at the woman beside me, "it's my favorite part of the day."

She smiles back at me, and in this moment, it feels genuine.

My feelings.

Our relationship.

Dennis gives me a nod, obviously happy with my response. He reaches for his drink and holds it up. "To Jillian and Kameron. To growing together, even when life wants to pull you apart."

My throat is thick as I grab my water glass and clink it against the other three. As I take a needed sip of the cold liquid, my eyes seek her out, watching as she takes a drink of her margarita.

We enjoy the rest of our meal, and the mood feels much lighter than it did at the beginning. It's as if I received their blessing, and perhaps with my little speech, I did. I don't know if Jillian believes what I said, but I meant every word.

It wasn't something to say to make her dad happy.

They were real.

Every reason for embarking on our original agreement seems to have long faded away until there's only me and Jillian left. Not the other bullshit. In less than three weeks, I went from barely knowing the real her to craving her every second of every day. How wild is that?

I'm desperate again, but for an entirely different reason.

I'm desperate for her.

CHAPTER
seventeen

Jillian

I groan and wipe my mouth with the back of my hand. This is the second time I've thrown up today and yesterday wasn't much better. The difference was yesterday I was at work. And we were incredibly busy for a Saturday. It was horrible, but Emmalynn was a trooper and was able to handle everything on the front end while I tried to hide in back as much as possible. The last thing I needed was to share whatever bug I have with my customers.

Surprisingly, after about eleven or so, I started to feel better, which was a welcomed reprieve, and I was able to figure out how to power through the rest of my day before I closed. I skipped dinner with Kameron, however. He invited me to come by the restaurant and grab a bite to eat with him, but I was afraid of whatever sickness I have rearing its ugly head once more, so I passed. I also passed on meeting him at his place, opting to cuddle up on my couch and watch a movie.

Did I miss him?

Hell yeah, I did.

Terribly.

But the distance was necessary. Not only would I feel horrible if I got him sick, but I've felt this overwhelming draw to him the last few days. Ever since dinner with my parents on Thursday night. His touches felt...different.

Real.

That's why a little space was needed. I was entertaining all sorts of ideas I had no business entertaining. Plus, we fell into an easy routine of me going to dinner at the restaurant or him cooking for me at his place, me spending the night, and going to work the next morning, only to do it all again. As amazing as it's been, I was in desperate need of a reminder of what we really are.

Temporary.

Fake.

And now here I am, with my face in the toilet on Sunday morning, grateful I'm able to throw up in the privacy of home.

When my stomach finally settles, I flush the toilet and move to the sink to brush my teeth. I'm completely exhausted, even though it's barely after nine in the morning, so once I've cleaned myself up a bit, I head to the kitchen to grab a drink. I find a Sprite in the refrigerator and a sleeve of crackers in the pantry. Despite getting sick, I'm surprisingly hungry, so I take my treasures to the living room and find something to watch on TV.

I settle on a cooking competition show, finding them much more interesting than I ever have. That's the Kameron effect. He's been teaching me little things in the kitchen, and while he's preparing dinner, I find myself completely engaged. Obviously, baking has always been my thing, but I've discovered cooking isn't so bad...when you have someone in the kitchen alongside you.

Maybe that's the big difference. It's been a pretty long time since I lived with someone, and even then, Davis was rarely in the kitchen with me. He preferred video games, believe it or not. He said it was how he unwound after a long day in the office, and he had a small group of three or four others from all over that would play together via the gaming system. I never got into it, not really understanding the appeal, but I never complained. Who was I to say how he should and shouldn't relax after work?

But when those games started creeping into all hours of the night and monopolized our weekends, a wedge was driven between us. Not to mention the fact I swore my biological clock was ticking so loudly the entire state of Wisconsin could hear it. I wanted a baby, to celebrate our love and grow a family, but he kept putting me off. Finally, nine months after we were married, he told me he changed his mind and walked away.

Now, I've experienced a whole new side of relationships. Sure, it might not be legit, but it feels like it, and I genuinely enjoy spending time with Kameron. I love helping him in the kitchen, relaxing together in the hot tub, and falling asleep in each other's arms. Even if I have to get up before the birds, he still rises with me and makes sure I get off to work okay. He's sweet, caring, and incredibly attentive, all entwined with a touch of alpha.

Very romance novel worthy.

I wish he were my real boyfriend...

Lying down, I take a few bites of cracker, grateful when it seems to calm my stomach instead of hurting it. I absently watch some of the show, not really retaining any of the challenge playing out on the television. They're making some sort of dish only using the provided ingredients, but my brain isn't in it. Instead, I try to run down the list of ingredients I need to purchase for my own shop.

I should be making a list.

Closing my eyes, I feel myself relax.

Maybe a nap is just what I need.

Then, when I wake, I'll go do my shopping.

I wake with a start, my eyes flying open and scanning the room. There's a new show on the TV, but the sun is still bright in the September sky. I reach for my phone to check the time, finding a few text messages from Kameron.

Kameron: Just checking on you. Hope you're getting some rest today.

Kameron: Thinking of you.

Kameron: Your parents were just here for lunch. They raved about their dinner Thursday night and suggested we do it again soon. I definitely won them over.

I can't help but smile, thinking about how much my parents talked him up after our dinner. My mom was positively thrilled by the news of me dating, but when they heard it was Kameron, it elevated her delight to a whole new level. She's practically picking out china patterns and ordering the invitations.

I fire off a quick reply before climbing up from my comfy position on the couch.

Me: Just took a nap. Apparently I was exhausted.

He doesn't reply, but I don't expect it. He's working and will get back to me when he can.

I stretch my arms toward the ceiling and yawn. I can't believe how tired I am. I'm definitely coming down with something, with the queasy stomach and exhaustion. I just hope it passes before I return to the bakery tomorrow morning.

Taking a moment to fill up my tumbler with water, I take a seat at the kitchen table and grab my notebook. I always make notes in here when I start to get low on baking supplies, so they can be added to my next order. I learned quickly after opening, the easiest way to not forget anything was to write it down as soon as I noticed I was low. After running out of butter and falling dangerously low on sugar once, I knew I needed to keep better track of my supplies. This notebook is a lifesaver. It goes everywhere with me and sits prominently in the kitchen. Plus, my employees know to write things down in there when they realize something is running low, especially serving or to-go supplies.

I pull up the app for the super center in Hudson and start adding the items I usually get from there. I purchase at the local grocery store when I can, but unfortunately, some of the stuff I need is a larger bulk size, and I just can't get that from our locally owned grocery store.

I make a separate list of the fresh items I'll be needing from Pine Village, including different fruits from the market, and then switch over to making a separate order for my own personal needs. Walking through the kitchen, I add a few things for the pantry and refrigerator, not going overboard, since Kameron seems to be content cooking most of the time. But since I do enjoy making a few dishes, I add those ingredients to my list, vowing to invite him to eat at my place either Monday or Tuesday night, since his restaurant is closed.

Before I complete my order, I go to the bathroom and check my stock there. I add a tube of toothpaste to my order, as well as a package of toilet paper. I have some, but both items are things you never want to be caught without. Needing to check my cleaning supplies, I open the cabinet below the sink and take stock of what's there. My eyes land on the open box of tampons and prepare to add them to my shopping cart.

But then something hits me.

My heart rate starts to climb as I click out of the shopping app and flip over to my calendar. I scroll back to the previous month and start counting.

"Oh, shit…"

Needing to recount, I scan the weeks and days and do the math all over again.

My breathing hitches in my throat when I come up with the exact same number.

I was supposed to start my period five days ago.

"Fuck, fuck, fuck," I mutter, jumping up and heading into the kitchen. I'm not sure what for, since nothing I need at the moment is there. I do grab my tumbler and take a healthy drink of water, my brain spinning.

"Okay, Jillian, think."

Exhaustion, check.

Upset stomach and feeling nauseous, check.

Reaching down, I gently press on my chest. Yep, tender, swollen boobs.

Check!

"I'm pregnant," I mutter aloud, the words echoing in my brain like a blaring train horn.

My legs feel wooden as I make my way to the living room and drop onto the couch once more. I glance around the room, as if it might give me some magical insight or the answers to the burning questions peppering my brain.

How?

When?

Why?

Well, I know exactly *how* it happened, and I'm pretty sure I can even answer the when. That first night we slept together, the condom broke. I had done the math, but apparently I was wrong. You *can* get pregnant around day twenty-one, because that's the only logical explanation. We've used protection every single time, and even though it's not completely foolproof, it decreases your chances of pregnancy tremendously.

Yet here I am...

My foot starts to tap on the floor as I try to figure out what to do. I'm so overwhelmed, I'm not sure what the appropriate next step is. Do I call Kameron? No, not yet. I'm not even sure I'm pregnant, even though the signs are all pointing that way. Maybe I really am just battling a stomach bug or viral infection. The last thing I'd want to do is tell him I'm pregnant and I'm not.

I reach for my phone, my finger hovering over his contact. In just a short amount of time—a matter of weeks—he's become my person. The one I want to share all the things with, from the small stuff to the giant news.

And this definitely qualifies as something enormous.

But I don't call him.

The phone rings twice before Blair picks up. "Hey, Jillian."

"Hi, Blair. I'm so sorry to bother you on a Sunday afternoon. I'm sure you're busy with your family," I say, feeling terrible for interrupting her day.

My legs start to bounce even harder.

"You're not interrupting anything. Actually, you are, but it's only laundry, and that's a welcome reprieve," she says with a chuckle.

"Oh. Okay. Well, I don't want to take any time away from Gabe and Wrenlee."

"You're not. He ran to the grocery store to grab something for dinner and took her with him. What's up?"

"Umm, well, I think I need your help."

"What's wrong?" she asks, all serious and businesslike.

"I think...Uhh, I might be pregnant," I whisper, as if the walls will overhear my words and blab them to the world.

"Oh. Oh, shit. Okay." I hear the dryer door slam. "You need to take a test?"

"Yeah, I guess."

"Well, the last thing you want to do is go to the grocery store or the pharmacy to purchase one, so why don't you meet me at the clinic."

My entire body relaxes, as if just hearing her words and her quest to keep everything private are exactly what I needed to hear. "I can do that."

"Meet me around back. There's a small parking lot for staff behind the alley. I'll be there in ten minutes, tops."

"Okay."

After a pause she says, "It's going to be all right, Jillian. Everything will work out."

"I know," I murmur, hoping I start to believe it myself soon.

"See you in a few," she replies before hanging up.

I set my phone down and look around the room. My head is swirling with the implication of being pregnant, and what that means moving forward. Not only will I have to tell Kameron, but it'll alter our relationship.

This changes everything.

Knowing I need to get going, I grab my phone and head for the kitchen. My purse is still on the counter, so I quickly collect it and make my way outside. It's a decent day, the sun hidden behind a few clouds, but the temperatures are holding steady for the second half of September.

I climb inside my vehicle and head for the clinic. It's not too far, only a handful of blocks to Main Street, so it only takes a couple minutes to reach the small back parking lot Blair mentioned. Her SUV is already there, and the moment I park beside her, she climbs out.

"Hey," she says, offering me a small smile.

"Hi."

As soon as I step beside her, she pulls me into a big hug. "Come on, let's go find out."

We walk to the back entrance, and she uses her key to unlock the facility, followed by a few taps on the keypad to disable the security system. "I really appreciate you doing this," I murmur as we step inside.

"It's what friends are for. I would have offered to just grab you a pregnancy test, but I figured this was quicker and more private."

I nod in response, glancing around the back of the clinic just to give myself something to do. Blair flips on a light for a small room in the hallway. "Come on," she says, stepping back so I can enter the room. "Have a seat."

But I can't sit. I have all this nervous energy, and taking a seat is the last thing I want to do. "This is okay, right? I mean, coming in here? I know you own the clinic, or your dad does, but..."

She offers me a friendly grin. "Yes, Jillian, this is fine. One little pregnancy test isn't going to break us."

I watch as she moves to a cabinet and pulls things down. She spins around and hands me a urine sample cup and a sanitary wet wipe. "You know the drill, right?"

I nod. This is most definitely not my first urine sample. When I was younger, I was plagued with a string of UTIs and it took a couple rounds of antibiotics before they got the right one to take care of the issue.

"Just bring the sample back here when you're done."

Moving across the hall, I go into the restroom and close the door. I stare down at that small cup, knowing what needs to happen next. I take a deep breath and get to it. I try not to think about the results, but it's hard. I want to think about what the results mean, whether the result is pregnant or not.

After providing the sample, I wash my hands and retrieve the cup. Blair is waiting in the small room we started in and takes the cup when I join her. She dips a pregnancy test in the sample and sets it aside on a paper towel.

"Are you going to be okay if this is positive?" she asks, glancing my way while we wait for the results.

I know instantly my answer. "Yes."

She grins widely. "Good, because you'd be a fabulous mom."

My throat is thick with emotion as I truly consider those words for the first time. It's not just the shock of being late, but it's the realization I might very well be a mother in just nine short months.

What I've always dreamed about.

Tears fill my eyes and I'm pretty sure I'm not breathing as Blair grabs the test and looks at the screen. Without showing any emotion, she holds it up so I can see the small display area. A strangled cry erupts from my throat as I realize my future is about to change.

Everything I've always wanted is happening.

The confirmation is right in front of me.

I'm pregnant.

Oh my God, now what?

CHAPTER eighteen

KAMERON

I smile when I see Jillian's reply. I'm glad she took a nap and is relaxing on her day off. She's been working tirelessly all week and deserves a little downtime. I only wish I were taking it with her. I wouldn't mind curling up beside her on the couch, enjoying a mid-Sunday afternoon nap.

Instead, I take a second to return a message.

Me: Gonna be the usual time getting out of here, but you're welcome to stay at my place.

Is it bad I want to fall asleep with her in my arms and wake the same way? Hell no. It just feels right at this point, and it's one of the moments I look forward to the most.

I set my phone to the side and finish cleaning up the grill from the last order. It's approaching dinnertime, and I'm sure it'll be picking back up soon. Sunday afternoons are usually somewhat steady, with customers enjoying meals at any point throughout the day. It's why we're open eleven to nine. We generally pick up after we open, thanks to the post-church crowd, and then also again midafternoon. Sunday nights are usually our slowest evening of the week, most people heading home to get ready for another workweek the next day, but we do have the occasional late-night diner or small group party. That's why I haven't shortened the hours on Sundays to closing before nine. I probably could shut down at eight, but I never want to miss an opportunity to serve food.

Maybe I'll consider it during the winter months.

The thought of spending even just one hour more with Jillian has a lot of fucking appeal.

Except...you're not really dating her.

But I want to be.

Real.

That's how this feels to me, and I need to get off my ass and tell her.

My problem is, I'm afraid she doesn't feel the same. I can assume my feelings are somewhat reciprocated, since she seems to be enjoying our time together as much as I am, but we all know enjoying time with someone doesn't equal love. It only proves our friendship is on point. But I know what I feel for her is more than just friends, and it's a hell of a lot greater than this fake relationship plan we devised.

Well, I devised.

My point is she could easily not feel the same, and that would suck.

Bad.

I'm certain that's exactly why I keep hesitating when I consider sharing my feelings with her. The last long-term relationship I had didn't end well, and I'd hate to go through that again. Not that a few weeks is considered long-term, but I definitely have strong feelings for Jillian. Maybe even greater than I ever experienced with my ex.

It's early evening by the time my phone chimes with her reply. I practically drop what I'm doing and dig my phone from my pocket.

I make sure everything is good for a few seconds before reading her message.

> **Jillian:** I'm just going to crash early here. Still drained and blah. Don't want to share my germs if I don't have to.

My gut twists when I read her words. She's been battling this stomach thing since Thursday. At least it's not severe, but the constant upset stomach and tiredness isn't good, especially when she has the job she does, up before the sun to head to her bakery.

I feel a wave of guilt that I'm even considering begging her to stay anyway. As much as I'd love to hold her and take care of her while she's under the weather, maybe this is exactly what she needs. Her own bed and a lot of rest. My own desire to be near her will just have to take a back seat right now.

> **Me:** I hate that you're still feeling under the weather.

Just as I hit send, an idea pops into my head. I turn to see if Marlin is still here, happy when I spot him over by the sink. "Hey, can you do me a favor?"

He nods. "Sure, what's up?"

"On your way home, can you drop something off at Jillian's house?"

He gives me a look, one single eyebrow shooting toward his hairline. "Uhh, maybe?" he teases.

"She's not feeling well, and I'd like you to take her some soup," I state, already moving toward the side station where the steam table is kept. I scoop two hearty ladles full of baked potato soup, and instead of adding the toppings, I choose to place them inside a small container, just in case she doesn't want them.

When I place the sealed containers inside a bag, I add a handful of cracker packets and fold it closed. I want to write a little note inside, but I know my attention is needed back over at the grill. So instead, I set the bag aside and glance to Marlin. "It's ready."

"Great, I'll drop it off on my way home."

I nod. "You know her address?" I'm pretty sure he does, considering most of the town knows where everyone lives, but I want to confirm anyway.

"Yeah, I'm good."

"All right, I'll send her a message to let her know you're coming, but if she doesn't answer the door, just leave it on the small table beside the door."

"Will do, boss. See you Wednesday," he says, giving a quick goodbye to the rest of the kitchen team.

"Later," I reply, retrieving my phone one last time.

Me: Marlin is bringing you dinner. If you don't answer the door, I told him to leave it on your table. Get some rest, sweetheart.

I click send, not even worrying about the term of endearment. Because of the circumstances surrounding our relationship, the use of the word might seem unnecessary. No one is witnessing it. It's not for show or because someone is watching. It's because I feel that term in my heart. *Sweetheart.* So timeless and simple, but yet so meaningful and perfect.

Now I just have to get through the rest of the evening without worrying or fretting over her. Easier said than done, that's for sure, but submerging myself in work helps. For so long, work is where I truly feel at peace. Behind the grill, preparing food has always been my lifeline, my solace.

But I feel the shift.

Jillian is causing it, and it doesn't feel like such a bad thing.

In fact, it's quite the opposite.

I just have to figure out what to do about it.

She's ignoring me.

It's Tuesday afternoon, and for some reason, she's not communicating.

Of course, it could be exactly what she says it is. She's busy. But even when I dropped by yesterday to say hello and invite her to dinner, I felt the disconnect. The distance. The shortness between us as she told me she had too much work on her plate to have dinner with me, and she really needed to focus on her cake orders.

So I left, even though I didn't want to. I would have rather stayed and helped her, like I did the week before when I was off work. Hell, even if it was just to sit back and watch her decorate cakes, I wanted to do it, because witnessing her create her masterpieces is so much better than sitting at home, alone. I still worry that something's wrong. She still looked tired and maybe a little pale yesterday when I dropped by, and I don't fucking like it.

Now here it is. Tuesday. And she hasn't responded to my text asking about her afternoon. Not to mention the one she replied to earlier today was a short "thanks" when I told her to have a great day.

I toss my phone onto my couch and glance around the living room. I can't sit here anymore. I've already mowed my yard and cleaned up the back patio. I even ran to the grocery store to grab some necessities for my own fridge, all with Jillian in mind, in hopes I could cook for her tonight when she gets off work. Maybe even fall asleep in my arms later.

But I don't see that happening when she's not responding to me.

Sure, I could drop by the bakery, but I'm not sure I want to. If she's as short today as she was yesterday then I'd feel like I was bugging her, and I don't want that. Flour Power is technically closed, but I'm sure she's there, prepping what she can for tomorrow and working on orders. I was hoping to discuss our first dessert collaboration, which is coming soon. First of October is when Jillian will officially start making sweet treats for Prime.

Needing a change of scenery, I grab my keys and phone and head out the front door. I don't live too far away from our small downtown area—not as close as Jillian—but it's a beautiful day for a walk. So, I walk. I find myself reaching Main Street, and since it's nearing the end of the workday, I spot several people I recognize on the sidewalk and offer polite greetings as I go.

The bakery is just up the street on the opposite side, but instead of heading there, I find myself entering a different business. A bell chimes over the door and a familiar face looks up from the reception desk and smiles. "Well, if it isn't Kameron Markley. What brings you in?" She glances at her computer screen. "I don't see your name on the schedule for an appointment."

"Hi, Stella, and no, I don't have an appointment."

A look of relief flashes across her face. "Okay, good. I was worried you got deleted or moved somehow." She stands and offers a smile. "What can we do for you?"

"Actually, I was wondering if Dr. Rhodes was available for a few minutes. It's a personal call, not professional," I tell her, realizing this was a bad idea. I can't just drop by my friend's medical practice at the end of the workday just because I want to chat.

"He's in with his last patient, Kameron. If you want to have a seat, I can let you know when he's done," she informs me politely.

With a nod, I walk over to one of the chairs in the corner of the waiting room and have a seat. There are two televisions in the space, one over by a children's table with blocks, books, and a few small toys showing a cartoon, and the other on the opposite side of the room with a news program on. I can't help but smile at the stark difference between the two halves. For as long as I've been coming to the Pine Village Medical Clinic, they have always taken care of patients from birth to one hundred, but ever since Blair joined the practice, as a pediatrician, I've been seeing a lot more for the younger patients. And from what I've been told, their practice has grown considerably, thanks to having her on staff. Her father, Dr. O'Connor, started the practice and has since retired, but he's still very much a part of the business. He fills in for Gabe and Blair when needed, especially when she was off after having their daughter. It's very much a family business, and I know they're all happy and proud of what they've built and continue to grow.

The sound of voices in the hallway catches my attention. As I look up, I see an older gentleman exiting the area where the exam rooms are housed, and before he makes it to the front door, Stella says, "Kameron, you can go on back to his office."

I nod in appreciation and head for the doorway the older man just walked through. A few of the doors are closed, letting me know there are still patients in the building, and I quietly pass by them and make my way to Gabe's back office. One of the nurses, Makenzie, is in the small room known as the nurses' station, and as I pass, she offers a polite wave. I return the gesture but keep my feet moving to where Gabe is.

When I reach the threshold, I find him already inside, moving a small stack of folders from his desk to the credenza behind it. "Hey, this is a nice surprise," he says as I step into the room.

"Yeah, sorry for just dropping by like this," I reply, feeling guilty for interrupting his workday.

He waves off my comment. "Close the door. I just finished my last patient, so the only thing you're keeping me from is the notes I need to enter into the patient's chart."

I close the door and walk over to one of the chairs in front of his desk. The room is much more crowded than it used to be. Since he and Blair married, they moved her desk over to this office. They wanted to be together in the same room. The other office is used by her dad when he's here, but also for more space for the office staff.

The moment I sit in the chair, he asks, "You okay?"

"Yeah," I reply quickly, running my hand through my hair. "It's not me, it's…Jillian."

He seems to sit up a little straighter in his seat, but he doesn't say a word.

"She's been, I don't know, tired a lot lately. And her stomach has been a mess for a bit. Like, probably a week or better? I know you can't talk to me about someone's medical stuff, but I was just wondering, as a friend, should I be worried?"

Because I am.

Worried as hell.

"Could she be pregnant?"

His words catch me completely off guard. I open my mouth and nothing comes out.

"That's the first thing that comes to mind," he says, leaning back in his chair, "And by the shocked look on your face, I assume that's a possibility?"

I nod, my mind going back to all those times we've slept together in just a short amount of time. Especially that first night. The one where the condom broke. She said it wasn't the right time, but what if she was wrong? What if she's pregnant?

"Of course, there are lots of other reasons she could be tired and sick too. There's a pretty rough strand of Influenza lurking around. We've been seeing a lot of patients with it. Takes anywhere from three to seven days before a patient starts to feel better. There're also other things like stress, menopause, endometriosis, medical side effects, IBS, anemia, diabetes, thyroid problems—"

"Okay," I interrupt, holding out my hand.

"My point is, if she's still a bit under the weather, she should see someone, even if it's just a lingering case of the flu. If it's been more than a week, I'd suggest sooner rather than later."

I nod.

"You care a lot about her." It's not a question.

Meeting his gaze, I give him a confirming chin lift. "More than a lot."

He smiles back at me. "'Bout time. I've been waiting years for you to fall."

My throat is thick as I think back over the last decade. Hell, longer than that. Not many people know about my time in Chicago, but Gabe does. Not because he was there, but simply because I shared the details with him one night right after my restaurant had opened over a bottle of red wine. He was complaining about his ex-wife, Amara, and I let all the dirty details about my time in the Windy City fly.

"I have to tell her."

His eyebrows shoot toward his hairline. "How you feel?"

"Well, yes, but I need to tell her about Chicago."

Realization sets in. "Yes."

I stand up, determination setting in. Just as I reach for the door, I turn and say, "If she's pregnant, I wouldn't be upset in the least. In fact, I'd be elated."

Gabe grins widely. "Go get her, buddy."

I open the door and take off down the hallway. Blair is stepping out of one of the rooms and turns, surprised to see me. "Kameron. What are you doing?" Then something that looks like worry transforms her face. "Jillian? Is she okay?"

"She's fine," I reply, hoping that's true. "I'm on my way to see her now."

Blair nods and smiles. "Okay, good."

I continue down the hall and wave to Stella before walking out the front door. Then, with the sun setting off in the west, I set out toward Flour Power Bakery. If she's been avoiding me the last couple of days, well, she's not going to be able to do it any longer. I want to see her.

No, I *need* to see her.

She's the oxygen I need to survive, and it's time she knows it.

CHAPTER
nineteen

Jillian

I sigh and rub my temple as I take a few calming breaths. I didn't sleep well last night, mostly because my brain was all over the place. I think I've come to terms with the fact I'm pregnant, but then the fear settled in. Since I'm thirty-seven, I'm considered high risk. Blair gave me some great information about geriatric pregnancies, and I've spent the last two evenings devouring it all. She encouraged me not to get too worked up, but it's hard. Both Blair and Hallie were thirty-six when they conceived, and they both had normal pregnancies and deliveries.

Of course, that still doesn't completely take away the worry I carry in my heart.

The fact that I'm even here, pregnant, is unbelievable. Though I've always aspired to be a mother, I've also given up on that dream. After my marriage failed spectacularly, I put all aspirations of children on the back burner. As the years passed, the flames on that burner eventually went out, and I figured I'd spend the rest of my life alone. Maybe I'd be lucky enough to find someone in my older years, but I didn't believe parenthood to be a part of that. At least having my own kids. Perhaps I'd be lucky enough to marry a man with kids from a previous relationship. I'd be perfectly content being a stepmom.

But this...

I wasn't prepared for this at all.

And I still don't know what to do.

The first thing I need to do is tell Kameron. I know it's not convenient, but I've decided to tell him this weekend. I need just a few more days to get my ducks in a row, as I often do when I'm facing big decisions, especially those that are life-changing.

A knock sounds at the back door of the bakery, and even though it could be any one of my friends, my Spidey-sense is tingling and tells me it's the man I can't seem to stop thinking about. Tears fill my eyes as I make my way toward the door. I take a few calming, deep breaths, preparing to face Kameron.

No amount of preparation could do my head—and my heart—any good. The moment I open the door and see him standing there, my entire body reacts. I *long* for him, crave him like a person wandering the desert craves water. He looks so beautiful, if you can really call a man beautiful. But he is. His jaw houses a little more stubble than normal, as if he hasn't bothered to shave today or maybe even yesterday, and he's wearing a casual T-shirt untucked and blue jeans. He looks positively gorgeous, and so far out of my league.

That only causes my heart to bleed even more.

I've fallen for my fake boyfriend.

And I'm carrying his baby.

Could this possibly get any more complicated?

"Hey," he says, offering the hint of a smile.

The compassion and tenderness in his eyes have my own tearing up. I blink hard and look away, stepping back to grant him entrance. "Sorry I've been so busy lately," I say lamely as I close the door.

"It's all right," he replies walking over and leaning against the counter. "I'm sorry to just drop in on you like this, but, well, first off, I wanted to see you. To make sure you're okay."

My throat is thick and dry and makes it hard to get words past it, but somehow, I manage. "I'm all right," I confirm.

"Good. I know you haven't been feeling well lately, and you've been working extra."

I shrug. "It's not really extra, Kameron. This is part of my job, what I do."

"I get that," he quickly adds. "I understand, probably better than most." He sighs and levels me with a look. "There's something I need to tell you."

The hairs on the back of my neck stand up as an uneasy feeling settles in my stomach. "Okay..." I reply, drawing out that one word.

He glances down for a second, as if digging deep for his resolve, and then levels me with a look. It's intense, full of worry and hesitation. "I was married once."

Okay. I wasn't expecting that.

My mouth opens, but nothing comes out.

He quickly pushes forward, as if determined to tell me what happened before I can say anything. "I was young and dumb," he adds, a look of sadness crossing his face. "I was committed, but to the wrong thing."

I'm still trying to wrap my mind around the fact he was married. And I didn't hear one chirp about it. That's very un-Pine Village-like. Usually, marriages and divorces are at the top of the gossip chain, so to find out he was married—*and divorced*—is a bit of a shock to the system.

He gives me a small smile, as if understanding my question without even vocalizing it. "Honestly, I'm surprised more people don't know about it. Gabe does, but only because I told him about it after I moved back here. My parents knew, but they promised not to say anything."

"You didn't want them to say anything?"

He shrugs. "Not really. I had been living in Chicago for about six years by that point, and I was so submerged in the city lifestyle, I didn't want my old life to mix with my new one. In Chicago, no one cared who you were or where you came from. Most people barely knew their neighbors or coworkers." He exhales loudly and shakes his head. "It's not that I didn't want them to tell anyone, but I just preferred to keep it private. They understood that and respected it. Besides, it's not like we ever came home. I was so damn busy with work, starting at the bottom and working my ass off in the industry." He levels me with a look filled with anguish and sadness. "I should have come home more. I'll always regret that."

A single tear slides down my cheek. "You couldn't have known," I find myself telling him, taking a step closer and reaching for his hand. It's part to comfort him, sure, but a piece of that contact is for me too.

"You're right," he agrees, his eyes full of emotion. "I couldn't have known. But it was more than that. Lilly—that's my ex-wife—she didn't really care to ever want to visit Wisconsin. She was born and raised in a Chicago suburb, and that was where she always wanted to be. Especially since I was working so much, she wanted to be near her family and friends. My parents had come to visit a few times, but it was always a little awkward. I worked six days a week, ten to twelve hours a day, and Lilly was stuck entertaining them in my absence, and I don't mean that to be harsh. She didn't know them." I pause and take a breath.

"On top of that, she wanted to start a family. And I didn't."

My heart practically falls out of my chest and dies a slow, painful death right here on the old tile floor. "What?" I whisper, the tears threatening to fall in earnest now. I do everything I can to hold them back, but it's becoming increasingly more difficult the longer he talks.

"We got married when I was twenty-four and by the time I was twenty-six, she was pushing hard for a baby. I was working so fucking much, barely having time to sleep. I just couldn't imagine bringing a baby into the relationship, at least at that point. I barely saw her. The last thing I wanted was to never see my child too."

I don't know when I truly started to cry, but his words—this realization—is like a dagger to my already bleeding heart. I empathize with his ex-wife, Lilly, because not that long ago, I was that woman. I was married, anxiously planning for a future that would never come. At least I found out after only nine months of marriage.

"Anyway, I told her I wanted to wait, and she didn't want to. Just before our fourth anniversary, she left. That was it. Our marriage was over. Two years later, my parents were killed in a car accident, and I moved back home. You know the rest."

I close my eyes, trying to figure out my next move. I still have to tell him about the baby, even if that's not what he wants. He has a right to know. But I'm suddenly prepared to take these next steps alone, and I'll do it with my head held high.

"Jilly," he whispers, pulling me into his arms. That single act makes me cry even harder.

My emotions are all over the place. Last night, I cried at a commercial for toilet paper. I know it's the onslaught of pregnancy hormones but come on. Something has to give, because all I want to do is cry. And then I get nauseous because I'm crying and crying because I'm nauseous. And here we are, as women, eager and ready to go through this time and time again. Thank God it's a short-lived issue, because I'm not sure I could deal with these emotions and the threat of vomiting forever.

The worst thing he can do is pull me into his arms. They're strong and warm and so perfect, and all I want to do is stay there, surrounded by his scent and his strength, forever. But no, the big stupid idiot had to go and prove he's just like every other man who makes a promise to a woman and then breaks it.

I push myself off this chest at the same time I pull back. I can tell he doesn't want to let me go, but he does. "What's wrong?" he asks, completely beside himself that I'm so upset.

The care and worry in his question only make me cry that much more.

My shoulders are shaking, and I can tell by the look on his face he has no idea what to do. *Well, neither do I, buddy.*

"I can't do this," I insist, hastily wiping tears from my face.

"What?" he asks, his confusion obvious.

"*This!*" I declare as my shoulders drop, and I start to cry again.

It's all too much. Finding out about the baby. The morning sickness. The fact I bumped into the side of a shelf with my boob earlier and it hurt like hell. The pregnancy hormones that are quadruple the normal amount, bringing on tears. The exhaustion. Learning about his ex-wife and why they split. Realizing he most likely won't want to be a part of our baby's life, at least for the right reasons. I want him to *want* to be a dad, not obligated. Oh, and let's not forget the lie. How about the fact our relationship isn't even real to begin with.

It's all that.

Too.

Fucking.

Much.

He opens his mouth, but no words seem to come out. He looks shocked by my outburst, and maybe a little bit of myself is too. I'm not this person. I'm not the one to react wildly, but I don't seem to have control over it right now. The best thing for him to do is leave so I can collect my thoughts and get everything under control.

"I hate this," I whisper, but I can tell he hears it.

"I'm going to fix this, Jillian," he states—or maybe he demands? It's a very determined, pointed statement, and his conviction is like a physical touch.

"It's fine, Kam," I murmur, wishing I weren't so overly dramatic right now. I feel like I can't even think straight.

"No, it's not. I did this," he says, stepping forward and placing a gentle hand on my arm. "I've upset you, I've caused you pain, even if it's not physical." He closes his eyes, and when he opens them, he looks every bit as anguished as I feel. "I'll make this right," he insists.

Recalling a previous conversation, I blurt out, "I need to wash my hair."

Confusion sweeps across his face. "What?"

"I need to wash my hair. You have to go," I insist, referring to the time he told me I could say that and he'd leave, no questions asked.

Realization sets in. "The code phrase," he whispers. "I'm going to fix this," he insists once more.

Before I can ask him what he's going to fix, he leans forward and brushes his lips against mine. "I'll make this right, Jilly, I promise. Please don't worry one more second about anything. I've got you." His words are tender, sweet, and full of emotion, and before I can say another word, he walks to the back entrance and exits, closing the door behind him as he goes.

I'm left standing there, fearing I've lost him for good and not really understanding why that hurts so much, especially because he doesn't want kids. It's not like I can say I don't want them either, all things considered. I'm having a baby. A very wanted baby. And if he doesn't want that, then that's his decision.

I shake my head and try to calm myself down. A headache is starting, and I know any work I was hoping to get done tonight isn't happening. Thank goodness I didn't really have anything on my plate. I was preparing for a couple of cakes I'll need to make and decorate for a Saturday pickup, but I don't have to worry about it now. The whole reason I was still here was because I hate being home alone. When I'm there, I long to be with Kameron, and last night was especially difficult. I knew he wasn't working, which was why I stayed late at the bakery and got a few things done. Tonight was going to be much of the same, but right now, all I want to do is go home.

I'm exhausted.

Emotionally spent.

I want to grab a tub of ice cream and lie on my couch watching terrible reality TV. I pray sleep comes easily and quickly tonight.

Just as I start to pack up my things, my cell phone chimes from an incoming text. I pull my phone from my pocket, both dreading and secretly hoping to see Kameron's name on the screen. Unfortunately—or fortunately, depending on how you're looking at it—it's my friend, Ryan.

> **Ryan:** Hey, wondering what you're up to tonight? Marcus is working late on one of the school buses. He has to get it finished for school tomorrow. Wanna grab dinner?

My stomach churns, and with the state of my emotions, I know going out to eat isn't in my best interest.

> **Me:** Haven't been feeling the best so I'll probably just head home and eat there.

The bubbles appear immediately.

> **Ryan:** Want company? I can bring food. Whatever you want. Some soup and grilled cheese from the diner? I'm not worried about catching anything.

I can't help but snort. The only way she's *catching* this is if she has unprotected sex with her boyfriend.

My stomach growls, as if it can hear the message on the screen. I haven't been vomiting much, but the constant state of nausea has kept me from eating too much. In fact, my main source of nutrients has come from different soups Kameron has made and sent to me. However, the thought of a big grilled cheese with soup has hunger pains filling the room.

Me: Actually, that sounds pretty good. I'd love a grilled cheese and some soup.

Ryan: Great! I'll grab whatever's on special from the diner and be over in about thirty minutes. Any requests or dislikes?

Me: No chili.

Ryan: You got it. See you soon!!

I slip my phone into my pocket and grab my purse. Making sure all the lights are off, I slip out the back door and head for my vehicle. It's getting dark out and the air holds a distinct chill to it, a sure sign of fall setting in.

Once I climb into my car, I stare at the back of my building and sigh. I'm going to have to worry about my hours soon. Maybe not before the baby comes, but definitely after. I might have to adjust the times I'm open, especially if I have a newborn to care for. But I refuse to look at this pregnancy as anything but a blessing, and there's no need to worry about any of the other stuff today.

Everything will fall into place.

It has to.

Right now, all I need to worry about is feeding myself and my baby. Will I tell Ryan about the baby? Perhaps, though I'd really wanted to tell Kameron first. However, I just might need some advice, and even though Ryan is around a decade younger than me, I could really use a friend tonight.

I guess we'll see how it goes.

CHAPTER *Twenty*

KAMERON

Seeing her cry has shaken me to the core.

I didn't even get a chance to finish telling her about Lilly, because I witnessed the weight of our lie suffocate her. She's been slowly sinking, our fake relationship tied around her ankle, and I'm done. I can't watch it consume and change her, and that's what's happening. She said she can't do this anymore, and I'm the asshole who made her do this in the first place.

Well, I can fix this.

I can fix us.

Because that's what I want to do. I don't want a "fake" relationship with her. I want a real one. I just hope it's not too late, that the damage isn't irreversible. I pray there's an *us* to salvage.

Pulling out my cell phone, I pull up the contact I'm searching for.

"Hello?" the older voice comes through the device, a grandmotherly, friendly sound.

"Mrs. Krokus, it's Kameron Markley," I offer.

"Oh, Kameron, what a lovely surprise. How are you?"

My heart is pounding in my chest, and it has nothing to do with the clipped pace I walk as I head back home to get my vehicle. "I've been better," I answer honestly. "Listen, Mrs. Krokus—"

"Dorothy, please," she interrupts.

"Dorothy," I reply. "I was hoping I could stop by and steal a few minutes of your time. There's something I need to discuss with you. Are you available right now?" I refuse to do this over the phone. Face-to-face is the only way to say what I have to say.

"Actually, I'm not. I just left to meet a few ladies at the diner for a late dinner."

My heart falls.

I really wanted to do this now.

"Why don't we meet at the building? I can steal a few minutes with you. We're so close to the signing date, and I'm getting anxious. I can't wait to see your vision come to life. Well, yours and Jillian's."

And there it goes. My heart sinks lower than ever before. It's like it dropped to the ground and everyone is walking all over it with high heels and track cleats. Clearing my throat, I agree, "I can be there in a few minutes."

"Great!" she bellows, obviously pleased by my offer. "I'll see you there, Kameron. Can't wait."

I reply something that sounds like goodbye, but my mind is already three steps ahead, the plan forming in my head. I make it home rather quickly, and instead of running inside and changing my clothes, since I'm dressed so casually, I opt to just go as is. The quicker I get to the building, the faster I can fix this mess I've created.

My drive back to downtown is swift, since it's only a few blocks. I probably could have just walked to the opposite end where my restaurant and the building I was planning to purchase are located, but I want my car there so I can go find Jillian afterward. Instead of driving around back where I'd generally leave my car while at work, I pull beside the one I know to be Mrs. Krokus's along the roadway. She offers me a quick smile as I climb from my vehicle, and she slowly does the same.

"Here," she says when I approach, handing me the key to the front door.

I take it, and even though I'd love to run up and get the door open right away—move this whole thing along—I hang back and offer my arm to the older woman. She graciously takes it and together, we make our way to the front door. Unlocking the old wood-framed glass door, a wave of sadness washes over me. I'm about to walk away from the expansion I always wanted.

But I'm walking toward something greater.

That sadness quickly transforms into calmness.

I know I'm making the right decision.

Dorothy reaches over with a shaky hand and flips the switch, bathing the dusty, old space in light. She smiles at the space, taking it all in. "I love it here," she whispers before closing her eyes. "I feel his presence."

My throat is thick as I try to swallow over the lump. I know she's referring to her late husband, and the guilt I feel sours my stomach.

Taking a deep breath, I turn and face Mrs. Krokus. "I have a confession to make. I can't buy your building."

If she's surprised by my statement, she shows no indication, just continues to watch me.

Knowing the only way to move forward is to walk through the shit-mess I created, I lay my confession at her feet, right here in the middle of her empty space. "I lied to you. I'm not in a relationship with Jillian. I told you that to get the building."

She finally reacts, cocking her head a bit to the side. "Why?"

"Why did I lie? Because I was selfish and I wanted this building. I didn't want you to sell to that other couple."

"There was no other couple, Kameron," she replies with a hint of a grin on her lips.

"What?"

She shrugs and releases my arm, taking a few hesitant steps forward. "You're not the only one who can lie, young man."

I'm completely flabbergasted, my feet rooted in place. "Why?"

"Why did I lie?" she asks, looking at me over her shoulder. "Same reason as you. I wanted something."

"What did you want?" I ask, trying to understand.

"I wanted you to see what was directly in front of you all along."

I look around the vast room.

"Not that, Kameron. Jillian."

My mouth falls open, but no words come out.

Dorothy chuckles and spins around, surprisingly agile for a woman of her age. "I was there that night, you know."

"What night?" I ask, confused.

"The night you prepared tacos for her and her friends."

I think back on that night not too long ago when Jillian asked me to return a favor. She had made a few last-minute desserts for me, and I told her I'd be happy to reciprocate at some point down the road. When she made that call, it was for something quick and easy she could take to a girls' night over at Blair's house. She didn't care what it was, just wanted finger foods.

I agonized over what to make all day, until it hit me. I prepared a huge taco bar spread, something I had never really done before, at least not since college. And when it came time to deliver the food, I wouldn't let her pick it up. I drove it all over to Blair's house myself, refusing to send one of my employees to do it. Veronica gave me a hard time over it. I remember catching some flack when I went up front to tell her I was leaving for a few minutes to deliver the food. There were a few customers in the restaurant. Was one of them Mrs. Krokus?

"I saw the look in your eye when you said you were taking it all over to the Rhodes's house. It wasn't anticipation for seeing Gabe or Blair. It was to see Jillian."

My throat is thick as I try to swallow.

I remember the way my heart kicked up a few beats when I saw her standing in Gabe's kitchen, waiting. She seemed thrilled by what I came up with, knowing the tacos would be a huge hit amongst her friends. But I was more enthralled with her eagerness and happiness over something as simple as tacos.

I smiled the whole way back to my restaurant.

Closing my eyes, I recall exactly how she looked standing there, helping me set up the feast I delivered. The soft curls in her hair, the pretty sundress she was wearing, the way her scent seemed to reach around me and squeeze. I remember every detail as if it had happened moments ago and not a few months back.

Same goes for the night I showed up on her doorstep and told her I needed a pretend girlfriend.

And every moment we've spent together since.

"You realize it now, right? There has always been something lingering between you two. I just helped push it along."

I gape at the older woman, who now wears a pleased smile on her face. "You set me up?"

She shrugs. "Perhaps."

I run my hand over my face in annoyance and shock. I can't believe she did this. "So, now what?" I find myself asking, desperate for a little bit of direction here.

"Well, now you go get the girl, Kameron. She needs tacos."

That makes me pause. "Excuse me?"

"She needs the man you were the night you came over with tacos. The one who dropped what he was doing to help her out." She gives me her full attention and reaches for my hand. "You love her, right?"

I want to nod, to confirm what we both already know, but when I finally say those words, it'll be her ears hearing them.

"It's okay, you don't have to tell me. I can see it in your eyes."

I shake my head, doing all I can to wrap my brain around the last few minutes. Hell, the last hour or so. "What does this mean?" I find myself asking, desperately looking for a little guidance right now.

"It means I know you lied, and I understand why you did it. I could have called you out, but chose to let it ride. Why? Because I was secretly hoping you'd realize your true feelings for Jillian."

Damn, I wish I had a chair right now, because the floor seems to be falling out from under me. I slip my hands through my hair and listen as she continues.

"Have you? Realized your true feelings?"

I nod. "Yes."

"Good," she replies proudly, a satisfied grin on her face. "Now, what are you going to do to win her over? There was a reason you came clean, right?"

"Yes. Not only was it wrong to continue the charade, but it's created unnecessary stress for her. She hasn't been feeling well lately, and this lie and the anguish it was creating isn't worth it."

She waves off my comment. "Jillian is fine, I promise."

I don't exactly share her blasé attitude where Jillian is concerned. She was anything but fine a little bit ago. The tears were very real, and I felt every single one of them as they slid down her cheeks.

"I'm afraid," I find myself confessing, the words just sliding from my mouth.

"Of?"

"Of messing this up again."

"Oh, Kameron, we all make mistakes. I've made plenty. But something tells me you're referring to a very specific one, right? I know about your marriage back in your twenties."

My eyes widen in shock. "What? You do?"

"Oh, yes," she says, placing her hand on my arm and walking farther into the room. I have no choice but to follow. "Your mom mentioned it to me once. She was so excited for your upcoming wedding but understood and respected your need for privacy. She told only a couple of people, me and her friend, Helen, included."

"You never said a word," I reply, trying to wrap my head around the fact she knew.

"I do indulge a bit in the occasional gossip, but that wasn't mine to tell."

I exhale slowly. "My ex, Lilly, left me because I wasn't ready to start a family."

She nods.

"She's happily married, with three kids," I add, smiling. I'm truly delighted Lilly found her happily ever after.

"As you should. It led you to yours."

My heart does this weird skippy beat in my chest. "Jillian's divorce sort of mirrors mine," I state, realizing how it must have sounded to hear about my former marriage and the cause of the demise of it.

"Sometimes it takes losing what you thought you wanted to gain what you truly needed."

Her words hit hard and when I realize we've stopped moving, we're standing at the back of the large space.

"This is going to make a beautiful restaurant, Kameron. I know you talked about adding more kitchen and storage space, which I'm sure you need, but I think you should add a little extra office space here," she informs me, indicating to the spot at the very back of the building I was just planning to use for more storage. She turns and holds my gaze as she adds, "This way, you can raise your family here too."

A mixture of longing and hope bursts in my chest like a Fourth of July firework. She paints a beautiful picture; one I want nothing more than to grab on to and hold close.

Clearing my throat, I ask, "You're still selling me the building? Despite everything?"

She smiles and brings her aging hand up to cup my jaw. "Of course I am. This space was destined for you. I'm certain it will again be filled with the sights and sounds of a growing family. *Your* family, Kameron."

I admit, I have to blink a few times to keep the sudden rush of moisture at bay. The vision of walking into my office and seeing

Jillian and a baby or two is vivid. It's like a beautiful painting hanging in a museum, one I could stand and stare at all day long and never tire of the scene.

"I have to go," I blurt out, turning panicked eyes her way.

Dorothy smiles. "Yes, you do. Go get your girl, Kameron. I'll see you Monday morning at the title company. We have a transaction to complete."

I throw my arms around her, giving the older woman a firm, warm hug. "Thank you," I whisper.

"Of course."

I turn and head for the door but stop in my tracks.

"Go. I can lock up. I want to spend a few more minutes taking this all in."

A smile stretches across my lips. "I appreciate all you've done for me—for us, Dorothy."

She grins the sweetest motherly smile, and I swear, I see my mom reflecting back at me. "You're very welcome, young man. The next time that door opens, it'll be to welcome new life within these walls. A new family. I can't wait to watch it thrive again."

I'm moving before I even realize my legs are carrying me back to Mrs. Krokus. I throw my arms around her once more and place a gentle kiss on her cheek. "I promise to make you proud."

She grins, her eyes reflecting moisture. "You already have. Now, go get the girl, tiger."

Just as I reach the door, I holler, "On opening night, you get seated first."

"There's nowhere else I'd be," she informs me.

"You sure you're okay here to lock up and get down to the diner?" I'll gladly stay an extra five minutes to help the older woman.

"Of course," she confirms. "I might be old, but I'm not dead yet." She throws me a wink and turns her attention back to the large, empty room that once housed her own business. I witness love and joy washing over her as she closes her eyes, reliving the past.

Maybe someday that'll be me. When I'm ready to turn the keys of Prime Steak House over to the next owner. The person who will love and care for it, helping it grow and thrive just as I've been doing for the last decade. Then maybe I'll be this person, the one standing in the middle of the room, taking it all in one last time.

Hopefully, I'll be doing it with a certain woman by my side.

What started out as a fake relationship, a desperate plea for help, turned into something bigger than I ever could have imagined.

It turned into love.

Now it's time to go get my girl, as Mrs. Krokus instructed. I'm ready. I just pray she will hear me out. I have a lot to say, and it's time I said it.

Hold on, Jilly.

Ready or not, I'm coming for you.

I'm coming for us.

CHAPTER
Twenty one

Jillian

Ryan just gapes at me, unmoving and silent for several seconds. "So...wait. You're telling me you and Kameron were fake dating so he could get the building next to his restaurant, you're pregnant, *and* you fell in love with him?" Her wide eyes stare back at me as she asks, "What did you get out of the deal?"

Instantly, my own eyes drop to my still-flat stomach, which makes her giggle.

"Well, besides that." Leaning forward she whispers, "It was good sex, right? Kameron just looks like the type of guy who knows his way around a kitchen, if you know what I mean."

I snort a giggle and shake my head. "Stop."

"No, you stop. I'm being serious. At least if there's a possibility of you having to parent this baby alone, it better have been good sex. Not that terrible grunting and slamming into you like they're jackhammering the sidewalk with one of those little plastic hammers."

My eyes widen to the point of pain before I burst into fits of laughter. "Oh my God," I giggle, letting the sound wash over me.

"True story. My ex. He might have been a movie star, but his bedroom skills were seriously lacking. You know what I'm talking about, right? Those little plastic tools that kids play with? It was like being pounded with one of those for two minutes, while sweat dripped on you. Seriously, it wasn't that great. Now, Marcus, I tell you, does *not* have one of those little plastic baby hammers. I'm talking..." She holds up her hands, indicating Marcus's...hammer...is much bigger than her ex's.

Of course, I blush.

"Anyway, we're not here to talk about Marcus. We're here to discuss you and Kameron." She exhales, watching me intently. "So, when are you going to tell him?"

I close my eyes, recalling the words he said about not being ready to have a baby with his ex-wife. "I was planning on telling him this weekend."

"You might just want to rip off the Band-Aid, especially after he told you about his ex-wife. But don't do it for him, do it for you," she says, leaning against the back cushion on my couch and watching me closely.

"I know."

"Now that you've had a couple of days to absorb the news and figure out your next step, it'll be a huge weight off your shoulders when you tell him. Plus, you'll know whether or not he's going to be a part of the baby's life."

A boulder sits in my stomach, disguised as the dinner I just consumed. While it went down easily—she brought grilled cheese and homemade tomato soup—I worry it may make a reappearance at some point. Ever since we started talking about the hard stuff, the queasiness has slowly increased.

Tears fill my eyes as I look up at my friend. I haven't known her long, but it's as if she's been part of our lives for years, when in fact I've only known her four months. It doesn't matter there's an age gap either. Despite being more than a decade older than her, I still cherish her friendship and find value and comfort in our talks.

"What if he doesn't want to?" I whisper, already knowing the answer to my own question but needing to hear someone else say it.

"Then fuck him!" she bellows, catching me by surprise. "No, seriously. You're awesome, Jillian, and if he can't see that, then screw him. And if he doesn't want to be a part of your child's life either? Then screw him again. But not literally. That's what got you into this mess to begin with," she says, making me giggle once more.

"That's true." I take a deep, calming breath. "I just...I really like him, Ryan. Like *more than like him* like him."

"I know you do, and the thing is, I'm pretty certain he *likes you* likes you too."

I start to shake my head and reach for the bottle of ginger ale she brought with my meal. "That's fake."

"No," she quickly insists. "No way. You can't fake that kind of emotion, Jillian. Anyone who saw you together could see it. Hell, probably feel it."

I close my eyes, trying to keep my mind from conjuring up every time he'd touch me in public, but what I see isn't what I expect. Sure, I know all the instances where he'd make a big public show of affection when eyes were on us, but I can't help but remember all the little things. The time he held my hand under the table where no one could see, or when he'd show up at the bakery and help me work, even after closing. That wasn't for show or for anyone's eyes.

What does that mean?

Could what Ryan is saying be accurate?

I don't want my heart to feel hope, because what if we're wrong? What if he's just that good of an actor? I mean, let's be honest, he went to pretty desperate lengths to be able to purchase the building by securing a fake girlfriend. I'm certain he would do whatever necessary to ensure the ink is signed on the paper. Not that I blame him. I completely understand having a dream and doing whatever's needed to get it.

My hand instantly moves to my stomach, as if to protect the baby inside.

My dream.

But this isn't how I wanted to get it.

I always envisioned being married and having a cute little house with a garden in the backyard and a tire swing hanging from a big oak tree. Of course, a big piece of that puzzle is the fact I would be in love with my husband, the man I would share those dreams with. Sure, I might have really—*really*—strong feelings for Kameron, but that doesn't mean he feels the same. In fact, just about two hours ago, he confessed a big piece of his past with me, including the fact he didn't want kids. At least he wasn't ready at that point. But now?

I guess I'm going to find out, right?

"You don't have to figure it all out today, Jillian. I don't know Kameron well, but from what I've seen, he's compassionate and trustworthy, and I truly believe his reaction will surprise you. I just can't picture him not wanting to be part of this baby's life."

Up until a couple of hours ago, I would have said the same, but right now, I'm not so sure. "We'll see," I mutter, leaning back against the couch and closing my eyes.

"How are you feeling?"

"Okay. Only slightly queasy. I'm just hoping to get a decent night's sleep," I tell her, even though my heart tells me that won't happen. I'll be replaying the conversation from earlier, dissecting every detail and wondering what I could have said or done differently.

Ryan stands up and stretches. "I should get out of your hair so you can relax and get ready for bed."

I nod, even though I've enjoyed her visit. Despite the fact we were talking about some pretty heavy stuff, it was comfortable and welcomed. She's a good friend, and I'm so glad she and Marcus are together, and she moved to Pine Village. "Thank you for dinner," I say, pulling her into a hug.

"Anytime," she insists and meets my gaze. "I'm serious. I can bring soup or vitamins or whatever you need. Just call me."

My eyes fill with tears as another wave of extreme hormones crashes into me. "I will."

"Good."

Before she can head toward my front door, there's a loud, insistent knock on the other side.

Turning her attention to me, she asks, "Are you expecting someone?"

"No," I say, trying to ignore the way my heart skips a beat with hope and anticipation.

I take a few steps, but Ryan beats me to it. She pulls open the door, and even though her face remains neutral, her lips tick up in a slight smile. "Hi, Kameron."

"Hey, Ryan," he replies, his voice sounding anxious and uncertain.

One step closer brings him into view through the doorway. He's still wearing the same jeans and T-shirt he was wearing earlier, and his hair is even more messy than before. His blue eyes are a bit wild as they settle on me, but immediately they relax. "Hey," he says softly. "Can we talk?"

I glance at Ryan, who is clearly waiting for me to take the lead. She's prepared to leave, stay, or possibly throw down with Kameron if I so much as give her an indication. I can't help but smile.

That's a friend.

"I'll be all right," I tell her. "Thank you for coming over and hanging out with me." I walk over and give her another hug. "And for dinner."

She squeezes extra hard as she whispers, "Just tell him, and let me know how it goes, okay? And if I need to kill him, just say the word."

I snort a laugh, knowing she's kidding. Or at least I hope she's kidding.

"Be good to her, Kameron, or you'll answer to me," Ryan announces before walking past him and exiting my house.

The polite thing to do would be to make sure she gets to her SUV, but my eyes are glued to the man at my door. "Can I come in?" he asks hesitantly, waiting for me to nod.

Kameron steps inside and closes the door behind him when I give the green light. The moment he's standing in front of me, all I can think about is the last time he was here. Was that really the last time he was at my house? We've spent a lot of time at his place, the restaurant, and the bakery, but we rarely come here. It feels like both a lifetime ago and mere days since he showed up on my doorstep and asked me to be his fake girlfriend.

"Can we sit?" he asks.

"Sure," I reply, leading the way to my couch. I take a seat on the same side I recently vacated, while he sits on the opposite side where Ryan was. The moment his ass hits the seat, he shifts and moves closer.

I catch his scent in the air. His masculine, fresh soap mixed with the musk of his bodywash or deodorant. It's my favorite smell in the whole world, and I didn't realize it until right now. I used to adore the scent of freshly baked bread, hydrangeas, or even vanilla and sugar, but now? All I want is to inhale Kameron all day, every day.

Weirdo...

"I have something to tell you."

My heart falls a little in my chest. The last time—just a couple short hours ago—he needed to tell me something, he practically broke my heart without even realizing it. What damage could he possibly do now?

"Okay," I whisper, steeling my spine and lightly grasping my knees. My left leg starts to bounce, betraying the cool and calm front I'm going for.

He notices and smiles before reaching out and placing his palm against my knee. Even through the material of my jeans, I can feel the searing heat of his touch.

My leg stops bouncing, his hand having a calming effect on my entire body. But then he speaks again, rendering me completely speechless and tense.

"I went to see Mrs. Krokus. I told her everything."

I feel my eyes widen and my jaw drop. All I can do is gape at him as I try to process his words. "What?" I finally spit out, unsure I heard him correctly.

He gives me a slight grin. "I ended it, Jillian."

My heart falls to the floor as a fresh wave of sorrow hits me hard in the chest. "Oh."

"I told her about the lie. I couldn't let it continue to destroy you, and that's what was happening. I'm the reason you are so stressed and upset, and I just couldn't keep doing it. Seeing you hurt, watching our lie make you sick and emotional will forever be one of my biggest regrets in life. I never meant to hurt you, Jilly, and that's why I came clean to Mrs. Krokus."

All I can do is stare at him as realization sets in. He told her it was all a lie? That means only one thing. Now that she knows the truth, the deal is off. He won't get the building.

He won't get his dream.

"Kam, no," I whisper, more tears filling my eyes as guilt consumes me.

He thinks I've been sick and emotional for the wrong reason, and while I haven't enjoyed lying to my family and friends, that wasn't the reason for me acting the way I have been.

"Oh, God," I groan, hating the situation we're in. I bury my face in my hands.

"Hey, hey," he says as he moves to crouch in front of me. He gently pulls my hands from covering my face, his blue eyes so full of worry. "It's okay. It needed to be done."

"No," I cry. "Now you won't get the building! Your restaurant!"

He gives me a soft, gentle smile and wraps both of my hands in his. "I'm still getting the building."

Okay, I wasn't expecting that.

"What? How? Why? What?"

He chuckles and brings my hands to his lips, placing tender kisses against my knuckles. "She says she knew I was lying and wanted to see how it played out." Humor dances in his eyes.

My jaw practically unhinges. "Seriously?"

He snorts and nods. "She claims she knew but saw something between us, so she went with it. She says there was no other family interested in the building. It was something she just said to push me."

I feel my eyes blink several times before I ask, "Push you to do what?"

The corner of his mouth curls up. "Push me to ask you out."

"I, uh, don't know what to say," I confess.

"That was my reaction too. Apparently, she caught on to the fact I might have developed a little crush on you when I was taking you the taco stuff for your girls' night. That's when she cooked up her little scheme to give me a...push."

"I don't believe this," I mutter, realizing we were played by a sweet old woman. "So, she knows it wasn't real."

"No, she knows it started off fake but turned very real." He swallows hard and holds my gaze. "At least it did for me."

My mouth is suddenly so dry, it's hard to push words out. "It feels real to me too," I confess, hoping those words don't come back to haunt me.

"Thank fuck," he mutters before pulling me into his arms and squeezing me tightly against his chest. Then, he pulls back enough to brush his lips against mine. The kiss immediately turns heated, his tongue coaxing my lips open to delve inside.

I have no idea how long we kiss, but by the time we finally pull apart, we're both breathless and gasping for oxygen. "Is this real?" I find myself asking, desperate to hear those words again.

"Yeah, Jilly. It's real." He clears his throat and moves to sit beside me on the couch. This time, he pulls me up onto his lap, my legs positioned on the cushion beside him. "I do have something else I want to tell you," he says.

"Okay, yeah, I have something to tell you too."

"Can I go first?" he asks, earning a nod in return. "I know hearing the fact I was married before came as a shock to you. Well, I didn't get a chance to tell you the rest of it."

My stomach churns once more at his words, the soup and sandwich I ate not long ago suddenly growing heavy. "Okay," I say, wiggling where I sit and wishing I were on the cushion beside him instead of directly on his lap.

"Don't worry, Jilly," he gently instructs, placing his warm palm on my leg to keep it from bouncing. "So, you know I was married and Lilly wanted kids. At that time, I was so focused on building my name, my credibility, I wanted to table the discussion to have a family. I felt if I could just get to the top, where I wanted to be, it would all finally click into place."

He pauses and exhales before meeting my gaze. "She left because she was ready and I wasn't. I felt terrible, like I had failed, but to be honest, I was a little...relieved. That probably makes me sound like a bastard, but looking back now, she's happily married and has kids. Just like she was meant to. And I'm not in that picture because I wasn't supposed to be." He gives me a sad smile.

"We went our separate ways, and it felt right. But the older I got, I realized I was missing something. Not her, particularly—and again, I'm not trying to be an asshole, but we just weren't right for the long haul. Something more. I started watching all my friends get married and have kids, and I realized I would never have that. I'm forty, and while work and building my business has always been what I wanted, I missed out on other things in life. Someone to share all the joys with, and maybe a kid or two."

My chest constricts with tightness and my breathing hitches. "You want kids?" I whisper, praying I didn't misunderstand him.

He gives a sad, sheepish grin. "I wouldn't have minded it. But again, I'm forty. Not exactly prime age to start a family." He's trying to be lighthearted, but I can feel the weight of his words.

"Oh my gosh," I whisper, tears starting to fall down my cheeks once more.

"I know you were married, and it ended because he didn't want kids anymore." Kameron closes his eyes and shakes his head. "If I could, I would, Jilly. I want to give you everything you want. I want to give you the world."

A choked sob erupts from my throat as I lean against his shoulder, my arms wrapped tightly around his neck. I hold on for dear life, mostly because I'm afraid he's going to up and disappear on me.

"Don't cry, honey. I hate it when you cry," he murmurs, gently pulling me back and wiping the wetness from my face.

"They're happy tears."

His eyebrows pull together in confusion. "They are?"

I nod, knowing there's only one thing left to say.

"I'm pregnant."

CHAPTER
Twenty Two

KAMERON

"You're...what?"

I swear I must have heard her wrong. No way was I telling her I regret not settling down, getting married, and having kids...and she's pregnant? Carrying my baby? I'm going to be a father?

And here I thought that ship had sailed.

"I'm pregnant," she whispers, smiling through the tears. "I know it's unexpected, Kameron."

I move, pulling her farther into my embrace and crashing her chest against mine. Considering she's sitting across me, it does make the hug rather awkward, but I don't care. Then, I find her lips with my own, and it's not a gentle kiss. It's full of everything I feel for this woman all wrapped in one big excited bow.

"I can't believe this," I mutter against her mouth. "You're really pregnant?"

She nods, her face sobering. "I found out Sunday," she confesses, but quickly adds, "but I swear I was going to tell you. I just, I don't know, needed time. Time to process everything. When Blair told me the test was positive, I was so overwhelmed. She suggested

I take some time to let it sink in. I knew I wanted this baby, but I...well, I wasn't sure what you wanted."

Linking my fingers with hers, I give them a gentle squeeze and rest our hands on her thigh. "I want this baby. I want to be a part of his or her life. I want to be a part of your life."

She seems to relax with relief right then and there but worries her bottom lip with her teeth. "We haven't been together very long, and even then, it was fake." That last word comes out a whisper.

"I can't change how we started, but I can promise you I'll do everything in my power to show you how much you mean to me every day moving forward."

I'm rewarded with a brief smile before she moves, straddling my lap and threading her fingers into my hair. Cupping her ass, I pull her against me, my erection hard and ready between us. I claim her mouth, reveling in the way she fits so perfectly to me, like a puzzle piece.

Her fingers start pulling at my shirt, and I rip my mouth from hers only long enough to help her remove the offending top. The touch of her fingertips against my chest sears me, branding me forever. I'll always feel them, see them. It's as if she's part of me.

Jillian rocks her hips against my erection, sending bolts of lust straight to my groin. My balls already tingle, ache for release. It's been too long since I've held her, touched her, been inside her pussy, and it's all I can think about.

Making her mine.

Forever.

She grabs the hem of her shirt and lifts it up and over her head, throwing it behind her. Her glorious tits seem to be overflowing from her bra, fuller and rounder than before. Looking down, she seems to notice where my attention is focused and says, "These things seem to have their own zip codes lately."

Leaning forward, I brush my lips across the swell of her right breast, followed by the left. "I don't think I mind," I murmur, gently pulling her bra down and exposing one rosy nipple.

My lips wrap around it and before I can even draw it into my mouth, she cries out and grinds down on me, hard. "Holy shit," she murmurs. "They're so sensitive and...oh God," she whimpers as I run my tongue around the outside and suck it hard between my lips.

"Sensitive and bigger," I add unnecessarily.

"Yes," she murmurs softly. "And tender. Don't be too rough."

My cock twitches between us. I'd never do anything to hurt her or cause her discomfort, but I do like the idea of watching her squirm beneath my touch. I'll just make sure not to push it too far and cause her pain.

Everything else happens quickly. She jumps up and strips off the rest of her clothes, and I try to do the same. Except, I'm only able to get my pants and boxer briefs around my ankles before she's climbing back on me, her naked body covering mine. My cock is ready, oozing precum like it hasn't seen a naked woman in years.

I reach up, taking her jaw in my palm and brushing my thumb over her bottom lip. "You sure?"

"That's the wrong question, Kam," she replies, rising up and grabbing a hold of my dick. "You should be asking me how quickly I can put this inside my body."

And then she lowers herself onto me, taking me all the way to the root in one long, slow motion. We both groan and something hits me. "Shit, Jilly, I'm not wearing anything."

She pauses her movements and meets my gaze. "Kinda late for that now, isn't it?"

I can't help but grin at her quip, but then she flexes her internal muscles, and I see stars. "Fuck, don't do that," I insist on a hiss.

"This?" she asks, squeezing my cock once more. I almost lose it right then and there. My hips flex upward, even though I'm already buried to the hilt. The friction is fucking glorious.

"Yes, that," I retort through gritted teeth. In my head, I start counting backward from twenty.

"I'm clean, Kam," she says softly, "and I'm pretty sure you are too."

"I am."

Seventeen, sixteen, fifteen...

"Then, since we're both clean and we don't need condoms to prevent pregnancy, I think we're okay."

I meet her gaze, mentally stopping my count. My hands are cupping her ass, and I lean forward enough to take her lips with my own. The kiss is chaste, but still full of meaning and intent. "We're okay."

With that, she lifts herself off my cock and slowly sinks back down, and all I can do is hang on for the ride. Sex with Jillian has always been spectacular, but removing the protective barrier between us is out of this world. Like hitting the game winning grand slam in game seven of the World Series or catching the perfect spiral football to win the Super Bowl.

Except, this is better...

Her pace starts to pick up a bit, and all I can do is hang on and enjoy the show. Her perfect tits bounce, begging for my mouth, so when I move forward and claim one nipple between my teeth, I make sure to do it gingerly.

"Oh God," she moans in pleasure, rocking her hips and gyrating against me. "Do that again."

So, of course, I do. I take the other nipple in my mouth, swirling my tongue around it before gently biting down just a bit.

She cries out and shivers. I shift my hands beneath her ass and help her move. When she lifts, I thrust up, filling her tight pussy over and over again. Her internal muscles start to squeeze, and I know I won't be able to hang on much longer.

Jillian rolls her hips and grinds her clit against my pubis, sending her over the edge. She comes hard, milking my cock for everything I have and triggering my own release. "Fuck," I groan as pleasure rips through me like a tidal wave. It consumes me, makes it hard to breathe.

My body moves on its own, pumping up into her and chasing every ounce of bliss I can get. She collapses against my chest, and I reach around to hold her close. We're sweaty, our bodies molded together in the best way, and even though I'm completely sated, all I want to do is kiss her...and maybe do that all over again.

She turns her head, resting her cheek against my shoulder and brushing her lips against my neck. "Wow."

"Mmhmm," I practically sing, ignoring the fact I have cum seeping down my balls and probably staining her couch.

"I'm a fan of sex without a condom," she murmurs, her warm breath tickling my flesh.

I snort a chuckle. "Me too. But I should probably get up and grab something to clean up with. I think we made a mess on your couch cushion."

"I don't care," she mutters softly, the contentment evident in her voice.

"You will when your friends come over and see a big white stain. They'll know exactly what it is," I tease, trying not to move and make a bigger mess.

"They probably all have white stains on their couch, Kameron. Every one of them has had couch sex," she insists.

"Quite possibly true, but I don't think I want it brought up as a conversation next time your friends visit."

Jillian giggles the sweetest sound and rests her hand against my chest. "I'm going to tell all of them exactly what we did here, even if there's no stain."

I bark out a laugh and shake my head. When she sits up and I see the happiness reflecting in her eyes, I know I have to say what's on my mind. Clearing my throat, I start, "I know this probably isn't the ideal time for this. I swear I'm not saying it because I'm in a sex coma. I can't go another second without telling you I fell in love with you. Hard. I think I was already on my way before we even agreed to that fake dating ruse."

She gives me the softest smile, one that reaches in and squeezes my heart. "I'm not saying this because you just rocked my world with some pretty impressive sex moves. I've fallen in love with you too."

Hearing her say those words is like a balm to my chest. To old wounds I've always carried deep inside me. So much loss in my life, and now here I am, creating a new one and finding love.

"We have a lot to talk about and figure out, I know, but tonight, I thought maybe I could just hold you. We can figure out the rest tomorrow."

She rewards me with the softest smile as she leans forward once more. "I'd like that. Can you stay here tonight?"

I nod, even though she can't see me. "Yes. I don't have any clothes, but I can get up with you and head home in the morning."

"Ahhh, the ol' walk of shame. Nice."

A chuckle slips from my lips. "Ain't no shame here, Jilly. I will walk proudly out your front door in the morning wearing today's clothes, with my head held high. I want everyone to know where I was, who I was with," I insist with a peck on the cheek.

"Well, that's good, because my neighbors are extra nosy, so everyone will know by lunchtime."

I give her a little extra squeeze with my hug and run my lips across the corner of her forehead. "Good. I want the world to know I'm with you."

She shifts against me, and unfortunately, her movement dislodges my cock. With it, comes a flood of mess. "Eww," she says with a giggle.

"I told you," I insist, pressing a chaste kiss to her forehead once more. "Stay here, and I'll go grab a towel."

"There's some in the hamper in the bathroom."

"On it," I say before carefully slipping out from under her and off the couch. My entire groin and thigh area is covered in our mess, but I don't care. I'll wear it like a badge of honor, if I'm being honest.

In some sort of caveman, twisted way, I have pride in knowing there was nothing between us as I made her come on me.

I slip into the bathroom and grab the towel on top of the hamper. I quickly wipe off most of the moisture, but some of it's already starting to dry and become sticky. I take in her tub and shower unit, hoping we'll end up here very soon. I want nothing more than to help clean her up and then get her dirty all over again.

And just like that, my cock is already at half-mast...

Retrieving a second towel, I return to the living room to help Jillian clean up. She's lying on the couch with her eyes closed, a faint grin spread across her kissable lips. As I approach, my eyes trail down her naked body and land on her stomach. It's still flat, of course, but a rush of pride and love washes over me, nonetheless.

"You're staring," she murmurs, reaching for the towel.

I drop to my knees beside the couch and gently wipe off her thighs. "I was just admiring how beautiful you are," I tell her, allowing her to take the towel and clean between her legs. As soon as she's done, I lean forward and place my lips against her stomach. "I can't wait to watch you grow our child."

Glancing up, I find tears in her eyes once more and my heart hitches in my chest. "These are happy tears," she assures me before I can ask what's wrong.

Reaching over, I take her hand, linking our fingers together. Then, I settle on the floor beside where she lies. "Hello there, little one. I'm your daddy. I can't wait to meet you, but you have to marinate and bake just a little longer. But I'll be here, talking and waiting for the day I get to hold you in my arms."

I don't know why I said all that. I know it's cheesy. But when I look up into Jillian's tear-filled eyes, I know I spoke from the heart, and it wasn't just for our baby. It was a message to her too. I'll be here, always.

No, I can't see the future, but what I can see has her in it. "We'll take it slow, okay? This is new for both of us, but I want you to know and understand my intent. I plan to date you, to shower you with love, and help you in any way I can. I'm in this for the long haul, Jillian, and it's not because you're pregnant. That's just the icing on the double chocolate with salted caramel swirl cake," I say with a big grin.

She sits up and throws her arms around my neck, pressing our naked chests together. "I like that idea, all of it."

"If you're not feeling well, I want to know so I can help, even if that's just to hold your hand or your hair until it passes. I'm going to be at every doctor's appointment, rub your feet and your back after the long workdays, and make sure you eat something other than a cupcake or cinnamon roll. I'm probably going to drive you absolutely crazy, but I promise I have the best intentions."

She brushes her lips across mine and slides her fingers into my hair. "I've been single for so long, I don't really remember what it's like to have someone by my side like that. Don't get me wrong, my parents are super supportive and a little too attentive, but they mean well. And this is different."

I press my lips to hers but stop before letting my tongue delve inside. "I can't wait to date you for real," I insist.

"Me too." Her words come out all breathy, and my cock takes notice.

"Now, first thing's first. Do you need to eat anything else?"

She shakes her head and reaches down, palming my dick. Of course, that one touch has me fully erect and ready to go. "I'm not hungry for food."

Noting the wicked intent in her green eyes, I ask, "What are you hungry for?"

Jillian smiles and licks her lips. "You."

"Well, Jilly, that seems to work well for the next part of my plan," I tell her, carefully helping her stand up, considering she's holding my manhood in her hand.

"And that is?"

"A shower. I thought you might want to clean up a bit before bed." My hands reach around and grab the globes of her ass, loving how perfectly she fits in my palms.

"Are you suggesting we clean up…and then get dirty again?"

"That's exactly what I'm suggesting," I say before taking her lips with mine in a searing kiss. It packs a punch too, like all our kisses seem to do, and my desire for her increases tenfold.

"To the shower, Kam," she whispers, taking a step toward her hallway.

"Start the water, and I'll meet you there."

She nods and heads for the bathroom. My eyes are glued to her delectable backside, mesmerized by the sway of her hips. I can't wait to see her body change as our baby grows.

I move to the door and make sure it's locked. As I flip the mechanism, I pause and smile. I'm one lucky son of a gun, that's for sure. Right now, I have everything I could possibly need. A beautiful woman I adore and a baby on the way. Not to mention the restaurant expansion is still happening.

But I realize instantly I would have, and still would, give it up to be with her. If Mrs. Krokus told me the deal was off when I confessed my lie, I would have walked away with my head held high, because being with Jillian and how I feel about her is more important than a building. I still have my dream—the restaurant—but now that dream has changed. It includes her and our child.

The idea of seeing a little girl or boy who looks like Jillian toddling through the expansion, hanging on to the backs of chairs for stability, is as vivid as if I'm actually seeing it happen in front of me. I can feel the peace and happiness that image evokes.

Mrs. Krokus was right.

That building was made for a family.

Mine.

And I'm going to do everything in my power to make it happen.

"Kameron?" she hollers from the bathroom, causing my feet to start moving.

But first, a shower...

CHAPTER
Twenty Three

Jillian

I took time off Monday so I could be with Kameron when he went to the title company. I've rarely done that over the years, taken time away, always putting my heart and soul into the business I've nurtured and grown. However, today is different. I want to be there as he signs his name on the line, purchasing the old brick building beside his own.

I wouldn't miss it for the world.

Or the celebration I have planned after.

Why? Because after today, I know he'll sink every waking hour into turning his dream—the vision he's had for the building next door—into reality, and I wouldn't want it any other way. I know it's going to be hard work, and I certainly know it's going to take a lot of his time, but I don't begrudge him of any of it. In fact, if I can help, I will.

Anything I can do to contribute to the success of his dream.

I reach down and place a hand on my flat stomach. Speaking of dreams...

We decided to hold off a bit on telling everyone. Of course, Blair knows, and I'm pretty sure that means Gabe does too. Ryan knows, since I told her last Tuesday night, so there's also a good chance Marcus is aware. I'm itching to tell the rest of the group and my parents, but I want to give it just a little bit longer. I'm excited beyond words, but I can't help but feel just a little nervous that it'll be ripped away from me.

Kameron pulls into a parking spot in front of the title company in Hudson. "Ready?" I ask once he's turned off the engine.

He flashes me an easy smile. "Definitely."

I start to climb out, and before I can close the passenger door, he's there, taking my hand and shutting the door behind me. We head for the glass front door of the title company, where Kameron will first meet with the loan officer at the bank. Then, Mrs. Krokus and her attorney will join us, along with a representative from the title company, to finish the paperwork.

Just as we approach the entrance, he pauses and faces me. "I'm glad you're here with me today."

I give his hand a gentle squeeze. "No place I'd rather be."

"You feeling okay?"

He asks me that often. I receive text messages throughout the day, checking in, but it doesn't feel overwhelming. It shows how much he cares about me and the baby, and the fact he isn't a fan of me being nauseous. Fortunately, that's all it is. It comes in waves and doesn't usually hang around too long. I'm tired a lot, but the fact I'm not throwing up is a blessing. I'll take a bit of nausea over actually throwing up any day.

"I feel great. I'm excited for you," I tell him, offering a big grin.

He seems to relax, as if hearing I'm doing okay has a calming effect on him. "This is it," he adds, bringing our joined hands to his lips and placing a tender kiss on my knuckles.

"Let's do this."

We enter the building, and forty-five minutes later are walking out with smiles on our faces. He sighs, taking a deep breath of the cooler, Wisconsin air. "I can't believe that happened." He turns to face me, a look of pure relief on his face. "Now, the real work begins."

"But you've been planning and prepping for this moment since Mrs. Krokus told you she'd sell you the building."

He snorts and nods. "Longer than that. I've had the plans drawn up for years."

"And now you get to use them. It's going to be a lot of hard work, but you've got this."

He nods again and levels me with a look. It holds his eagerness, his fears, and everything in between. "I've got you, so I can do anything."

My heart melts into a pool of goo at my feet. He's been saying the sweetest things lately, and it never fails to make me blush and swoon. Maybe it's just the pregnancy hormones, but I don't think so. I've been like this since he showed up at my door and asked me to be his pretend girlfriend.

"Where to now?" I ask as the door behind up opens.

"Why aren't you two already heading back to Pine Village?" Mrs. Krokus asks as she steps outside with her attorney.

"I was just taking a few minutes to tell this beautiful woman how much I appreciate having her beside me," Kameron says with a wink, feeding right into Mrs. Krokus's tender heart.

"You two," she coos, stepping forward and placing an aged hand on Kameron's arm. "I know I said so before, but I truly am happy you've purchased this building. I felt my Louie smiling down from the heavens above as I signed my name on those documents. That place is in good hands with you and Jillian, and I'm so excited to know you'll be welcoming a new life into the fold in the near future."

My mouth falls open, as does Kameron's. Her attorney doesn't say a word, just politely waits to escort the older woman to an awaiting car.

"Ho—how did you know?" Kameron asks, confirming the fact he wasn't the one to tell her.

She just grins and winks. "I just know, dear. Now, both of you go, enjoy, and most importantly, don't forget to always come together in love at the end of the day. It's what will carry you through when it gets hard."

I lean against Kameron's side and offer a small smile. "Thank you."

She turns to her attorney and takes his offered arm. "Let's leave these two to it. They have some celebrating to get to," she says with an ornery glint in her eyes.

Kameron chuckles as we watch the older woman walk away. "I take it you didn't tell her our news?"

I shake my head and turn to face him. "No. I suppose one of the others could have told her, but I doubt it," I reply, referring to the couple of friends who are aware we're pregnant.

"Hmm," he replies, watching as the attorney helps Mrs. Krokus into the passenger seat of his car. Finally, he turns to me and smiles. "Ready to get back to town?"

"Yes," I reply, and together, we walk to where he parked his vehicle. "When are you meeting the contractor?"

"Not until tomorrow morning," he says, shocking me.

"Really?" I stop before getting into the passenger seat. "I would have thought that would be the first thing you'd do after this appointment."

He shrugs. "He had another appointment later, so we opted to meet in the morning. This gives us more time for the walk-through of the building and to finalize the plans. He wants to start Thursday."

A huge grin spreads across my face. "I'm so excited for you."

He leans forward and brushes his lips across my forehead. "Us, Jilly. This is all for us. Our future."

My hand goes to my belly once more before I climb into the front passenger seat of the vehicle and the door is closed behind me. Maybe that's how Mrs. Krokus figured out I was expecting. I have been placing my hand on my stomach a lot, mostly because I'm still in shock that I'm pregnant. Perhaps I absently did it during the meeting we just left.

We drive back to Pine Village, discussing the building and the changes he has planned for the restaurant. His menu will remain mostly the same, but he's wanting to continue some of the new updates from the new building into the current one. His business loan was increased enough to change the lighting and move a few walls to accommodate the changes to the added space.

Kameron parks behind my building and turns off the ignition. "Are you coming inside?" I ask.

He flashes me a grin and retrieves his phone from the cupholder. "I thought I'd stay and help you this afternoon. Plus, it's nearing lunchtime, so I'll go grab us, and Helen too if she wants, something to eat from the diner and bring it back."

A smile instantly breaks out on my face. "You're too good to me."

He presses his lips to mine in a short, chaste kiss. "Never, Jilly. I could never be too good to you. If anything, it's quite the opposite."

Shaking my head, I say, "We'll just have to agree to disagree there, mister."

"Let's go for a walk," I say, my heart starting to beat a little harder than it was just a few minutes ago.

He gives me a slightly confused look but nods quickly. "Of course. You're feeling okay?" he asks, clearly referring to my bout of nausea that hit just after lunch.

"I'm fine," I insist, trying to hide my excitement so he doesn't get suspicious. Fortunately, I don't have any cake orders for tomorrow, so everything I had to work on this afternoon was in preparation for the next day.

Lacey Black

I make sure the back door is locked and take his offered hand. We make our way to the front sidewalk and toward the opposite end of downtown. The restaurant is just down the way, and with each step we take in that direction, I get more excited for this surprise. I have worked with both Mrs. Krokus and Ryan to make it happen, both eager to offer their assistance.

When we reach the block that house's Prime Steak House, I take notice of the vehicles in the area. I recognize most of them, especially the few in the parking lot beside Prime.

"Huh, seems to be a lot of activity here," Kameron notes, but doesn't say anything more about the additional vehicles.

"Maybe the bank is hosting an after-hours event," I suggest, even though we just passed it and clearly the lights were off.

"What do you want for dinner tonight?" he asks as he pass the front door to his restaurant.

"Umm, I'm not sure," I blurt out, catching his attention. My voice is a little wobbly, which he notices, but before he can ask me what's wrong, we're standing in front of the empty building next door.

The first thing he notices is the white paper covering the front windows. It wasn't like that before, but we decided to do that to not only enhance the surprise, but also because the contractors will do it before they begin to work. "What is going on here?" His voice is firm with a wave of uncertainty sweeping through it.

He's reaching for the door handle, realizing it's unlocked, and pushes it open.

"Surprise!" everyone yells, catching him completely off guard.

"What the hell?" he whispers, running his hand through his hair as he takes in the group of people gathered in the vast space.

I feel his palm start to sweat as he turns his shocked gaze to me. All I can do is smile. "Surprise!"

"You did this?"

Nodding, I confirm, "I had lots of help."

He looks around the room before returning his blue eyes to me. "Why?"

"Because we all wanted to celebrate *you*, silly. Everyone here is proud of you, and they wanted to show how excited we all are for the expansion of Prime."

His eyes turn a little misty, and it's not lost on me that while he's had support from friends and townspeople in the last decade, he hasn't had many people truly in his corner. Not since his parents passed away, which is why I wanted to show him how much we all love him. He has a tribe.

All of us.

He moves, pulling me into his arms and kissing me soundly right here, in front of our family, friends, and employees. I taste the sweet vanilla icing on his tongue from the cupcake he saved for dessert after our lunch.

I hear the catcalls and the cheers from our friends, and as he breaks away, he gives me a wide grin. "Thank you, Jilly. I love this, and I love you."

Before I can reply, my parents rush up, my mom throwing her arms around Kameron's neck. He lets go of me to hug my mom, followed quickly by a handshake from my dad. Mrs. Krokus is here too. She's the one who unlocked the door for Marlin and Veronica so they could set up and promised to turn over the final key at the end of the evening.

Speaking of Marlin and Veronica, they have an amazing spread of food set up on a table toward the back. I gave him free rein to serve whatever he wanted. He opted for simple finger foods, along with a few desserts he insisted on making himself too. Besides setting the ball in motion, they took care of everything, ensuring all I had to do was get Kameron down here at the end of my workday.

There are a few small tables and chairs brought over from next door, and as I look at them, I can't help but visualize how this place will look when it's complete. He's been so excited the last few days; we've talked extensively about the remodel and ultimately what he wants when it's finished.

"I think he was surprised," Blair says, grabbing my attention.

I give her, Hallie, Ava, Ellie, and Ryan each a hug and a warm smile. "Thanks for helping gather the troops. He was definitely not expecting this."

"When does he think he'll be open?" Ellie asks, sipping on lemonade.

"I think the plan is three to four months. A lot of the main dining room is going to stay original, with the exposed brick and old hardwood floors. The kitchen expansion and remodel will take the most time and work, but the contractor is confident he can get his part done in twelve weeks," I tell them.

"Logan already has a big order placed for materials, but I think some of the special-order stuff they were waiting on until the papers were signed, just in case," Hallie adds.

"Fortunately, all the current kitchen stuff they'll be using in the updated space, but he's adding more freezer and refrigeration units. I think he was waiting to get those ordered until today," I inform the small group, knowing he spent about thirty minutes today placing a few orders from my office at the bakery. When I suggested he go to his office at the restaurant, he refused, stating he wanted to be with me and he only needed a little time to make a couple of calls.

"I can't wait. I bet this place is packed opening night," Ava says, glancing around the large room.

"Can we make reservations now?" Ryan asks, making us all chuckle.

"I promise, you'll all be invited to our opening night celebration," Kameron states, pressing a kiss to my cheek. "I want to do a big event the night before we officially open to the public, and you'll all be there."

My friends give hugs to Kameron and congratulate him on the building purchase. All I can do is smile proudly, so stinking excited for him.

When he turns his gaze back to me, he asks, "Did you get something to eat? It looks like Marlin's been busy."

"Not yet, but I will," I assure him.

He levels me with an intense look. "Make sure you eat, Jilly," he murmurs privately, though I'm certain my friends overhear.

"I will. Promise."

"You good? I was gonna run over and talk to Veronica and her husband and Marlin and his wife, Rebecca."

"I'm fine," I insist.

He gives me another kiss, this time on the lips. When he straightens up, he turns to my friends, who are all standing there with dreamy looks on their faces. "Make sure she eats, all right?"

I roll my eyes as they all chime in with reassurance. "I'm perfectly capable of getting myself something to eat when I'm hungry."

He flashes a grin. "Humor me."

I huff out a deep breath, even though I secretly love his protectiveness and extra attention. "Whatever."

He leans in once more and gives me a chaste kiss before walking over to greet his employees.

"You two are so stinkin' cute," Hallie says, pulling my attention away from the man I was following with my eyes.

"It seems to be going well," Ellie states, clearly referring to my relationship with Kameron.

I blush, thinking of the fact they don't know it wasn't real from the beginning. Of course, Ryan knows, but everyone else doesn't know about the arrangement. Yet. I'm sure I'll tell them eventually. Now we're dating for real, it doesn't feel like such a big deal, but the fact remains, I lied to them, and friends don't lie.

I just pray they're all as forgiving as Ryan was when I told her.

I spend the next hour visiting with guests, talking about the restaurant plans, and snacking on food. Kameron ended up bringing me over a plate of delicious food and has been watching me closely to make sure I'm, not only eating, but feeling well afterward.

Surprisingly, I am. I feel great, actually. I'm surrounded by family and friends, and we're all here for the same reason.

To show Kameron our support.

Kameron walks to the middle of the room and holds up his hand. "If I can have everyone's attention, please?" When the room quiets down, he continues, "First off, I just wanted to say thank you. This wasn't what I was expecting when Jillian suggested we go for a walk," he comments with a chuckle. "But I appreciate it."

He turns to his employees and says, "Thank you for being here, setting this up, and for the delicious food. I have the best staff in town. Thank you to our friends, Jillian's family, and, of course, Mrs. Krokus for not only selling me this building, but for believing in my dream as much as I have."

My throat is thick with emotion as I glance over at the old woman, sitting happily at a table and enjoying her second plate of refreshments.

"And to my Jillian," Kameron starts, turning his blue gaze my way. My heart skips a beat when our eyes meet, just like it does so often. I still can't believe he's mine.

My hand drops to my belly as I think of the life we've created.

That's when I hear the gasp.

I look over and realize it came from my mom.

My eyes fly back to Kameron, who realizes exactly what I've done when all eyes seemed to be focused on me. A soft smile spreads across his lips as he extends his hand to me, indicating he wants me to join in. My legs feel heavy as I make my way to the center of the room to stand beside him.

The moment I'm there, he presses a kiss to my forehead and gives me an easy smile. "And a huge thank you to the woman I love. She's been a sounding board, a friend and confidante, and the brightest light on my darkest days."

This time when he kisses me, it's on the lips, and it's not exactly PG. His tongue dives inside my mouth, making my toes curl as I throw my arms around his neck and raise up on my tiptoes. The kiss only lasts a couple of seconds though, and when we break apart, he gives me a content little grin. If I had any question about how happy he was, it's gone now. I see it reflecting in his eyes and feel it in his touch and kiss.

Kameron places a featherlight kiss on the tip of my nose and then blurts out our secret. The one we had planned to keep for just a little longer. The one I probably ruined the moment I placed my hands on my stomach just a minute ago.

"Jillian's pregnant."

CHAPTER
Twenty four

KAMERON

It's been just over three weeks since I found out I am going to be a dad, and I don't think I've ever been happier in my life. Not just the pregnancy, but Jillian too. Proving to her this is real, making her mine, is what dreams are made of.

We see her obstetrician on Friday, just two short days away, and I'm ready. I've been anxious since the moment she told me she was pregnant, and fortunately for her, the nausea hasn't turned into vomiting. A few bouts of queasiness, mostly after she eats, and the fact she's super tired are the major symptoms she's dealing with right now. Her normal eight to eight thirty bedtime has turned into even earlier lately, or at least naptime. She's stayed at my house, waited for me in my bed several nights throughout the week, and it's the best feeling ever, coming home and finding her there.

I want that every night.

When I got home this evening, I found her asleep on my couch, a nineties chick flick movie playing on the TV. Instead of waking her or carrying her to bed, I sat beside her and just breathed her in. She shimmied closer to me, but didn't wake up, and even though it's late and I need to crash myself, I take a few minutes to relax.

I've been working extra lately, thanks to the restaurant remodel. The building next door is coming along nicely. The large entrance between the two buildings was cut out and a thick piece of plastic was installed to keep people from walking into the addition while it is under construction. Of course, everyone asks about it. Veronica and the serving staff are fielding questions every day, but they don't seem to mind. It just shows how excited the town is for the larger space. And every night when I do a walk-through to thank those people for their support and make sure they are enjoying their meal, I get happy smiles and anticipation for what's to come.

Not to mention, kudos for Jillian and her sweet treats...

She's been providing the desserts for the restaurant for over two weeks now, and I'm pretty sure the increase in customers has been for that very reason alone. It's not my specials that bring them to the door, it's her decadent, delicious desserts. Word spread like wildfire that she was creating special desserts for me, and since they're specific treats not offered in her bakery, everyone seems to want to try them.

And why wouldn't they?

She's fucking amazing.

Knowing she has an early morning, I carefully reach for her laptop. It's still open and sitting off to the side on the arm of the couch, out of the way. When I move it, the screen wakes up and comes to life. I go to set the device down on the coffee table, but what's on the screen catches my eye. I realize instantly what I'm looking at.

A recipe.

But then I find myself scrolling and scrolling some more, and I realize it's not a recipe or even a couple. It's a cookbook. It's fascinating and enthralling and a wave of pride rushes through my body. The recipes are all for desserts and they appear to be categorized. Decadent chocolates, cakes, cupcakes, and cookies, no-bake treats, fruity options, and more. Some of the treats she's even featured in my restaurant. It's not a super big cookbook, but I can feel the love pouring from every page I read.

Why hasn't she mentioned this?

A cookbook? That's a huge deal!

I close the lid on the laptop and place it on the table. Then, I move in close and gently wake her up. "Jilly, it's late. I'm going to carry you to bed," I whisper.

As soon as I scoop her up, she wraps her arms around my neck and holds on. "You don't have to carry me," she murmurs softly, resting her cheek against my neck.

"I know, but I love the feel of you in my arms," I tell her, carefully walking to my bedroom and placing her down on the bed. I help pull the comforter back and cover her before pressing a kiss to her forehead. "I'm gonna run through the shower. Go back to sleep, love," I tell her, brushing the hair off her cheek with my hand.

"'Kay," she mutters as she burrows into the pillow and seems to fall fast asleep.

I stand here, watching, for a few more seconds before heading to the bathroom to shower. I'm quick, not wanting to waste a single minute with her in my bed. Someday, I'll make it *our* bed, but everything still seems so new. Even with a baby on the way, I don't want to rush it, even if getting my ring on her finger suddenly seems like the only option there is.

Someday.

It'll happen.

I'll make her mine forever.

After I wash the restaurant off me, I dry off and slip on a pair of cotton shorts I left hanging on the back of the door. Then, I return to my bed where I left the woman I love. She's fast asleep, curled on her side facing my side of the bed. I slip beneath the covers and reach for her. Even in her sleep, she moves toward me and settles against my side.

It's the best way to sleep.

The *only* way I want to sleep.

Exhaustion hits me hard. Not only was the restaurant open tonight, but I spent a big chunk of my day at both buildings, prepping to be open and meeting with the contractor to finalize a few last-minute changes. Knowing her alarm will be waking her up sooner rather than later, I close my eyes and settle into a comfortable position. Of course, as long as Jillian is here, any position is comfortable.

When her alarm goes off, I feel like I've only been asleep a couple hours, but that doesn't stop me from climbing from the bed. "Stay. Sleep," she murmurs, reaching out for me.

"I can go back to sleep when you leave. For now, I'll grab you something to eat while you jump in the shower."

This is our routine when we're together. I make her a slice of toast or an English muffin so she has something solid in her stomach, just in case her nausea gets worse. I also make her a mug of warm ginger tea. After researching on the internet for ways to help relieve her nausea, I found lots of information with different options to try. The ginger tea and something light and plain first thing in the morning seems to help her throughout the rest of her early morning.

When the tea and English muffin are ready, I take them into the bathroom. She's completing her shower, and I can't help but be a bit of a voyeur and watch.

Thank God for clear shower doors...

"You're being creepy," she says as she shuts off the water and opens the door.

I'm there, handing over a thick, fluffy towel. "It's not my fault there's a beautiful, naked woman in my shower," I tease, even though I'm not joking in the least.

"Hmm, you say that now. Just wait six or eight months when I've gained thirty pounds and can't bend over to tie my shoes. Nothing sexy about that," she states with a chuckle.

I'm moving before she can finish drying off her arms. Not caring about getting wet, I pull her into my arms. "Don't do that. Don't belittle the woman I love. She's growing a life and with that comes some body changes. I, personally, am looking forward to witnessing every one of them. In fact," I state, rocking my hips forward to show her how hard the thought of her being nine-months pregnant with my baby has me, "just the thought of it has me so hard I could cut glass."

She giggles, wrapping her arms around my neck and pressing a kiss to my bare shoulder. "I think you're silly."

"Nope," I insist. Even though I'd rather bend her over the bathroom sink, I take a step back and reach for the mug of tea. "Breakfast."

She flashes a grateful grin and wraps the towel around her chest before reaching for the mug. "Mmm, thank you," she murmurs after taking a small sip.

"You're welcome," I reply, propping my ass against the counter. "Can I ask you something?"

"Of course," she insists, taking one more sip before replacing the mug on the counter and grabbing half her English muffin and taking a small bite.

"Last night, when I moved your laptop, something came up on the screen," I start, keeping my eyes on her. That's why I notice the way she freezes and she tries to cover it with taking another bite of her breakfast. "Since you're not saying anything, I assume you know what I'm referring to. Why didn't you tell me you were writing a cookbook?" I ask, unable to keep the excitement out of my voice.

"I'm—it's nothing," she quickly insists, as if she can't get the words out fast enough.

"What do you mean it's nothing? It's fucking amazing," I encourage, trying to understand why she's not more excited about this.

She's already shaking her head as she reaches up and tightens her towel. "Kameron, you don't understand. It's just a...dream. It's not happening. I'm not producing a cookbook."

I try to keep my confusion off my face and my body relaxed. "But what if you did? From what I saw, it's fucking fantastic. I'd buy it."

Jillian rolls her eyes. "Of course you would. You're my boyfriend."

"Damn right I am. I'd buy a hundred copies and gift them to everyone I know for Christmas."

She shakes her head and cracks a smile. "I appreciate that, and I have no doubt you would, but it's not real. It's just something I've been jotting down for a while. It doesn't mean anything."

But there's no missing the look of longing she tries to hide in the depths of her green eyes. She wants this but is afraid to take the steps. Has she even inquired about what it would take?

Dreams are only achieved if you're brave enough to take the risk.

I let it go but have no intention of letting it drop completely. The last thing I want to do is upset her before she has to leave for work. Instead, I focus on making sure she has enough English muffin and ginger tea. She quickly gets dressed in a bakery T-shirt and leggings and rushes back into the bathroom to dry her hair.

Leaving the bathroom door open, I get comfy in bed and watch her. Even though I can't hear her over the noise of the blow-dryer, I can tell she's humming. She always hums when she's getting ready, and while she doesn't dance along, per se, she does occasionally sway her hips to whatever music she hears in her head.

I want this.

Every morning.

But I know it's too soon.

Not that there's some rule or timeline in which you can ask your girlfriend to move in with you, but about two months after you start fake dating seems a little rushed. Even with the addition of a baby on the way. I don't want her to think I'd be asking for any other reason than the fact I want to spend every minute of every day with her, and I would want that even if she wasn't pregnant.

And I'm not so sure she'd agree right now. We still have a lot to learn about each other, and over the last couple of weeks, we've fallen into an easy, content schedule. Of course, that schedule seems to change frequently and will continue to do so as I get closer to opening the restaurant expansion and she progresses through her pregnancy. Life will always be chaotic, but as long as she's by my side, I know we can work through anything thrown our way.

I want to do this right. This time, it's forever.

I'm not going to lie and say my age doesn't factor into things too, because it does. When she told me she is considered high risk because she's over thirty-five, I got a little panicky. Worried. For her and the baby. But she assured me her obstetrician is the best around and will take good care of both of them over the next nine months. She did deliver both Hallie and Blair's babies, so that gives me a little bit more comfort.

"Whatcha thinking about?"

Her question breaks through the noise in my head, and I realize she's already finished drying her hair and has moved on to a touch of makeup. A little eyeliner, some mascara, and a light dusting of loose foundation is all she wears. Honestly, she doesn't even need that. She's fucking beautiful regardless.

"Thinking about you," I answer truthfully, offering a smile. "And our little one."

Her hand instantly goes to her still-flat stomach. "Are you excited for tomorrow's appointment or nervous?"

"Both," I confess.

"Me too." She stands up a little straighter and swallows hard. "I just pray everything is okay."

That has me moving, climbing from the bed and heading in her direction. The moment she's in my arms, I reassure her, "Everything will be fine. Promise."

She nods, but I can see the hint of worry in her eyes. "I think until I see the screen tomorrow, I'll just be a tad bit nervous. Not that something can't go wrong after the first ultrasound, but...you know. I just want to see him or her."

"Me too." I press a firm kiss to her forehead and take a step back. "And tomorrow, we will."

Her smile reaches her eyes, lighting up her entire face. "I can't wait."

I step back and watch her finish getting ready. She drinks the rest of her tea and carries the last few bites of her English muffin toward the kitchen as she prepares to leave. With keys in hand, she grabs her purse and shoves the last bite of food into her mouth. I don't even wait for her to finish chewing. I press my lips against hers, making her giggle as she keeps her mouth firmly closed.

"Love you," I whisper.

She wraps her arms around my waist and mumbles, "Love you too." When she finishes swallowing, she goes up on her tiptoes and gives me a proper kiss goodbye.

"I'll drop by and check on you before I go to the restaurant," I confirm, even though she already knows it's part of my routine. I visit her every day.

"Sounds good," she replies with one more kiss before opening the door.

I watch as she walks to her vehicle and climbs inside. I stand where I am as she backs out of my driveway and heads toward the bakery just a handful of blocks away. Only then do I shut the front door and make sure it's locked. Usually, I'd return to bed to catch a couple more hours of sleep, but my mind isn't settled enough for that. Instead, I go to her laptop and open it. Her device isn't passcode protected, something I'm going to have to talk to her about, so it fires to life as soon as I touch a key.

Lacey Black

My eyes devour the cookbook she's compiled, and I can't help but wonder why she isn't more excited to submit it somewhere. In fact, she seemed downright scared, as if this is one dream she doesn't want to chase or fulfill.

Fuck that.

This thing is good.

Damn good, and it deserves to be in kitchens all over the world.

An idea forms in my head and before I can stop myself, I have my own laptop fired up and am doing a little research. I spend two hours online before firing off a text to Ryan. If anyone can help me, it's her. She may not know personally what I need, but I'm hoping she has enough resources to offer some insight.

Do I worry this'll piss Jillian off?

Yep.

Am I still going to do this?

Damn right, I am.

Why?

Because she deserves the world, and I'm the man to give it to her.

CHAPTER
Twenty five

Jillian

My foot is tapping a mile a minute. I can feel it. Kameron can feel it. Everyone in the lobby of the OB/GYN office can feel it. It practically shakes the entire building, but I can't seem to make it stop. Even when Kam reached over and placed his palm gently above my knee, it didn't settle down.

"Jillian," a polite woman states at the doorway leading to the exam rooms.

My heart leaps in my chest and my hand darts out to grab on to Kameron's. He takes it readily and stands up, escorting me to the waiting nurse. "Don't be nervous," he murmurs softly before we reach the doorway.

I snort. "Easier said than done," I comment.

"Ready?" she asks when I reach her side.

"Yes."

"Can you tell me your date of birth?" she asks, confirming my identity before we step back to the exam room area.

We stop in a little kiosk looking space, where the nurse asks me a few questions before taking my blood pressure and temperature. She hands off the little plastic cup. "Every visit you'll have to give a urine sample. Restroom is across the hall, and there's a door in the wall where you can place your sample when you're done."

I nod and take the wrapped plastic cup.

"You go on in, and I'll take Dad down the hall, room three on the left when you're finished."

I step inside the restroom and do my thing. As I wash my hands, I try to calm my racing heart, but it's no use. I don't know why I'm so nervous for today's appointment, but I am. And I'm so damn glad Kameron is here. He didn't balk for one second when I told him my appointment was on a Friday afternoon. He just made sure Marlin could cover his absence, which he did and mentioned he'd make sure he was available for every appointment Kameron needed to attend.

Taking a deep, calming breath, I unlock the door and make my way to room three. Kameron's blue eyes light up the moment I enter the room.

"Go ahead and have a seat, Jillian. We're gonna go through your medical history and then the doctor will come in and talk to you. She'll do an eight-week ultrasound, so you'll be able to get a first peek at your baby today," she informs me with a smile.

I hope up on the exam table, while Kameron remains seated in the chair beside me. He's able to reach my hand, which he does as soon as I start answering health questions. We go through my history and that of my immediate family. I blush a bit when she starts asking about my period history, even though I shouldn't be embarrassed. The man has seen me naked on many occasions. Hell, he's eaten buttercream icing off me naked. We're having a baby. I have nothing to be embarrassed about.

When we've gone over everything, the nurse pulls a paper gown from the cabinet and sets it on the counter, along with a paper drape. "Go ahead and get undressed from the waist down. Gown open in the front. Dr. Bergman will be in shortly," the nurse, Gina, informs me before stepping out of the room and closing the door behind her.

"You doing okay?" Kameron asks, bringing my hand to his lips and kissing my knuckles.

"Yeah, I guess. I mean, I have to do a pelvic exam," I grumble, carefully getting up from the table and walking over to the gown.

"I'll be honest, I don't envy you right now," he says, glancing down at the floor before meeting my gaze. "I know they're pretty invasive."

"Super, but I get it." I toe off my slip-on shoes before grabbing the waistband on my leggings and shimmying them down my legs.

"I'll give you some privacy," he blurts out, spinning around and looking at the wall. Of course, there's a graphic diagram of a woman's reproductive organs there, and watching him study it as if he's about to take a high school final on it is pretty amusing.

"Why did you turn around?" I ask, placing both my leggings and my panties on the empty chair and reaching for the paper gown.

"To give you privacy," he repeats, still examining the poster on the wall.

"You've seen it all, Kameron," I remind him, making my way back to the table. "All done."

"I know," he confirms, turning back around and holding my gaze, "But if I see you naked then I want to do naked-time things to you, and this is hardly the time or place."

My giggle comes out a snort, and I'm saved from having to comment by a knock at the door. "Good afternoon, Jillian. How are you feeling today?" Dr. Bergman greets when she opens the door and steps inside.

"Not feeling too bad," I tell the female physician who is in charge of my care throughout the pregnancy. I've always seen the nurse practitioner in this medical group for all of my lady bits care, but I've heard nothing but positive things about Dr. Bergman. In fact, that's who both Hallie and Blair used, and she comes highly recommended from Blair and Gabe's medical practice.

"Always happy to hear that," she replies pleasantly before turning her attention to Kameron. "Dr. Bergman," she states, offering him a hand.

"Kameron Markley. Dad."

Dr. Bergman gives a wide smile. "Pleasure to meet you, Dad."

That reference alone seems to brighten the room. Kameron beams with pride and excitement as Dr. Bergman returns her attention to me. "Shall we get started?"

We go over my history and she spends a few minutes talking about my age and what that means for pregnancy. "There are a few things we'll watch for, associated with an advanced maternal age pregnancy. There can be a higher risk for pregnancy complications, chromosomal abnormalities, and an increased risk of preterm delivery. We will monitor you closely and make any necessary care changes if something should arise."

"What kind of monitoring?" Kameron asks. I can tell he's listening intently to everything she's saying, and even though I've already talked to Blair extensively, I make sure to do the same.

"We'll stay on a regular schedule with appointments that'll include measurements and perhaps an extra ultrasound or two. You have an option to do genetic testing if that's something you're worried about, and we can go over the risks when the time comes. But I think it's important to say, while there *is* a risk because of Jillian's age, many women have perfectly healthy pregnancies and babies every day. The age is just a guide, and we'll use that guide to navigate you both through this."

I feel my heartbeat settle a bit as I give her a small, grateful smile. I know I'm in good hands with Dr. Bergman, and if something should arise that sparks concern, we'll deal with it.

"Now, are you ready for the uncomfortable part?" she asks, getting up from her stool and moving to the sink to wash her hands. "We'll do a quick pelvic exam today and then a transvaginal ultrasound. It's too early to hear the heartbeat on the doppler, but we should be able to pick it up this way."

A bubble of excitement erupts in my chest. Even though I'm about to be subjected to the dreaded pelvic exam, the fact I get to see and hear the baby's heartbeat afterward is a reward.

I lie back and the nurse comes inside. Kameron stays near my head, his eyes widening as Dr. Bergman helps my feet into the stirrups. "Should I leave the room for this?" he asks, panic laced in his voice.

"No, you're fine," I tell him. "Just stay up here by my head." The paper gown covers what she's doing down there, so it's not like he's going to get a front row view of the exam.

"All done," Dr. Bergman states after a couple of minutes, gently patting my leg with her hand after removing the gloves. "Stay just like this, and we'll take a peek at that baby."

I try to relax, but really, the only thing that seems to do the trick is when Kameron scoots up and takes my hand. Together, we watch Dr. Bergman wheel the ultrasound machine beside the table and prepare for this part of the exam.

"Okay, here we go," she says, talking me through what's about to happen.

It's not comfortable, but it's not uncomfortable either, if that makes sense, and fortunately, I have no time to dwell on what's happening down south because the screen fills with the first image of our baby.

"I'm going to take a few quick measurements," she informs me before tapping on a keyboard and rolling a mouse around. "Hmm..."

My heart catches before pounding hard in my chest. I look at the screen, trying to see what she's seeing, but it looks foreign to me.

"Is something wrong?" Kameron asks, his grip on my hand tightening.

"No, not wrong, really," she says, clicking and zooming in. "Look right here." She points to a bean-shaped little spot on the screen. "That's Baby A."

My eyes water as I lay eyes on our baby for the first time. My heart swells in my chest and through tears, I just watch the screen. I'm completely smitten, already so over-the-top in love with my child, and the sight of seeing him or her on the screen is almost overwhelming.

"Wait, Baby A?"

Kameron's words pull my attention away from the screen and crash with his wild, wide eyes. Realization sets in for both of us at the same time, and our gazes fly back to the screen.

Dr. Bergman is smiling. "Yes, Baby A. This right here," she says, pointing to the second little bean on the screen, "is Baby B."

"Holy shit," I mutter, my mouth gaping open at the sight before me.

"Congratulations, Mom and Dad. You're having twins."

We're silent the entire ride back to Pine Village, both of us lost in our own thoughts. The only thing keeping me grounded is his hand wrapped firmly around mine. Otherwise, I fear I might float away, part exhilaration, part shock, and part fear.

Twins.

Holy crap, we're having two babies.

"So..." Kameron seems lost for words and doesn't say anything else.

"Yeah..."

"I think I'm still in shock."

I snort, thinking about how big I'm going to get with twins. Will I be able to work the entire pregnancy, like I had planned before? What will I do with the bakery? Who is going to help me take care of two babies? Childcare wasn't something I was going to look into until closer to my delivery date, but now I feel like I need to figure this out right now. Who is going to have the space to take two babies instead of one?

Looking over to the driver of the vehicle, a faint smile reaches my lips. He's concentrating hard, and I can practically see the wheels in his head spinning, but there's also this aura of happiness surrounding him, and that brings me comfort in a moment of turbulence.

"I'm scared." The words are out of my mouth before I can stop them, not that I'd want to.

Suddenly, he's slowing down and pulling off the roadway into the lot of an old gas station that's been long closed down. He throws the engine into park and turns toward me. Reaching out, he pulls me into his arms as best he can, considering we're both seat belted into place.

Kameron brushes my lips with his and rests his forehead against mine. "I'm scared too, but do you know what? I know everything is going to be okay. Why? Because I have you beside me and we'll be doing this together. Every step, side by side. You and me."

"It's going to be pure chaos," I blurt out with a laugh.

"Oh, for sure," he quickly agrees with his own chuckle. "But, again, we'll figure it out. Besides, two babies, two parents. How hard can it be?" He's clearly joking by the look on his face.

"Double the diapers? The feedings? The crying?"

"Double the snuggling?" he adds, making my heart soar.

"That too," I reply.

He exhales deeply and brings our linked hand to his lips. After swiping a kiss across my knuckles, he pins his blue orbs on me. "It's going to be hard and scary, but it'll also be the most joyful, rewarding thing we've ever done. And the fact I'll have you at my side, figuring this whole thing out together, is what keeps my fear at bay. Don't get me wrong, I'm still worried. We have a lot to figure out over the next few months, but one thing I'll never question is how much I love you.

I'm honored to walk through this craziness with you, Jilly, and I'm so fucking glad that condom broke."

I blurt out a hard laugh and shake my head. "Twins. Can you believe it?"

"Actually, I can, because ever since I showed up on your doorstep and asked you to be my fake girlfriend, everything has sort of been this beautiful mess, you know?"

"I do know," I confirm, leaning forward and resting my cheek against the crook of his neck. "Thank you, Kameron."

"For what?" he asks, holding me tightly.

"For loving me," I whisper, lifting my head and meeting his gaze. "For loving me the way I've always dreamed of."

His hand pushes hair off my forehead as he looks deeply into my eyes. "That's the easy part, sweetheart. Loving you is as natural as breathing."

His words make me all swoony. "You're very charming, Mr. Markley."

He snorts a laugh. "Charming. That's probably not the term I would have used that night I showed up on your doorstep."

"Nope. Desperate would have been more accurate," I tell him, remembering the wild look of panic in his eyes when he asked me to play pretend.

"I was pretty desperate," he confirms. "But that's okay, because I got the girl."

"You did. And now two babies."

"I hope they look just like you," he murmurs, kissing the tip of my nose.

I return my head to rest against him and just breathe in his familiar, woodsy scent. "We should probably get back to town. You have to work."

"It can wait. First, I'm going to take you home and show you just how desperate for you I am." He wiggles his eyebrows suggestively, causing my nipples to pebble against my bra and a rush of moisture to flood my panties.

I brush my lips across the underside of his chin and murmur, "Less talking, more driving, baby daddy."

His eyes blaze with an intensity I've never witnessed before, just by saying those two words.

And that's how we end up getting pulled over for speeding...

But the moment we crossed the threshold of my front door, and I was being pressed against the wall, my clothes ripped from my body by a madman, it was his words that echoed through my head as he made me come on his cock.

"Best. Ticket. Ever."

EPILOGUE
epilogue

KAMERON

This is it.

The night I've been waiting for, working toward, dreaming about.

The night before we officially open the new addition to the restaurant, and those I love are here to celebrate.

I prepared a spread of food to feed an army, and my kitchen staff will be watching to make sure everything is stocked and taken care of. The bar is open, serving wine, mixed drinks, and beer, along with an assortment of non-alcoholic drinks. Jillian has been right by my side the entire night, as I've greeted guests and thanked them for their support. She's been a trooper, never once complaining about standing, but maybe that's because I'm keeping a close eye on her. I make sure she has something to drink, a plate of food, and a chair to sit in if needed. She's my top priority.

Her and our babies.

Speaking of which, Baby A and Baby B are both growing well. She's just over four months pregnant now, and finally past the nausea stage. Her appetite has increased tenfold and so has her sexual drive. Not that I'm complaining. Not in the least. In fact, I rather like her increased libido, especially now that she's showing. I can't keep my hands off her, especially the swell of her belly.

I'm practically a walking hard-on every time I see her.

"How are you holding up?" Jillian asks me, stepping up to my side and slipping her arm around my waist.

"I should be asking you that," I insist, turning so we're belly to belly and threading my arms around her.

"I'm fine, promise."

She's been feeling pretty good lately, but I still insist she takes breaks throughout her day. Tonight, she looks sinful in a black wrap dress that hugs her growing stomach and shows off the bump she's sporting. Just seeing her is an aphrodisiac, and the only reason I'm not dragging her off to my office to bend her over my desk is because someone in this room full of people would see and comment.

Everyone is here.

Jillian's parents, our friends, my staff, and a few townspeople who made this dream a reality. Mrs. Krokus shines like a diamond in her navy blue and gold dress. She sits at a table with the mayor and the loan officer I used to finance this building, and I can tell from all the way across the room, she's charming the men with her quick wit and smile.

"You about ready to speak?" Jillian asks me, drawing my attention.

"I think so," I reply, checking my watch and noting the time. I start to get a little panicky that my special guest isn't going to show up.

As if I conjured her from my brain, the door opens and a well-dressed woman in a business suit steps inside and takes in the restaurant.

"I wonder who that is?" Jillian asks, obviously noticing the new addition right away.

"I'll go find out. Why don't you grab me a bottle of water before I go up and give my speech?"

There's hesitation in her green eyes, but she nods and walks over to where we have the bar set up.

"Mr. Markley?" the woman I know as Janice asks as she approaches.

"Yes, and you must be Janice Decker."

"Pleasure to finally meet you," she replies, shaking my hand. "You have a beautiful place here."

"Thank you. I'm getting ready to address the room, but I hope you'll stay and have some refreshments before you head back to New York."

Janice explained to me she's on a tight schedule but wanted to personally stop in and meet Jillian following a meeting in Los Angeles. She has approximately an hour before she needs to leave to return her rental car in St. Paul and catch her next flight.

She gives me a warm smile. "It smells amazing in here. Hopefully I have a little time to enjoy some of your food before I need to go."

"Let's get this show on the road," I state before Jillian returns.

She glances around me curiously, eyeing the woman who just arrived, but doesn't say anything. "Ready, sweetheart?"

"Yes," she replies, handing over the bottle of water.

I take a quick sip before recapping the bottle and taking her hand. "Let's do this."

another EPILOGUE

Jillian

Kameron leads me toward the front of the room and raises his hand. "If I could have everyone's attention?"

He's not big on public speeches, but we discussed the importance of him speaking this evening. Even though he'd prefer to let the food and the ambiance do the talking, he knew this was the right way to express his appreciation to those in the room this evening.

The room begins to quiet down, and I can feel the eyes of everyone fall on us, including the newcomer at the back. I don't know who she is, but Kameron does. Perhaps she's an old friend from Chicago or someone he knew from his culinary school days. She's well dressed, in a dark blue business suit and designer shoes. Her hair is perfect, not a single strand out of place, and her nails manicured and red.

"I won't bore you with a long speech, but I do have a few things to say this evening. First off, every person in this room had a hand in tonight's celebration. I want to thank my staff, who always go above and beyond, the city and Mr. Mayor for his encouragement and patronage, Mrs. Dorothy Krokus for believing in me and granting me the purchase of this beautiful space. My vision has come to life because of her, and I will forever be grateful."

The older woman blows Kameron a kiss, making him blush and me laugh.

"My friends are all in attendance tonight, as well as Jillian's family. I appreciate you all being here tonight."

He takes a deep breath before continuing.

"There are a few people noticeably absent this evening. My parents," he states before clearing the emotion from his throat, "and my younger brother, Kelvin. I have no doubt all three of them would be standing here with us tonight. I just..." He clears his throat a second time and whispers, "I just hope I've made them proud."

My heart aches as tears fill my own eyes. I give his hand a gentle squeeze, letting him know I'm right here beside him and he's not alone in his grief.

"You have," someone hollers from the back of the room.

When I look up, I see Gabe standing there, holding up his beer bottle in salute.

"Thank you." Kameron gives himself a few more seconds to compose his emotions before he continues, turning to look at me. "And last but certainly not least, my Jilly. You are my everything. You've been my rock on the hard days and a sounding board when I needed to work things out in my head. You've put up with late dinners and even later nights at work, often going to bed alone until I get home. Our schedules don't always sync, but we make it work, and there's no one I want by my side but you."

He flashes a quick smile. "You and our babies."

The audience claps as he leans over and gives me a gentle, PG kiss in front of everyone. When he stands up, he turns back to the crowd. "I've done something she's going to hate, and all I can hope is she forgives me and knows my heart was in the right place. I love you, Jilly."

My eyebrows draw together in confusion as I consider his words. I glance over to where my friends are standing, and they all look on, equally perplexed.

Well, except for Ryan.

She's grinning from ear to ear.

"If Mrs. Janice Decker would please come up to the front," Kameron says with a grin.

I watch as the woman in the blue business suit steps forward and smiles. "Thank you so much, Kameron, and might I add a quick congratulations to you on your beautiful restaurant. I'd love to speak with you soon about featuring you in our publications."

My eyes dart to Kameron, who looks shocked by her statement.

Publications?

He squeezes my hand, and I admit, I'm glad he's holding it. Even with his fingers linked around mine, I know I'm trembling, unsure what is going on and dreading the spotlight I've been thrust into.

"As Kameron mentioned, I'm Janice Decker, CEO of Foodie Publications out of New York. A few months back, I received a rough draft of a cookbook. It was submitted by the boyfriend of the author and was everything we look for at Foodie."

My heart is trying to hammer out of my chest, and it's suddenly a little hard to breathe. I feel Kameron's hand on my shoulder, his thumb running over the back of my neck in a soothing manner.

"That cookbook was written by Miss Jillian Kirby, and if she'll accept our offer, we'd love to produce that very cookbook for world-wide distribution by next summer."

The room erupts into applause and cheers.

Did I hear her correctly?

I gaze up at Kameron, who looks both worried and proud. "You did this?"

He turns and pulls me into his arms. "No, Jilly, you did this. I only sent an email."

The tears filling my eyes spill out as he kisses my lips. "I don't believe this," I mutter.

"Well, believe it, beautiful. Janice has a contract for you to review and details to discuss." He stands up tall and places his hands on my stomach.

"But...th-this is your night," I stammer, still in complete shock.

"No, my love. This is *our* night."

And it is.

After stealing about thirty minutes in Kameron's office to discuss the offer, my name is signed on the contract and Janice is on her way back to New York, promising to email the final paperwork first thing in the morning.

"Is this really happening?" I ask when the guests start to leave and the cleanup begins.

"It is," he confirms, pulling me against him. My stomach isn't flat anymore, but he doesn't seem to mind. If anything, his hands are always seeking it out, as if he needs to touch our growing babies more than he needs air.

"I can't believe you did this," I say once more, reeling.

"I was worried you'd be mad, and maybe telling you about it publicly like this wasn't my brightest idea, but I'm hoping you'll be so happy with the outcome you'll overlook that indiscretion."

Shaking my head, I slip my arm around his waist and lean into his side. "I forgive you, Mr. Markley."

"Good," he states, leaning down and kissing the crown of my head. "Because the next course is going to be even better."

"Next course?" I ask, catching his culinary reference.

"You and me, Jilly. I see a little house where our children can grow and play. A swing set in the backyard and a huge kitchen where we can both cook and bake to our heart's content." He brushes his lips across mine. "I see a diamond ring on your finger, Jilly. One day, I'll make that happen."

I can't help but smile. It's only been a handful of months since we started dating—fake or otherwise—but to hear him talk about proposing, about getting married, about raising our twins and any more kids together, feels perfect.

No, not perfect, because life never is.

It feels right.

Very right.

I gaze into his eyes and smile. "I'll say yes."

I've never been more confident in something this major, this life-changing, as I am right now.

He clears his throat, his eyes turning a bit misty. "I know it's not the same as a new ring, but...I have my mom's wedding ring."

A lump the size of the Titanic forms in my throat, making it hard to breathe. "I'd wear it proudly."

"Yeah?"

I nod. "I always thought it would be perfect to wear my grandmother's engagement ring. It's timeless and classic and...yeah. I don't need a new ring."

"Good to know."

"And I love the vision of our future, Kameron. I don't want to rush either, but when you're ready, I will be too."

His blue orbs brighten with excitement. "I love you, Jillian Kirby. Thanks for agreeing to be my fake girlfriend."

I can't help but chuckle as I press my lips to his. "I love you, Kameron Markley. Thanks for asking me to be your fake girlfriend."

What a beautiful mess we're living.

A beautiful life.

I'm ready for the next course.

Don't miss a single reveal, release, or sale! Sign up for my newsletter.
http://www.laceyblackbooks.com/newsletter

BOOKS ALSO BY
lacey black

Rivers Edge series
Trust Me, Rivers Edge book 1 (Maddox and Avery) – FREE at all retailers
Fight Me, Rivers Edge book 2 (Jake and Erin)
Expect Me, Rivers Edge book 3 (Travis and Josselyn)
Promise Me: A Novella, Rivers Edge book 3.5 (Jase and Holly)
Protect Me, Rivers Edge book 4 (Nate and Lia)
Boss Me, Rivers Edge book 5 (Will and Carmen)
Trust Us: A Rivers Edge Christmas Novella (Maddox and Avery)
> ~ *This novella was originally part of the Christmas Miracles Anthology*

With Me, A Rivers Edge Christmas Novella (Brooklyn and Becker)

Bound Together series
Submerged, Bound Together book 1 (Blake and Carly)
Profited, Bound Together book 2 (Reid and Dani)
Entwined, Bound Together book 3 (Luke and Sidney)

Summer Sisters series
My Kinda Kisses, Summer Sisters book 1 (Jaime and Ryan)
My Kinda Night, Summer Sisters book 2 (Payton and Dean)
My Kinda Song, Summer Sisters book 3 (Abby and Levi)
My Kinda Mess, Summer Sisters book 4 (Lexi and Linkin)
My Kinda Player, Summer Sisters book 5 (AJ and Sawyer)

My Kinda Player, Summer Sisters book 6 (Meghan and Nick)
My Kinda Wedding, A Summer Sisters Novella book 7 (Meghan and Nick)

Rockland Falls series
Love and Pancakes, Rockland Falls book 1
Love and Lingerie, Rockland Falls book 2
Love and Landscape, Rockland Falls book 3
Love and Neckties, Rockland Falls book 4

Standalone
Music Notes, a sexy contemporary romance standalone
A Place To Call Home, a Memorial Day novella
Exes and Ho Ho Ho's, a sexy contemporary romance standalone novella
Pants on Fire
Double Dog Dare You
Grip
Bachelor Swap, A Bachelor Tower Series Novel
Perfect Kiss, Mason Creek Series book 9
Waiting For Love, The Love Vixen Series book 11
Quarterback Keeper, a surprise baby novella
Kissing A Stranger, book 4 in the multi-author The Kissing Games series

Burgers and Brew Crüe Series
Kickstart My Heart, book 1
Don't Go Away Mad, book 2
Same Ol' Situation, book 3
Wild Side, book 4
What's It Gonna Take, book 5
Home Sweet Home, book 6
Too Young to Fall in Love, book 7
Without You, book 8

Time For Change, book 9
You're All I Need, book 10

Pine Village Series
Pretty Remarkable, a free prequel short story
Pretty Incredible, book 1
Pretty Dependable, book 2
Pretty Drunk, book 3
Pretty Relentless, book 4
Pretty Wild, book 5

Co-Written with *NYT Bestselling* Author, Kaylee Ryan
It's Not Over, Fair Lakes book 1
Just Getting Started, Fair Lakes book 2
Can't Get Enough, Fair Lakes book 3
Fair Lakes Box Set
Boy Trouble
Home To You, a second chance novella
Beneath the Fallen Stars, Never Too Far book 1
Beneath the Desert Sun, Never Too Far book 2
Tell Me A Story
Royal
Crying Shame
Watch and Learn

ABOUT
lacey black

USA Today Bestselling Author Lacey Black is a Midwestern girl with a passion for reading, writing, and shopping. She carries her e-reader with her everywhere she goes so she never misses an opportunity to read a few pages. Always looking for a happily ever after, Lacey is passionate about contemporary romance novels and enjoys it further when you mix in a little suspense. She resides in a small town in Illinois with her husband and two children.

Website: www.laceyblackbooks.com
Email: laceyblackwrites@gmail.com
Newsletter: http://www.laceyblackbooks.com/newsletter

www.ingramcontent.com/pod-product-compliance
Lightning Source LLC
Chambersburg PA
CBHW060622260626
47161CB00008B/2780